THE WAY THE ANGEL
SPREADS HER WINGS

Barry Callagban — poet, publisher (of Exile Editions and *Exile Magazine*), editor, translator, television host and personality — has also spent time as a journalist in many troubled places, including a leper colony in Africa. He has been a war correspondent, a documentary film producer, a political prisoner in foreign jails, literary editor of the *Toronto Telegram*, and somewhat of a gambler, and is Professor of English at York University, Toronto. He has won numerous awards for his work. His acclaimed books of poetry include *The Hogg Poems and Drawings, As Close As We Came*, and *Stone Blind Love*, which Northrop Frye called ''...a most impressive achievement... A descent into the underworld, a dark, oracular sequence of variations upon mortally and metamorphosis.'' His stories have been widely published in the United States and England as well as Canada, and translated into many languages.

BARRY CALLAGHAN

The Way the Angel Spreads Her Wings

Little, Brown and Company (Canada) Limited
Boston • New York • Toronto • London

Little, Brown and Company (Canada) Limited
148 Yorkville Ave
Toronto, ON M5R 1C2

First published by
Lester & Orpen Dennys 1989
Vintage U. K. edition 1990
Little, Brown and Company (Canada) Limited edition 1995

Canadian Cataloguing in Publication Data

Callaghan, Barry, 1937-
    The way the angel spreads her wings

ISBN 0-316-12472-9

I. Title.

PS8555.A49W39   1995   C813'.54   C95-930548-3
PR9199.3.C35W39   1995

Printed and bound in Canada by
B.B. Manufacturers

To those days and nights
of our Jive talk,
and C-Jam to come

*The Way
the Angel
Spreads
Her Wings*

And startled God is taking
our pulse, grave, mute,
and like a father to his little girl,
just almost, almost, prises the bloodied cotton
and between his fingers hope.

VALLEJO

Own only what you can always carry with you:
know languages, know countries, know people.
Let memory be your travel bag. Use your memory!
It is those bitter seeds alone which might sprout
and grow someday.

SOLZHENITSYN

Let us look back to the past: it will be a step forward.

VERDI

Here I lie, taken from life.
Epitaph

ADAM WATERS
Photographer

Adam's mother sat braiding her black hair in front of a big oval mirror. She had bony fingers. A burning cigarette left a long ash in a glass tray, and then she lit another, watching the match burn, staring into the blue flame. She kept the flame alive, building a mound of charred matchsticks, and then she put on her glasses and turned and said to Adam, who was leaning against the leaded window, "Well, let me look at you. What kind of boy are you today?"

"A good boy."

"And what's a good boy?"

"I don't know."

"A good boy is a boy who loves his mommy."

"Why can't I love Dad, too?"

"You can, but sometimes Dad's a bad boy. Sometimes Dad doesn't come home. Now, let's pray and go to bed."

"Does god love me?"

"Of course he does. He died for your sins."

"Did I do some sins, Mommy?"

"No. No, you're much too young."

"Then he's not dead for me."

"He will be, you'll see when you get older."

She put him to bed and went down the back stairs. The stairs were lit by a bare bulb in a ceiling socket, and she walked out onto the porch and sat down in the dark in a white wicker rocking chair.

* * *

He wiped his hands with his handkerchief. He was sweating in the shade at a café table. The awning had been tattered by desert winds. There was no one else in the café, not in the afternoon heat; no sound, but only a rustle of dry leaves in the air and the *shloop* made by clumps of mud thrown into the river by children crouched along the bank. He picked up a postcard, a little lacquered map of the country: dark green with the main roads in fluorescent red, and a crescent of ocean blue with a white emptiness in the northwest, the desert. He licked two stamps, stuck them to the card, and wrote a short note. He read the note and turned the card over and stared at the map. He tore the card into tiny pieces and dropped them into his empty espresso cup. He stood up. A lean black waiter wearing a blue kepi and white tennis shoes said, "The heat mek too hot too much maybe." Adam shrugged, left some coins on the table, and went into the sun. Because he was wearing a creamy white suit, he seemed to dissolve into the glare of the heat.

* * *

Old Millicent Skinner, whose gardener wore pearl-grey gloves, stood out on her lawn watching the window lights across the street. She was drunk, standing in a pink lace slip, and she saluted when a light went out in an upstairs bay window. Itzak Klein, wearing torn leather slippers and a skull-cap, came out of the shadows of the trees and crossed the lawn and bowed to her from the waist.

"Delighted," he said. "Delighted Missus to make an acquaintance."

"I'm a Miss," she said sternly.

"Everything's amiss," he said and bowed again and went down the alley between the houses. He had a small hand press in his cellar and in the middle of the night he slipped pamphlets through the brass letter slots in the doors on the street:

PREPARE FOR REVOLUTION

He was an old man who had lived for years with his daughter above his printing shop on Augusta Avenue, but then he moved up from the side-streets of the market, buying a brick cottage, an old servant's house in the laneway close to the garages behind Adam's house, and every evening he went for a stroll on the sidewalk in his slippers. One day Miss Skinner said to Flo, Adam's mother, "It's awful, Mrs. Waters. He treats the street just like it was his living room, those awful torn slippers." Mr. Klein also collected butterflies. He chloroformed the butterflies in large fruit-preserve bottles and pinned them to plywood boards in the cellar room where the press was. He printed a pamphlet that said: AVRAHAM STERN –

RENEGADE – WHO OFFERED TO BARGAIN WITH THE NAZIS TO
GET PALESTINE FROM THE BRITISH IN EXCHANGE FOR A HEBREW
STATE. No one on the street knew who Stern was, but a week
later two truck drivers delivering cases of seltzer water beat
Klein up, chloroformed him, and stomped on his butterflies.
The next morning, the broken boards and tattered butterflies
lay scattered in the alley. About a month later, Klein was
arrested for stabbing automobile tires in the night with an
ice-pick.

*   *   *

There was a sheen on the sluggish river water and fallen
saw-toothed yellow leaves seemed suspended in the sheen.
Adam walked across a narrow bridge, and an old blind man
wearing a wool cap sat in the shade of the bridge cradling a
harp made of charred wood covered with iguana skin. There
was a carved white mask on the bald end of the harp to ward
off evil spirits. He had the strange feeling that the blind man
was hissing at him, a snake's hiss, and then two mahogany-
skinned women, their lips tinted with papyrus juice, wearing
white face powder and long skirts, stepped out from behind
bushes and a barbed wire fence. Their husbands gave them
four ritual kisses and went into a Muslim prayer house where
they hunched forward on rugs in the rose-colored dust. He
caught a whiff of gunpowder and iodine on the stagnant air.
A child behind him said, "It's going to spill," but no one was
carrying anything, not that he could see, so he hurried down a
lane toward the hotel where a thin black girl whose several
beaded pigtails were tied into a crown on top of her head
stamped her bare foot in the dust. She had raced another,

taller girl to a board fence. There were posters plastered to the fence: militiamen aiming Uzis at the sky.

"My shadow mek it first," the tall girl yelled.

"It did not, Dainty."

"It did. It mek de fence first."

"Show me your shadow," she cried. "There's no shadow."

"I tank you stupid."

"De sun fled away, when we are running de sun fled away."

"I saw it," the braided girl screamed.

"It didn't get to there, I tank you got no shadow."

* * *

The bushes in the low hedge around the Waters' lawn had bright berries. Adam's grandfather, who lived in a war veterans' residential hotel, said, "Don't eat those berries. You'll die." Adam collected them in his pockets and crept between the houses at night and threw a handful at a bedroom window until a face appeared against the glass, staring with wary yearning into the dark. Miss Skinner, whose stone house was covered with ivy, caught him. She was wearing a white satin petticoat. "You do that again," she said, "and I'll smack you so hard you'll see stars."

That week his grandfather died and his mother said, "You're too young to see someone dead." She carried him to the stuccoed house of her friends next door. They gave him tea, poured his mother a Drambuie on the rocks, and as she went off to the hospital she said, "This won't be the last time in your life you're left alone." There were colored Easter eggs and a photograph of the neighbor woman on the mantel. The woman was naked and sitting cross-legged in an empty room painted white and black. She was a singer with a dance band. Adam always thought of her when he was on the altar at church, a choirboy in a black soutane and white surplice. He said, "I'd like to paint your breasts like those eggs." She put him to bed and in the morning her husband, who had a pencil moustache, said, "Hello, my name is Edmund," and he gave Adam a pocket watch. "Well, your grandfather is gone." Adam curled up in the strange bed and watched the sweep of the second-hand, and then he put the watch on the pillow and it lay there like a silver eye and he said, "I guess Grandpa ate some of those red berries."

When his mother came home she gave him a drawing book. The pages were blank except for black dots, and the scattered dots had numbers beside them, and using a stubby little pencil he learned to count and connect the dots. He clapped his hands with wonder when the dots became a horse or a house or a man with big floppy shoes holding an umbrella. Then one day he drew a big black dot on the white wall over his bed and when his mother came home she was furious.

"Why did you do that, you terrible boy?"

"That's Dad," he said, backing away.

"What?"

"Dad's a great big dot and the wall's the sky."

She took off her glasses and began to cry.

"Adam, you're all I've got," she said.

"Sometimes you're all there is too, Mom."

He cradled against her belly and said, "I guess I sinned, eh Mom?"

"No, no it's not a sin."

"Why not?"

"Because it's not. Your dad's off playing wherever he is. But a dot on the wall that's your dad is not a sin," and she put her glasses on and gathered up his drawing books, slipping them between her garter belts and underclothes in her dresser drawer, and after supper she came back from the store with a big glossy book about the stars.

"You want to look in the sky," she said, "then you should know what you're looking for."

He studied the stars and tried to stay awake as long as he could in the dark. As weeks passed and his mother cut her hair and wore her glasses all day, he dreamed of winged horses and ships adrift in the sky and planets that wheeled around the spokes of the sun, and he drew the little points of light together on his charts. He sometimes thought that planets wheeled around his room, and he discovered he could squeeze his eyes so hard that he saw little dots of light. He told his mother, "I've got stars in my eyes," and she said, "No you don't. Your father does. You don't ever want to have stars in your eyes."

"Why not?"

"Because people who've got stars in their eyes hurt other people. They've got their heads in the stars instead of at home."

"But there's the Big Dipper, Mom, and follow your eye down the handle, there's the last star in the Little Dipper. The whole world's up there," he cried, holding her as close as he could, feeling the heat in the hollow of her thighs.

"Not everything," she said. "There's no cross. The fiery cross comes at the end of the world."

"What's the end of the world?"

"When everything's nothing, except we'll see fire in the air first."

"So, we should be down at the South Pole."

"Heavens, no," she said, laughing.

"Why not?" he said. "All they've got in the sky is a Southern Cross."

With his magnifying glass, he searched his glossy star maps, looking for points of light in the north that could connect into a cross, but finally he folded his arms at supper and said, "I give up. There's no cross where we live."

"Oh yes there is."

"Where?"

"We all carry a cross."

"I don't like that."

"You'll see."

*　*　*

At the Libreville hotel, Adam changed to a madras shirt and a light linen jacket. He sat at the small Five-Star Bar that was attached to the hotel, jutting toward the beach, open to the wind off the ocean. The skies were clear but the wind was strong. A salt spray coated the mirror behind the stainless steel and mahogany bar. There was a red, yellow, and green flag hanging from a stick in an empty water bottle, the black star of Africa at the heart of the flag. A dark brown lizard skittered along the bar and up to the water bottle. It stretched its wrinkled neck and slowly turned an albino pink, the color of the bottle.

"Perfect," he said to the barman.

"What that be, mister suh?"

Adam wagged his finger at the lizard. "Disappearing."

"We all make our perfections."

"Oh yeah?"

"The most perfect thing I ever see," he said, running a small towel around the lip of a whisky sour glass, "was a rat drinking the coconut water ..."

"I'll have a whisky ..."

"... and the rat, he go up the trunk of the tree and set out on the coconut and drill himself a hole to sip the water, so when he full up he turn around and whip the rest the water out of the coconut with his tail, so then he nibble the stem some and go in the hole where he don't drown 'cause enough of the water gone and he wiggle around until the stem break so the coconut fall and before the coconut hit the ground he leap out the hole and run off so the coconut break all to pieces without him, so he drink all his water full and take his elevator down, the rat being himself a rat."

A small boy carrying an empty plastic jug looked into the bar. He blew into the mouth of the jug ... three throaty notes ... and shuffled his feet. The barman laughed. "Move yur ass," he said. The boy jumped up and down and scowled and then went away, singing, making a rasping click sound in his throat, and the lizard scurried up the empty water bottle, swimming into the glass, creeping along the flag, settling into the black star. The evening sun was on the clouds. A lean, mangy dog appeared in the door to the bar. It stared and began to whimper, but while whimpering, it bared its teeth. It had a long pink tongue, and in the shadows it seemed to be screaming with laughter. The barman threw an ice cube at the dog, hitting it in the ribs. It ran toward the shore, toward the surf breaking on the sandbars. Adam sat in silence, staring at the water, at the falling light. A shabbily dressed soldier wearing high boots with spurs and a holster with the flap open began to walk toward them from the sandbars. "Good lord," Adam said, "he looks like he's liable to do anything."

The shabbily dressed soldier had come to the edge of the elephant grass, to a single palm tree. He stood jingling some old flat brown coins. His holster was empty. "He's not a soldier," the barman said, "he live in a house across from the cemetery. He sell the birds, fighting birds."

"Cocks?"

"Yes suh."

"How bad is it back in the bush?"

"The fighting come and go, suh."

"So it seems does the government."

"Yes mister suh, we got all kind of governments all the times and militias, they make freedoms we know very well."

"You know what I was just thinking," Adam said, turning from the violet haze that had crept in around the palm and the man with the empty holster and spurs.

"No suh."

"Livingstone."

"Who suh?"

"Doctor Livingstone."

"That old missionary man I tank he is a memory no one has no more," the barman said.

"He was trying to find the five fountains, the fountains of the Nile," Adam said, leaning forward. "He was sure they'd heal the five wounds of Christ ..."

"The world full of crazies for sure, mister suh," the barman said, building a pyramid of whisky sour glasses on the bar.

"... and it was wonderful when he was so sick and lost, he was trekking around the whole time wearing a pair of shiny French patent leather shoes that were too small, too tight, pinching his little pinkies, but he wouldn't take the damn shoes off, just like he couldn't get rid of the slavers who were paying his bills, and finally he just lay down and died with his little patent leather shoes on."

"Yur staying with us, suh?"

"No. Heading into the bush."

"It a bad time to go, suh."

"I got to go."

"Yur a journalist, suh?"

"Yes, but whatever this war is, it doesn't mean anything to me."

"It mean nothing to me either, suh."

"It's personal. I'm looking for someone, that's all."

"You got yur shiny shoes, mister suh?"

"Afraid not."

"I always leave myself a pair of shoes where I been, suh. So it mean I come back."

"It's funny, the woman I'm looking for once told me the same thing."

"Yes suh."

"She left her shoes in a room, too."

"Yes suh."

"She never came back."

* * *

Adam's father stood in the sunlight on the back porch.
"Give this man of yours a kiss," he said. "Give old Web
Waters a kiss." His mother laughed and took off her glasses
and kissed his hand. "Don't be silly," Web said. He had a long
face with deeply set hazel eyes, long arms and legs and big
hands. "This old toddling child has got to come home some
time," he said and swept her into his arms. He murmured a
low song in her ear.

Later, he told Adam stories about travelling. "Life's a
pilgrim road, boy, even for a poor piano player like me." They
were stories full of wonder, about a city in which there were
no roads but only canals, and a café in Berlin where raw rein-
deer meat was fed to piranha fish in a tank, but sometimes it
seemed that Web suddenly lost his wonder because he said,
"I'm just a nowhere man," sitting silently in a stuffed maroon
leather chair. Adam sat cross-legged in front of him and asked
why the round world was so flat, and he said, "Hell, I know
all about that, I know how things go flat." He laughed and sat
down at the piano. "To really play the blues like your poppa
does you've got to have big hands, you got to be able to hold
more than eight notes in your hands." He played a song.
"That's a little tune called 'Chopsticks'," he said, "except I
played it like they played it in the old sporting houses, what
they called ragtime, which was what they used to play in
Chinese sporting houses, I guess."

"What's a sporting house?"

"That's a house ... you pretend is wonderland, but it's not."

"Where's wonderland?"

"Inside your head. Sometimes it hurts, boy, sitting only
inside your own head, but that's where you find yourself
most of the time so make the most of it." But then he said, as if

talking to someone outside the window, "The thing that makes you feel at home in your city where nobody knows anybody is your dead, the ghosts you got buried that you can call your own, like Grandfather. It's the dead, once you've got them, who make you feel at home in your own town."

Web took Adam to the old cemetery, the burial yard where the Waters were scattered under oak trees, some side-by-side, others between crypts and cairns under chestnut trees, and in September the chestnuts were big as green apples, and in winter the black branches of the trees were sheathed in ice and his father threw snowballs up into the trees, shattering the sleeves of ice so that shards fell in the sunlight. "You know, I was standing here one day after a big snowstorm," he said, "the snow banked up around the stones, and these pall bearers appeared carrying this coffin with a big bell sitting on it, and some navy men and cadets followed along single-file through the snow, and it reminded me that back in the old days there'd only been a wagon track through these trees that they used for hauling boats up the hill on the portage through the bush to Clear Bay, and they say a huge elm fell across the trench and all the wagons went under it so that it looked like the crossbeam of a gallows tree, so this was called Gallows Hill, you didn't know that, did you? and also the blue clay was used to make the bricks for the first jail house, a damn blue jailhouse just like a jewel on the hill, and your great-great-grandfathers are lying down here under where those sailors went, just like they were in their own little cells."

Their family stones stood along the lane into the cemetery and some lay flat below ground with only the nub of an angel's head showing and letters that needed rubbing to be read, but the rest were lean elegant slate slabs or little stone steeples and turrets inscribed with dates and lists of names. "For me," Web said, "a burial yard is like a room full of notes left behind." His favorite stone was pale brown, between his grandmother and grandfather:

You passers-by, stay not to ask my name,
I'm nothing at present,
From nothing I came.
I never was much, am now less than ever,
And idle hath always been my endeavor,
Who, coming from nothing,
To nothing is fled,
Yet thought she'd become something once she was dead.
18 __ to 18 __

* * *

Adam stood in the shadows of the Five-Star Bar, and in the darkness he could see only the drooping ropes of casuarina trees close to the glass-enclosed restaurant that had been built out over the water on piles, like a small ship moored in the night air. Over the breaking of the sea he could hear laughter, men and women in galibayahs spreading their arms like birds, enfolding each other in wings. He felt suddenly chilly and put his arm around the tall girl in the white dress who had agreed to walk out to the hotel garden with him.

"You want to go there for supper?" he asked.

"No, no. I don't mek good time there."

"No?"

"No."

She wore a simple loose silk dress gathered at the waist by a thin rhinestone belt. She had long hennaed fingernails. Her hair hung in a curtain of narrow braids threaded with bone and ivory beads, and with her long neck and high cheekbones, she had a severe dark beauty.

"When yur happy with me, then you will only have to tank of me your happiness."

"Where would you like to go?"

"You come, okay."

She led him out of the garden shadows into a dimly lit service corridor in the hotel, past an empty hall where old flaccid party balloons still clung to the ceiling. He could hear the beating of a drum. She opened a heavy, grey steel door. A big steamy smoke-filled room was crowded with blacks seated in rows at long tables. They were being served by village boys dressed in kelly-green lederhosen, carrying wide aluminum trays filled with jug beer and sauerkraut and sausages. A big hand-painted banner was slung across the front of the room, with blue and white letters – BAVARIAN BEER – and five paunchy white men wearing mountain-climbing boots, lederhosen, and alpine hats were sweating and playing polkas, with the crowd hollering and singing – "Roll Out the Barrel."

"It is joy," she said. "You like?"

"Love it," he said, unbelieving, and suddenly wished he had his cameras, because that was how he captured what he couldn't believe in, how he held on to all the lone solitary moments, stealing them in black and white from the blurred sheen of light that sometimes seemed to be all he could see, as if a flooding reality always hardened into walls of clear ice filled with light, light that blinded him.

"I am good girl for hire, I mek happy time surprise."

She tucked a linen napkin into the bodice of her dress. She beamed as she stared at the sauerkraut heaped on her plate. The five bandsmen broke into another polka … *oompa pa oompa pa* … she ate and asked for more sausage and then led him onto the dance floor, pointing at the tuba, laughing, her silk dress clinging to her wet body, bouncing and leaping in circles, her shoulder strap slipping until suddenly her breast with its mulberry nipple was bare, and with stern childish glee, she cried, "Polka, polka …"

* * *

Adam sat on a needlepoint stool beside the piano and told his mother and father stories about the stars and the streets he roamed around on. "This is my downtown," he said, and told them about Mrs. Blasingame, who was so drunk one afternoon that her silk bonnet slipped over her eyes and she couldn't see that her slow-witted thirty-five-year-old son had let his trousers fall to his ankles and he was playing with himself behind a curtain of climbing sweet peas. His mother and father laughed, but a few weeks later, the slow-witted son killed his mother with a rake. "These are wild times," Web said. "Everyone has a boil about to burst," and he waved his folded newspaper. "We're all on the loose with boils about to burst. I like that." He wrote it down in a little notebook. The desk and dresser drawers in the house were filled with notebooks he'd kept over the years, things he liked hearing himself say, and he said that Adam could have them when he was dead. "You'll be lucky because you'll learn something about your father, which is more than I can say about my father."

"Well, your father was afraid of red berries."

"Life is the berries," and he laughed and poured himself a drink of bourbon, and after a while, a little drunk, he said, "Come on kid, Web's gonna take you for a walk down to his downtown."

It was nine o'clock at night. There were girls in white plastic boots and miniskirts along Isabella Street, and old guys with the stink of sleeping all day in movie houses stood staring at billboards on the walls of Starvin' Marvin's Stripperama ... breasts and buttocks and whips and pearl-handled pistols and women on their knees kissing each other on the mouth. The sidewalk was crowded and they walked around the bodies of young boys and girls stretched out and slumped against the buildings, grey and tattered children. Someone had propped up a sign: REDEMPTION IS LOVE. Adam only caught whispers and low laughter as he and his father side-stepped the panhandlers and *Watchtower* preachers and then a pale girl with round black eyes lifted her head and saw Web and Adam coming and said, "Hey kid, how about if I drop my strides and take your picture for five bucks ..." The bare-footed boys and girls stretched out on the concrete had tied long strings to their toes, and there were white balloons floating high in the air like distress signals. The white balloons drifted in a night filled with rippling electric stars, and he wanted to lie down, too, and tie a string to his big toe, except he wanted to fish in the sky the way he'd read boys used to lie down and sleep beside a river and let a string trail from their toes in the water, trying to hook catfish.

* * *

A mist rose from the river, an acrid musty smell from the elephant grass. Black-and-yellow birds planed from the tree tops. Though he hadn't opened his eyes the morning air had the heavy close feel of the summer heat-lightning days back home, corrosive yet lulling days, and he tossed, half-asleep *naked legs catching the light, your arms thrown back, and put to bed with kisses all over your breasts and belly. The whole room recedes and then explodes in my eyes ... the salt warmth of your flesh, and during that caress of your cunt with my tongue, the salt of your love. I cannot feel you. I want to feel your breath against my neck* and then he opened his eyes and saw the room and saw the black girl who had showered and was standing naked in the open window with water beading on her body, opals of light on her dark skin (the first time he'd bedded a black girl, she'd said, "Turn on the light, man, so's I can see you," and she'd run her long fingers across his belly and his rib cage. "You got no shadow in your skin, man ... White folk is like pork fat, all pork fat and no meat. You's scary in a sorta sweet way, like I got a real live ghost in me when you're in me."), and she was holding up one of the cameras as she said, "How do you have so much cameras?"

"I take pictures. Wherever there's killing I take pictures."

"You tek my picture?"

"If you want me to."

"No. Picture no good. You steal me inside."

"I wouldn't steal you."

"You tek me when I sleep?" she asked suspiciously.

"No."

"Good. So why you tek pictures?"

"It's what I do."

"Here?"

"No, in the bush."

"So bad in de bush now, big fighting."

"I'm going to the leper camps."

"It no good to see sick people too many."

"It's a woman I love, that's all. She's called Gabrielle."

"She sick?"

"Who knows ..."

"And you love?"

She stepped into her high heels and stood brazenly with her hands on her hips. She had a young girl's pointed breasts.

"Yes, very much. It's almost a year since I've seen her."

"Too long time."

"Maybe."

"I tank you love me too."

"A little."

"You go out with me, your girl for sunshine."

"My mother," he said, laughing and taking her hand, "she told me to never step on sunlight ..."

"Why?"

"She said I'd break my heart."

* * *

Some homes on the street had been turned into rooming-houses filled with working couples who were always in a hurry. On Saturdays the unshaven men stood on their stoops wearing baggy trousers and old hats or gabardine skull-caps, staring wryly at the elderly gardeners unbuttoning their paisley vests before they polished the family cars. Other men sat reading the newspaper in aluminum chairs on the lawns or sprawled over the hoods of their cars. They talked about baseball or fishing. Edmund, who had given Adam the silver pocket watch, told Web that he wanted to take Adam fishing. "It's the first spring run. The sap's coming out of the trees just like candy."

One morning, Adam got into the car with Edmund and two of his friends who were sportswriters and they drove north to the Black River. It was a wide shallow river that emptied into Clear Bay. "On a good day you can see right to Clear Bay," one of the sportswriters said staring blankly downriver. "Do you work in a sporting house?" Adam asked. They all laughed and the man said, "No, but I'd like to," and they set up camp, making a fire in a circle of stones. They sat on their haunches and passed around a bottle of rye whisky, talking about hooks and bait and how to fillet a fish, depending on whether it was perch or pike, and how carving a duck was not like carving a turkey: "You got to take your shears and scissor right through the breastbone to quarter the bird. My father was a tailor," Edmund said, "and I got his shears. The only damn thing of his I got and they're perfect for scissoring ducks." They put Adam in men's high rubber boots and led him out into the white rushing water, a long pole in his hand, and Edmund helped him cast. Adam looked around and couldn't find them. They'd gone around a bend. He stood in the river a long time, bewildered, holding the pole straight out in the air, with no idea where the end of the line was, scared and cold, so he began to sing a song his mother had always sung in the dark when he was a child: "It's a grand night for singing ..."

He liked to sing. He was in the church choir. All the boys dressed in black soutanes and stood close to each other in the stalls. Sometimes he closed his eyes as if he were alone, letting the lights that flashed in his eyelids look like stars again, and the other voices rippled through him, and as he stood singing alone in the river he suddenly felt the boys were all there with him and his voice was linking the little stars that fell like stones into the rush of white water in his ears. He sat down on a big stone and waited. He was calm. He loved stones. The colors were startling when they were wet. He wondered why the colors were hidden and why the water made them alive. The priest, Father Zale, said the water was the grace of God, His gift, and Adam leaned against the church walls listening for voices inside the stones, sure the iron stains were the tears of trapped voices.

He had made his first confession in that church, kneeling in the dark and waiting for the grate to roll away from the wire screen, trying to think of something terrible he had done, and since he'd seen a girl lift up her skirt and spread her legs, he'd blurted out: "I f-u-c-k-e-d, Father." He'd heard a chuckle in the dark. The priest had whispered, "How old are you, my son? You mustn't try to be bad, my boy, that'll come soon enough, so say the Stations of the Cross for a penance and try to remember Our Lord died for your sins." Adam had suddenly been happy. God at last was dead for him. But when the grate rolled shut he'd become angry, as if he'd been coldly cut off in the dark from a sudden kindness, and he'd pounded on the grate, whispering, "Open up, I got more sins."

Wearing a starched collar with a white silk bow, he'd taken communion at the marble altar rail, opening his mouth to the pale disc pinched between the puffy white fingers of the priest who had told them they would swallow the Word of God and that the Word would always speak in them no matter their silence. In the late afternoons, before he had joined the choir, he used to lie down in a pew in the empty church and listen to the choirmaster at the organ. The gently vaulted blue ceiling was covered with hundreds of gold stars as if all his spinster school teachers had filled the sky with their approval. The rumbling notes shivered his bones and he wanted to sing as loud as he could so the choirmaster would see him, but he had only a little voice so he began to pound his feet on the pew to the beat of the music, staring at the stars, and then the music stopped and he heard the choirmaster coming down the aisle and he held his breath, trying to shrink into a corner of the pew.

* * *

Stop traveller, and know
that here lie the remains
of Edgar
son of Maurice and Margaret Waters.
Before he was a year old,
he arrived at puberty and was four feet
before he was three years old,
endowed with great strength,
exact symmetry of parts,
and a stupendous voice.
He had not quite reached his sixth year
when he died, as of an advanced age.
Here he was born and here he gave way,
September 3d, 1907.

* * *

Gabrielle had disappeared. When he'd woken in the morning, she had been gone, just like she had said she wanted to disappear. "Remember when we were kids, in the comics there was this invisible man. He would just appear and disappear. He didn't die, he just didn't have to be there. Think of all the times with your mother and father when you were a kid and you said you wished you could die but really you just wished you didn't have to be there." She left behind only a pair of shoes the way she always left shoes behind so that she would come back. "The only place I never left shoes was in my house, when I left my father. I was never going back there." Her lip was curled. "You look like you're going to spit," he'd said. She had laughed wryly: "My mother told me ladies don't spit, but maybe she'd have saved herself a lot of trouble, saved her own life, if she'd just learned how to spit."

He knew she was not coming back. He was enraged and then shaken by the hollowness he felt, the loss, because he was sure he had drawn all the pain out of her, their joy together had been so clean, so unexpected. "It's like we're six thousand miles from everywhere," he'd said, and only been a little surprised when she'd sung in a nasal country twang, "*Only six thousand miles from everywhere and that much closer to hell.*" She'd then begun to dance in the hotel room by herself and he'd laughed as she'd spun on her toes, her arms reaching up. But now she was gone and at first he could only find friends at the Casino hotel who said, "Yes, she was sitting right here but only for a few days since she said she was going somewhere." How, he wanted to know, could she have stayed with him all those days, so full of affectionate silence, saying *you swallowed my soul, swallowed my sins* with those eyes that seemed to well up out of sorrow with wonder, or was it disbelief? He loved her with a wonder that left him speechless in disbelief, shouting in his sleep, "You're not leaving me here on the front porch of the dead." When he opened his eyes in the morning, he expected to find her sitting on the window sill, the tree behind her and the hummingbird that came each morning, hovering, sapsucking. But the bird never came back, as if it had never really been there, and now she was gone, too. He pieced together every conversation they'd had, because he knew that sometimes, in his exuberance, he got so swept away by his own pleasure that he said sardonic and unthinking things, wounding things, but he could remember only her joy, her ease, and those eyes that haunted him. "Yes, she had wondering eyes, you never forget those eyes," but no one knew where she'd gone. She had just disappeared, until a plump brown woman who had worked for a while as her dresser in a nightclub said, "She told me she be going to the village of light."

"The who?"

"That ain't what she called it. She called it the *village lumière* but I be asking someone who might know what that meant, her friend Mio, and he says it's light, it means light, and she told me it's where lepers be living, they got the light that shines in their wounds. I won't never forget her saying that, and then she said, 'God help the child who doesn't begin by being crazy.' She just up and let me have a last sorrowful look and she be gone."

part TWO

It snowed steadily for three days. Schools were closed. The snow was nine feet high along the roads. Some roads were only footpaths. "It's like walking in ancient tombs," Adam's mother said.

On the third day, he began to tunnel into the snow in front of the house, carving out a long hole shaped like a hook, and then several short dead-ends off the hook, smoothing the walls so they had an icy sheen and he could slip easily around turns. It kept on snowing. Flo had no idea how deeply he had wormed into the snow until she noticed the flashlight was missing. "It's pitch black in there," he said. "And cold."

"You've tunnelled all that," she said, staring out the front window, the snow up to the window sill. "Where in the world did you think you were? It could have collapsed on you, suffocated you, and we'd never have known you were in there."

"I prayed."

"I should say so."

"I thought I was in god's mind. I heard Harry singing."

Harry O'Leary, the choirmaster, was a lean wiry man Adam had first seen in the church yard under a weeping birch, pacing like a quick long-legged bird. He had straight hair and wore black straight-last shoes with tooled leather toe-caps, like the street hustlers and pimps who stood outside the pool halls on Queen Street. He had an easy laugh and loved trumpet voluntaries, Verdi, and the horses. He also played military marches on the organ for hockey games at Maple Leaf Gardens, but in the afternoons he wore a banker's blue serge suit and a pearl-grey fedora and went to the racetrack. "A horseman," he told the choirboys, "is the next best thing to a gentleman."

He had a daughter. Gabrielle had black eyes and long black hair, and though she was only thirteen she sometimes wore high heels. On Saturday mornings she sat in the choir listening to her father play. She wet her lips, keeping still in the stained-glass light, and then, when he was finished playing Bach or Gounod, Harry stood up and bowed. She covered her face with her hands like a shy girl who has been told to blow someone a kiss. Adam wondered what her bare thighs looked like because she had full breasts and one day she kissed him on the cheek and said, "Pretty soon you'll be big enough for a girl like me."

In the choir, he learned to read music and medieval chant. He stood beside a white-haired boy who had white eyelashes and pink eyes, the boy's whole face suffused with light. They learned the *Panis Angelicus* and then the pink-eyed boy disappeared. "He read all the words backwards," Harry said. "He was going backwards when we were going frontwards. His brain was all switched around." Later that year, the white-haired boy played the Christchild at Christmas, an overgrown angelic boy sitting in a huge crèche. Adam laughed and Harry cuffed him on the ear and took him outside and left him in the snow under the leafless weeping birch. "You stand out here until you switch your brain around, until you learn that some folk sing just to keep from screaming and some folk scream because they can't sing." When he was allowed back into the choir room he stood with the other boys and listened to Harry explain that Verdi's name had been a cry for freedom, had been graffiti written on the walls by ordinary men, meaning Victor Emmanuel Re d'Italia. Harry beamed. None of the boys knew what he was talking about. He didn't care. He was busy writing on the chalk board:

VERDI

In the sacristy, Father Zale blessed the starched linen shirts. He dropped sheaths of colored silk over his shoulders, green and red, or requiem black, and the angular lanky boys filed onto the altar, bowing toward Harry seated on the bench behind the organ. He released the ivory-headed stops and shuffled his feet over the pedals. "All together now," he called across the altar. The boy beside Adam was a doctor's son who regularly took off his shoes for a quarter in the schoolyard and showed the boys his webbed toes and once Adam went home and asked his mother why there were webbed feet.

Her hair had grown longer and she was smoking cigarettes in front of the mirror, staring into the flame of the matches, lighting one from the other, and she said, "It's where we come from."

"What d'you mean?"

"We come out of the water. We were all webbed things once. And the fire's where we're going."

* * *

A rusting diesel engine slowly shunted an empty flatcar onto a railway bridge over the river. The engine moved to the centre of the bridge and stopped, suspended in silence. The driver pulled down his cap and went to sleep. Big black birds flew low over the greasy brown water. Two men sat in the mud of the river bank, their shins crossed. There were small houses behind them, bamboo frames and open lathing packed with maroon mud. Blue smoke leaked out under the eaves of the corrugated roofs. The road along the river was pitted with holes and in places there was no tarmac at all, only mud corded and crimped by rain water. There were big logging trucks on the road, enormous tree trunks chained together, the lime-yellow sap running out of the black rings in the trunks *and maybe going off into the bush like this after her is unwanted, like the screech of a bird in the sky, though she had said, "Wherever I've gone, no matter how long it's been, I've always wanted you a little, though we were just kids then, and maybe it's a kind of nostalgia, and if it is, then the nostalgia's just made it better, knowing that a sweetness I've kept close to me can be even sweeter," and she had let out a cry, lifting her hips off the bed, her eyes full of tears but laughing through her tears, suffused, she said, by light, by a clarity in which she could remember nothing, not a thing in the room except the light that left her joyful because she felt cleansed, that much was clear* in the immensity of the forest edging in on everything, the muddle of shacks making the narrow road seem like a scar half-healed in a wall of vegetation ... a mass of branches, leaves, boughs, vines, and towering trees with delicate umbrella tops like monstrous parsley stalks beyond the litter of shacks on the outskirts, a wall of ennui, a tangled weight of green with holes tunnelled into the wall, paths and trails, but holes that only went deeper into what seemed endlessly the same, and from the bridge – the angled arch of rusted girders over the river – the immensity increased. "There's no perspective," he thought. "Nowhere's every-where, you swallow your own voice."

The city spread back over gullies and the slopes of hills, the roofs of the plastered one-storey shanties all tinted by the red dust that hung in the air like a screen wavering in the light winds so that it seemed a city of rose and russet light. "But your point of view, your angle on things that point to possibilities or conclusions ... you've got to have a point of view, some perspective, without that we're lost ..." and Adam, feeling a little shudder of panic, held his finger down on the camera trigger, seeing nothing ... *click click click click click* until it was empty, as if he had somehow caught moments that meant something ... and as he walked over planks laid across a ditch, two albinos smiled at him. They were holding hands, and after he got up the grade to the truck route along the river, he looked back to make sure that their pink flat noses and pink wool hair had not been an apparition, but he couldn't see them. The ditch lay behind a grassy knoll.

Covered by red dust from the logging road, he went down into the twisting market streets where there were tiny shops and shacks and the Budget rent-a-car depot, an old Silver Cloud touring trailer set up on concrete blocks, the tires gone, with six Mercedes parked under trees in the small lot. It was late afternoon and the lot was crowded with men dressed in slacks and sneakers or rubber sandals and galibayahs. The young women had their hair gathered into rococo braided crowns. Across the road, hand-clasping boys stood in front of beer parlors and pinball joints and one, wearing Elton John sunglasses and a big gold furry peaked cap, was sitting beside a big man with the limp little legs of a six-year-old who suddenly crossed the road and went by Adam in a box on wheels, pushing himself with his gloved fists toward a small Barclays bank where a man with his head shaved except for a pillar-like tuft of hair sat primly behind a sewing machine surrounded by women on their haunches under black umbrellas, one smoking a pipe the size of her thumb.

Adam rented a Mercedes 300 from a man who meticulously filled out several forms and then, when Adam said he wasn't leaving till the next morning, lost interest and let the papers fall into a waste basket, though he still gave Adam the key.

As dusk fell, a huge electric cross came on, pinheads of light in the dark green hillside *pin stripes of light under water in the dark and Gabrielle swallowing water, swallowing light, luminescent in the rippling casino lights holding the dice, said each moment and each memory hangs like a veil over the edge of the next to meet again to part once more* where it was suddenly overcast, unraveling thunderclouds moving through the valleys, decapitating the hills and obliterating the cross and in their wake came a solid sheet of pewter cloud and a downpour so heavy the city was flooded in rain and mist. A few men and women hunched over tables in restaurants open to the wind, the tails of the tablecloths blowing up into their faces. On a dimly lit street a

drunken soldier in a great-coat and one sole slapping loose on
his boot whistled and hooted at passing cars.

* * *

One night, Flo told him that when she was young she had
danced on a table in a restaurant, the night she had met his
father. He'd come out of a crowd and said, "How you doing
angel eyes?" and she'd said, "Just watch my angel dust." She
had taught Adam to sing sad songs that could be danced to
with gaiety. "The blues are what give you a little smile when
you're all alone, and your momma's alone too much ... but
those are your nights to remember ... your memories of
yourself are what keep you going, keep you alive in your
mind, and that's what love is ... the memory you hold of
someone in your head since when the love dies the memory
dies and if you've got lots of memories you've got lots of love
... and if you keep hatred to your heart, if you keep it ... then
that's a love too, and it may be the only love you've got, which
is too bad, but memory's what makes us. That's the whole
story and without the story we don't even know if we've been
here." She taught Adam the songs she liked:

> Wrap your chops
> Round this stick o'tea,
> Come along, get high with me.
> I'm twenty-one, I've just begun,
> I'm viper mad ...

She also taught him another song:

We're poor little lambs who have lost our way,
Baa, baa, baa ...
Gentlemen songsters off on a spree
Doomed from here to eternity,
Lord have mercy on such as we,
Baa, baa, baa ...

"My little lamb, my doomed gentleman songster," she said sitting with him on the back porch, and sometimes she told him about the doomed in their family: a cousin, J. Sledge Waters, a young lawyer who had fallen in love with a woman in Quebec City; he had lived with the woman for a year, speaking only French, but then he had come home to his mother who'd wanted him to herself. He had wakened one morning unable to speak, his tongue swollen, and he sat in a daze as his mother fed and nursed him for two years, dumb-mouthed, but his mother told everybody that her love, her special love would bring him back to talking, and he woke on a summer morning and began speaking, only in French, his tongue tied in English, and he never spoke to his mother in English again and he went to live and die in Quebec. Flo said she'd seen the tomb once, a tall, wind-pocked stone angel wrapped in its own wings. "Its wings were like a cocoon," she said as they sat looking at the rows of garage roofs. "One morning," she said, "I thought I saw him, the same angel standing right over there on the peak of that roof, the peak of Mr. Klein's house, moving his lips. It must have been a message or the play of the light."

"Does light play?" he asked.

"The light plays all sorts of tricks," she said. "So you never know what's going on."

He loved the garages, the slopes and tin gullies and rain-gutters, and often after school he sat on a pebbled asphalt roof and stared at the glare of the sun against the rows of windows. Sometimes, he sat alone with a deck of Bicycle cards Web had given him and he played solitaire. "If the Queen of Spades comes up too soon you always lose," Web had told him. With other boys and bandy-legged girls he sucked the sweet nectar out of lilacs, hidden by over-hanging branches, and when the maple trees went to seed – their lime-yellow propellers spinning through the air – they peeled the seed-pod propellers apart and wore the pods on their noses and took off their clothes to look at themselves and put the seed pods all over their bodies. They were uncertain, shy, and a younger girl – Marybeth Dignan – said to him, "Well, look at this." It was white and hairless, a vacancy. "But you've got nothing there," he said. "My mother told me every boy wants what's there," she said. "Well, I've got hair," he said and they lay unclothed and watched squirrels. "My father told me," Marybeth said, "that squirrels are only rats who look good because they live in the trees." They made a sound like squirrels by sucking air through their back teeth. Down below, a couple of men who thought they were alone stood in the dark in an empty garage. They were hiding, too, and then they laughed, and Adam knew it was Al, the Acme Farmers milkman who had let him ride in the truck early in the morning, shifting the wire-and-wood milk cases, but now Adam was too old for that. Al had strange wet eyes. "Vaseline eyes," his mother said. Some older boys sometimes slept overnight with Al and they whispered about Al kissing them and Al's whisker-rubs and how he gave them cases of milk for their families. After Grandfather Waters had died, Adam's mother had given him the dead man's long-johns, the dead man's underwear, but he secretly handed them over to Al because Al said his legs were always cold in the wintertime. Adam had seen them drying one afternoon on a laundry-line, flying in the wind, the cod-flap open, empty, and he stole them back because he loved flying things, like the kites he flew from the garage roofs, and balloons, so runty and flaccid until the boys blew life into them, batting them in the air, letting them dance on their fingertips. One hot day, a boy brought fistfuls of balloons to school and they all blew them up while a nun wrote on the blackboard ... THE EXPLORERS OF THE NEW WORLD – PONCE DE LEON ... when she turned around, the air over their heads was filled with balls of bouncing color, their hands outstretched, and she stood there stricken, and then she ran to all the windows, throwing them open, and she waded into the balloons, trying to gather them toward the windows, trying to clear the air, but they caromed away from her until all the students were laughing and she fled from the room.

He studied Ponce de León, the short man in a floppy hat that he'd seen standing in a book beside a drawing of a waterspout that looked like a giant celery stalk. He studied him because he had come clanking across the sea in an iron suit, sitting down on a poop deck under an umbrella, scowling over old scouting maps of islands and rivers lined with gold pebbles. He had read the stars and crossed the ocean and Web said that what was wonderful about him was he loved the hills of his own illusions. Web liked that so much he wrote it down in his book. "Yep," Web said, "he sailed the ocean that men full of good sense and fear said was flat and told him he'd fall off, sailed into the abyss that is always filled with possibilities, and then years later he looked into a mirror of polished gold and gagged because he wanted only one thing ... his youth, and when cannibals told him there was a miraculous fountain in the islands, he packed up, smiling and full of hope, and discovered the front porch of the dead, Miami Beach." Web laughed and slapped his thigh. "And then Ponce disappeared."

The next day Adam asked his mother, "Did you ever worry you were going to disappear?"

"Disappear? We're all going to disappear."

"I don't mean die. I mean disappear."

"Where to?"

"I don't know."

He was standing in front of a mirror, and there was another full-length mirror on an open closet door behind him. He could see tens of images of himself down endless oblongs of reflected light.

"It's like I'm a hundred me's," he said, "a whole bunch of me's I don't know, and maybe they're nobody because they all got no shadows."

"Everybody's got a shadow."

"They don't. They're just me, disappearing."

"But you're right here."

"They make me feel empty, like I'm leaking away into wherever you go inside mirrors."

He stood against the glass facing him and breathed on it. He drew his finger through the mist, and then the mist disappeared, leaving the faint trail of his finger, a faint smudge.

"I like having no shadow," he said. "A shadow's like having a reminder."

"Of what?"

"I don't know. All the things you and Dad remind me about, you're always reminding me."

"Of what?"

"Of you and Dad."

* * *

His hotel and the Five-Star Bar were surrounded by drunken soldiers. Their great-coats looked as if they'd been made for Polish winters. Two sallow-faced white women sat behind a wire mesh screen on his floor in the hotel. One wore her hair in a bun. It held pencils. She was brusque: "Coffee in the morning, six-thirty – room service quits at six-forty-five, you're on your own after that." In the murky half-light, he looked back down the semi-spiral staircase to the lobby; doors were ajar with single men sitting back-to-the-wall staring out; in stringy undershirts, they were having a last cigar before bed, blue smoke layering the rooms, framed by the doorways, as if he had taken their photographs – lonely men posing like prostitutes he'd seen in Hamburg sitting in the windows of whore houses, the same brazen, defiant loneliness in the eyes, and when whores winked at him as he worked around the world he wondered if they saw the same loneliness in him, that same reckless dislocation in his pale blue eyes as he'd seen in the eyes of men just before they were shot, shot for terrorism in a stony field by politicians who'd seized power as assassins but now held press conferences and complained of a moral collapse in the free world. When he brooded this way he felt alone and solitary, and lucky to be solitary. His room had a steel frame bed and a thin felt mattress. The room was so desolate he was sorry he didn't have the black girl and her laughter with him again, so he opened up his camera cases and set up a little aluminum stand at the foot of the bed, positioned a camera on it, set the timer and lay down with his hands linked behind his head and took his own picture. "There," he said. "There you are." It was about eleven o'clock. He could feel the *boom boom boom* in the walls from the polka band *and in my blood your laughing eyes* Gabrielle's eyes that haunted him, *and your mouth like a wound I've tried to suck free of all your past loves that went into my innards like a worm, but had to be taken in, bloated and killed in the blood of my love for you, and so now there is only the present ... a silence in the courtyard of my waiting ... and your voice, a whisper I cannot quite hear, yet I feel it in the streets of our childhood, so little distance really travelled with everything telescoped in my mind, in the dark, in the quiet of midnight when I went walking, houses as a child I thought were evil, houses in which old ladies lived, left behind with their dead dreams ... and my mother (and yours: how do you learn to live with your mother killing herself?) destined to end up sitting alone on a stoop staring at the sun filtering through the trees ... or maybe someday discover the mystery of her and my father, the little revelations, as if each word between us in the phosphorous bay were a song, and each time I told you I loved you, it was a song, a song against the sorrow of the heart, a song against the withering, the way I keep my mouth from going dumb with loneliness, with the dumbness of death that lurks off in the distance ... I sing yet with the honey of the honey sac of your cunt in my throat ...* and he heard footsteps in the hall and then a knock on the door.

"Who's that?"

"The police, come to the door."

Naked and suddenly cold, he opened the door. Two black men offered no identification. They were in their thirties and casually dressed. One, with a moustache and a plump belly, stood back smiling, as if his presence were a mistake. The other, self-assured, taut, wearing dust-pink jeans, spoke as if his jaw were locked at the latch. There were no accusations. He wanted Adam's passport and said, "We'll be back."

Adam felt a sudden lethargy, as if sapped of all his blood, and he fell back into a half-sleep, dreaming that his sleep was a dream, that he was never going to sleep again and he would never know why and Gabrielle would never know he had come after her. When they returned, he sat naked on the bed.

"Yur under arrest."

"You're kidding."

"Get dressed, mek yur bags together."

"What for?"

"I jess tell you."

"You mean I'm going to jail?"

"Yes."

"Why not leave the bags?"

"Get dressed."

"But it's midnight for god's sake."

"Get dressed."

"I could sleep here, at least ... let's look after this in the morning."

"You wouldn't sleep."

The woman with her hair tied into a bun was at the desk. She had plucked a pencil from her hair and had prepared the bill. "Do you mean I've got to pay?"

"You must mek pay," the secret policeman said.

"It's none of my doing," the white woman said, smiling.

His bag and the camera cases were piled into the back of a Land Rover. They drove to a police checkpoint. Soldiers milled around the back of the Land Rover, and then two of them got up beside the bags. There was a little moonlight in the cloudy sky, a smear of light, and the soldiers grinned through the back window as they drove along the dark, almost unlit streets, leaving houses behind until they were driving into gaps and shadows in the nighttime bush, sitting in silence in the cab, Adam staring straight ahead, insects smearing against the windshield.

"I study criminology by correspondence," the driver, the man wearing pink jeans, said.

"Does it help?"

"Help what?" he asked coldly.

"Whatever ails you," he said, smiling.

"You think it is funny?"

"No, no," he said, suddenly wary and wishing he had said nothing. "Look, do you think we can stop for a piss?"

"OK. You mek pee, the river is here. Usually they pee fast, some time in your pants."

With the Land Rover parked aslant on the shoulder of the road, they walked through long grass wet with dew down to a sandy shore. They stood side-by-side, Adam pissing into the river, and then the policeman, saying very quietly, "This is not funny," punched him hard in the chest, a sharp right cross that sent him to his knees, hacking for air, pissing on himself. "Yur lucky I do not kick in yur face. You mek respect now for education."

He walked back up the slope, leaving Adam bent over on his knees.

"Come to the truck as you can be able," he said, "and do not run. Yur going to prison or my boys shoot you."

The cell was attached to a courtyard of twenty-foot stone

walls. It had an open window and a steel mesh door. The cold damp wind blew through the cell. The walls were painted black. The toilet was an open bowl. The wind picked up the smell of shit along the floor. The walls were covered with scrawled notes: a drawn skull, a dagger, and TELL THEM WHAT THEY WANT TO KNOW – THEY'LL FIND OUT ANYWAY ... "Probably scratched into the paint by the police," he thought, suddenly aware that he was humming the *Dance of the Sugar Plum Fairies*, and he remembered the peculiar smell of dust in his mother's living-room rug, a child marching tin soldiers across the floral patterns of the rug, and finding a sugar plum coated with dust caught in a corner behind grandfather's chair, grandfather's white hair, dead of an explosion of blood in his brain and his winter underwear still in his boyhood dresser, afraid to put on a dead man's clothes. He lay down on the foam rubber pallet on the concrete floor. It reeked of puke and the shit-scared sweat of other men. He dozed though the overhead light was kept on. They opened and slammed the steel courtyard doors to keep him awake. At first light, a young cop with a line of little pimples along his left jaw came and called out, "Graze time ..." He asked, "What's that?" The cop said, "You know, like animals, you graze ..." He put a tin plate of brown bread and a tin cup of thin coffee on the courtyard floor just as an old man in his late sixties came into the yard. He had a bemused smile.

"Can I see whoever's in charge?" Adam asked.

"The colonel."

"Can I see the colonel?"

"Colonel not here," the cop said.

"What have I been charged with?"

"Dey mek charge for you."

"Ich will mit dem herrn Kommandanten sprechen ..." the old man said quietly and shook his head as if he were tired and bored ... "that's what they all said." He walked away and then came back, taking Adam by the hand. "I thought you'd like to know, I'm a professor. I work with these people."

At noon, they came for Adam. He'd been standing close to the courtyard wall. Exhausted from lack of sleep, body clammy with sweat, he'd been trying to get heat from the sun that hardly entered the shadowed well of the high walls: he reached up, holding his hands into the sunlight, shivering in the damp, mildewed yard. As he walked out into the sun, blinded by the light, to his astonishment he heard himself thanking the guard, who said, "Don't blame me." Upstairs, in a main building, three sets of barred doors had to be unlocked, and inside a wire enclosure, two men waited for him. One was the sad-eyed, pasty-faced old professor with the rueful smile. The other, the colonel, was wearing smoked glasses. He had olive-brown skin tight on the bone, like a polished gourd. He said, "Our professor is here to record de record, but you have de right to say nothing if you want to say nothing."

"What would you like to know?"

"Tell the professor why you are in jail."

"Why?"

"A guilty man knows why he is guilty."

"Are you a cop, Professor?"

"I help out," he said. "I'm here to help you."

* * *

The old four-storey stone mansion, his school on the bluffs by the lake, had been the first insane asylum in the country, but then – after the war – when shattered men came home from the trenches, crowding into the halls with their camp cots – the parish had bought the house from the government and made it into a seminary. "We are the soldiers for modern sanity," the bishop had said, and the seminary had been filled with scholastics learning medieval logic, but then the study halls slowly emptied as fewer men wanted to be priests and so the bishop made the mansion into a school for boys. The old wooden stairs between classroom floors were worn. The plaster walls above the varnished wainscotting were painted pea green. The white porcelain latrines in the basement had a wide gutter that stank. There was a coal furnace beside the latrines. It was stoked by the caretaker, a silent man whose arms were tattooed, who muttered, "I am the man at the bottom of things," as he threw another shovelful of coal into the fire. Every day he swept the school floors with an inward look in his eyes, and then he went down to the furnace room and sat in front of the open damper and sometimes his face was red and covered with sweat as he leaned toward the flaming coals, smiling. Sometimes, in his first years at school, Adam stood so close to the fire that his face got red and the caretaker pulled him away. "Go upstairs where you belong," he said. "This is no place for a boy." He sent him out to the lane with a bucket of twisted cinders and clinkers and one cold winter day he said, "Maybe that's what little boys do in purgatory."

"What?"

"Carry souls out to cool in the snow. Maybe heaven is all snow. Maybe God is only a caretaker at the bottom of things."

part THREE

There was a small courtyard beneath the colonel's window and a brick hut with an open oven. The hut faced the graveyard. Two beautiful adolescent girls wearing mourning clothes cranked the oven bellows, selling baskets of bread, candy animals, and cookies. A path ran through the graveyard with grey wooden markers on either side. The path ended in a swamp where men tended grass fires. Black birds swooped out of the smoke.

The colonel and the old professor faced him, their arms folded. They said nothing, and then the professor asked about photographs, and had he ever taken pictures with one of those box-shaped cameras ... the kind that had hoods you dropped over your head ... and did he know what it was like to have a hood dropped over his head? The professor had small yellow teeth. "You mustn't worry," he said. "The colonel only has justice on his mind." They stood up and the colonel tucked a riding crop under his arm. "The question," he said, "is state secrets." They left the room.

Adam got up and went recklessly to the desk and thumbed through some papers: "Joseph Poni appears to have no political interests or involvements. We will therefore continue to keep him under surveillance." He went back to the window and sat watching the women and the graveyard. There were no trees in the yard. It was barren, the grass sparse. Some of the mounds were well kept, the earth raked, and there were strange icons on the mounds ... a small red sports timer's clock, a licence plate TJ 199-491, jars with dried roots tied to them, and an empty milk bottle ... and he remembered reading ... *those things which were the marks of subversion are now relics*, or maybe old Itzak Klein had said that, standing on the porch stairs in the early morning, wearing a skull-cap, a velour dressing gown, and his slippers, and whenever a car went by he gave a little wave as if he were saluting an old friend, or he waved at Miss Skinner standing on the other side of the street, drunk, her hair mussed and her skirt on backwards. She was scowling. "Adam," she called out. "You should come back to your side of the road."

"Leave the boy alone, now," Klein told her.

"You'd like me to call you a dirty Jew, wouldn't you," she yelled.

"I wouldn't like it," Klein said, drawing his dressing gown closed.

"You would, too," she yelled striding out into the road.

"It'd be a mistake, Miss Skinner," he said coldly. "A big mistake."

"Mistake. You think you can tell me about mistakes." She made two fists and pushed them into her cheeks, her eyes full of tears. "You've got it backwards, I'm the authority on mistakes."

"I suppose you are," he said. He sat down on the stairs and stared at the distraught woman in the middle of the road. "For you, Miss Skinner," he said quietly, "I will say Kaddish."

"And for me?" Adam asked.

"You! You should dream your youth. Over and over again," Klein said, clapping him on the shoulder, "but only after you go to school."

In the school music room, Miss McCorckle, one of his spinster teachers, used a long knitting needle to conduct the class. The spinster ladies were friendly but an aloneness clung to them. As a child, when he'd first come to school, they'd gently touched his cheek as if they'd forgotten something. "There was a child once ..." Staring out a window beside Miss Hamlin, he'd seen a sign that said ADANAC MIRRORS and he'd said, "What does that mean?" She touched his head and said, "That's the country spelled backwards." She was crying. She'd told him to sit in her lap. She was in charge of collections for the African missions, in charge of canned goods and used baby clothes, and one day Adam knocked over several cartons of canned soup and the cans rolled and banged down the stairs. "You've bruised all that food," a nun yelled. "How can you bruise soup?" he asked. It was the nuns, not the priests, who punished them, dour women who had the sour smell of springtime frost easing out of the earth. They gave boys the strap. Sister Saint Alban, her chins chafed by a starched wimple, curled her lip and made him wet his hands with snow to sharpen the pain. "St. Sebastian didn't cry," she said. They'd been taught all the lives of the saints and martyrs, and how the Indians had picked the flesh from Father Brébeuf's broiled bones with clam shells. There was a picture of Brébeuf in the hall, and also a tinted engraving of the lean muscled Sebastian tied to a pole with long arrows in his thighs, his loincloth loose, staring ecstatically at a gold star. Sister Saint Alban collected pictures of the martyrs and made them copy the pictures. One day, she gave Adam a prize for drawing, a tennis racket with all the strings broken. "You get your father to fix the strings," she said. "That's what fathers are for." Adam stood the racket up in his bedroom window and looked through the strings at the clouds, and once, with the racket close to his face, he looked at his father and said, "You're coming apart." Web laughed. "That's right," he said. "People are always coming unstrung. I'm unstrung, Harry's unstrung." But, to Adam, Harry had always seemed so sure of himself, standing up in the middle of mass as soon as the priest went into the pulpit, leaving the altar by the back door, a Protestant choirmaster in a Catholic church who refused to listen to the sermon. "I've a patchwork character," he always said, laughing, and went into the sacristy where everyone was sure he sipped the mass wine, and then his face appeared pressed against the glass in the door, peering out, his hand cupped to his cheek, a cigarette tucked in his palm. When the sermon was over, Harry hurried out to the organ. The choir sang the *Credo* and Adam thought it was wonderful that Harry didn't believe what they believed as he danced on the pedal notes.

"I think we can get this done quickly," the professor said, as he and the colonel came back.

The colonel laid his riding crop across the desk. Two very tall ebony-skinned men came in behind him. They were in long white dashikis tied at the waist with black and red cord. They sat down at the desk, and as the colonel sat down, too, putting on his flight glasses, Adam realized the colonel's jacket did not match his trousers. *How many goddamn armies has this guy been in?* and Adam straightened in the chair beside the window, aware that again in his life he'd been hopelessly foolish, wearing his disdain for danger on his sleeve: *You guys who go around so aloof like you can't get your asses shot off*, an old journalist had told him, *it's just a form of showboating. You'll get yours*, and as the old white professor, his hands covered with liver spots, flipped a wall switch, Adam wondered if this was it: was he going to get it here, wherever here was? A ceiling fan began to turn slowly.

"Our officials of the revolution," the professor said, "led by the colonel who you have already met, will review your case." He took out a notepad and pencil.

"What case? I only came to the coast three days ago, how could I have done anything?"

"That's to be seen. Among your papers is a police card ..."

"Sure. I'm accredited everywhere ..."

"Perhaps not."

"Where?"

"Here."

"But I'm not working, I'm not here to work."

"Which is suspicious. Is it not? Why are you here, why would you ever come to our country if you're not working?"

"Just passing through."

"Ah, what luxury, to just pass through ..."

"Look, I want to know what's going on."

"Do you now?"

"Yes."

"Don't we all."

The old professor smiled, but it was a smile of rueful menace.

"I guess you've seen a lot," Adam said drily.

"Life still surprises me," he said sternly.

Adam decided he would not show the old professor the small photograph of Gabrielle he carried, a photograph trimmed to the shape of a playing card and kept in his deck as a substitute for the Queen of Spades, a substitute for the black queen, so that when he played solitaire on the road she would suddenly appear, sitting by a table on the hotel room balcony in Puerto Rico, bare-breasted, head back and eyes shut, sunning herself after lunch, an almost empty bottle of Montrachet on the table. *Wouldn't you go after such a woman?* but he knew the professor would never dream of anything so foolish, let alone believe that Adam was a foolish man.

The colonel tapped his middle finger on the desk. Staring at Adam, he began to speak in a whisper, a guttural, unintelligible whisper that at last took on its own music to Adam's ear, and he realized it was Arabic ... that the colonel was talking to him in Arabic, making some kind of statement, and he wondered how he could be hearing Arabic this far south, but suddenly he heard the word REVOLUTION and the two tall men bristled and shook their heads and began to speak angrily to the colonel, also in Arabic, and Adam said helplessly to the old professor, "I can't understand ..."

"It is not important. But have you been to Chad?"

"No."

"It's not important."

"So why'd you ask?"

"It's not important."

"But ..."

"If anything is needed from you ..." The old man smiled,

and a dry tightening in Adam's throat became a sharp pain. He winced, and could feel the nerves gather and pull at the base of his scrotum, so that he had to lift slightly off the chair. *O Jesus, how the fuck could this happen* and he crossed his legs and tried to look calm, even bored, as bored as he had been sitting beside the hotel swimming pool in Cairo waiting for a telephone call from the Revolutionary Council in Amman, waiting calmly week after week. The waiting he'd learned to put up with as a journalist ... the pockets of inaction between surges of energy and exhilaration, the mind-sapping inaction as he watched Swedish airline stewardesses sun themselves while they read old Arthur Hailey novels, "The bland reading the bland," he'd said sourly to an Egyptian Jew who was the correspondent for *Le Monde*, and the correspondent had smiled and said, "Frankly, I find them astonishing ... I fuck them and look into those pale blue eyes and I know that in there is the light in the abyss, it fills me with hope." Adam had laughed and ordered champagne cocktails for the girls at poolside, waving to them gallantly. But one afternoon, the gull sails of the ancient boats on the river filled him with a melancholy yearning, and an absolute certainty that he was wasting his time, and because he'd known for over two months where Gabrielle was supposed to be, he booked a flight south, to the west coast, to confront his own wondering about what was still there between them, to assuage the loneliness that left him feeling distant when he was with other women, watching them, almost amused but seized by sorrow, a loss that always woke him when he was beside a woman early in the dim light of dawn, the same dim light as in the colonel's office, the colonel's glasses like pools of dark water, a black light under the water. "What do you think?" Adam said to the professor. The three men, seemingly so angry and gruff with each other, paused, disapproving. The professor touched his lips. "Shh ..." he said, and held out his hands comfortingly.

Adam slumped back into the chair, aware he was sweating, and he felt cold, afraid and determinedly indifferent to the voices, to the guttural lilt, as if he were not there at all and could therefore not be judged ... all his life he had refused judgement, the condemnation of himself, of others. He hated the easy righteousness of vindictive people, *all the finger-pointing bastards* (except he could not escape a dream that dogged him year after year ... an anxiety that bored like a bit of light through the blackness of his sleep, a night when he'd wakened sweating because it seemed a piece of his past had been dredged out of forgetfulness, a forgetfulness that he himself had willed, a forgetfulness that would leave him free from confronting the crime he had committed ... murder ... almost able to see the drifter, a faceless old man with big bony hands, bony shoulders in a loose jacket, grey stubble on the chin ... luring him underground into a parking garage, back between the cars, the long sleek fenders, and cracking an iron bar across that faceless skull, a tire iron ... and as the dream light shed itself on the shoulders of the unknown man, Adam woke up deprived of the face yet seared by the act, by the belief he had killed ... and that unbelievable moment was so real, so believable it left him shivering in his bed. He'd ransacked his memory, trying to find the face, the actual moment, the motive ... sure that he'd been so appalled by the death, the meaningless murder, that he had shoved the blow into the shadows of his memory. But the truth seemed clear, felt if not seen, because he could not shake the conviction that he had caught himself at last, and the more he tried to locate the face the more he shrank into terror, condemned, so that he leapt out of bed, panic-stricken, and rushed into the streets to be near someone, anyone. Standing on a corner with the lights changing from red to green to red he relaxed. But the dream came back time and again, the face almost clear, and though he knew he was innocent, he was afraid he was guilty, a fear in his marrow, and this fear, when he took it apart during the day, bemused him because he was not easily frightened. He did not easily show fear. When gun jockeys in the side-streets of Beirut had stuffed the barrels of their automatics up under his chin and hit the action bolts to see if he would flinch, he'd smiled, all the muscles in his abdomen drawn, that peculiar pull in the nerve endings in the scrotum nearly taking his breath away, but he'd kept still. And it was the stillness in him that fascinated people, particularly women, as if he had – with a casual recklessness – taken himself into corners and dead ends where only men aloof from littleness went ... men who seemed to side-step fear. And he'd come out of all those corners because he was not afraid. He'd hunkered down inside himself, sure that patience would prevail, that all he had to do was keep loose and wait out the confused maniacs of the world, like this tribunal trying him in a language he didn't understand as he sat like someone abandoned in dead space. He wanted to laugh but he knew with a cold clarity that all killers, like cops, hated laughter, and to resolve their confusion they might kill him, just to clear the air, just to stop the laughter. Maybe that dreamt murder was an act to clear the air, if only in his dreams ... to eliminate an act ... though no face was ever there, and it struck him that maybe the missing face was his own, that maybe going off unprotected down rivers and into jungle towns like this was only a death wish, maybe he was trying to kill himself and these dark men gabbling at him were accomplices in the act, driven men in their own sour sweat. Yet now he was not sweating. He felt lethargic, pointlessly innocent, and looking out the window he saw that in the early dusk the moon was already up before the sun went down. Why, he thought, does the moon come up before the sun goes down? ... *The shadow of what's to come*, and he wanted to yell at the sun still shining on the barren graveyard, outraged and suddenly certain that if the sun went down they would take him out and shoot him. That was the sign of the timer's clock ... men who'd been shot, and he heard himself whisper so quietly that even the professor didn't notice *Ponce ... you had all those tattooed ladies*, but suddenly the professor, snapping his pad open, said, "They want to know, since you were – according to your passport – in Beirut, did you know a man called Khassan Kanafani?"

"Yes," he said eagerly.

"How well?"

"Quite well. He saved my life, and ..." He hadn't thought of Kanafani for years. Not since he'd been arrested by the Saica commandos in Shatila camp in Beirut, and Kanafani had negotiated his release.

"They would like to know who his wife was?"

"She was Dutch. I forget her name, but she was Dutch. It was a little strange, his being with her and being ..."

"Such a revolutionary ...?"

"Yes."

"He was a martyr!"

"Well, the Mossad got him, and his niece too."

The colonel and the two men listened to the professor. They nodded and scowled, and the colonel took off his glasses and squinted as he leaned forward to look at Adam. Then he put his glasses back on, and the wrangling seemed to begin again, with one of the tall black men wagging his finger at Adam without looking at him. He suddenly wondered if he'd been too eager, too helpful; it was one of his weaknesses – an open helpfulness, a generosity – that seemed too often like vanity, like the casual grandeur of someone who assumed he had nothing to hide, and he knew some men, in a way he could never understand, hated his openness. Perhaps these men had hated Kanafani ... after all, the soldiers in the streets carried Uzis, and loyalty these days was only to your arms dealer, and again he felt a terrible tiredness ... *of old men pecking stones and picking the bones of beheaded fish*, and where had he read that, and *pain was a pearl of milk in mother's mouth* ... that was his mother, she'd said that as she sat scissoring paper squares and then she'd unfolded them into snowflakes that she'd burned in a dry holy water font beside the bedroom door:

ash is evidence
of the sacrifice we make,
absence of water
the pain in which we partake.

She had said that and laughed. Leaning his head against the window pane he, too, laughed quietly, watching the mourning women close down the bread oven and walk away with their baskets strung out on poles, past mercenaries at the gates eating candy animals, their faces reddened in the sun, *and that's what Ponce had told the Indians ... that he was the red-faced son of the sun and he'd set up a sundial so they'd know at exactly what hour they were going to die, and they'd believed him ... after all, they thought the mountain streams were the magic urine of spirits who spoke to them out of tree trunks* and at a hook in the Puerto Rican coastal road, through a stone arch in a wall, he had found the old Spanish cemetery by the sea ... poor Ponce's cemetery, poor old Ponce, his skin sapped blue under the eyes, gambling everything for his fabulous fountain ... the cemetery a rococo stone clutter commemorating the dead piled up on Ponce's dream ... the tang of salt on the wind off the ocean. Then Adam licked his upper lip, realizing he was sweating again, the taste of his own salt in his mouth. It was almost a year since he'd been in Ponce land, in Puerto Rico with Gabrielle, and had tasted the salt of her. Suddenly the colonel and the two tall men in white stood up. The colonel took off his glasses. He handed Adam's papers to the old professor, who shrugged and said to Adam, "You are free to go."

"Really?"

"Yes."

"Why?"

The professor smiled. There were gaps between his small yellow teeth.

"Those under arrest," he said, "never know what to say." The colonel and the two men left and the professor said, "It is not easy, being arrested, is it?"

"No."

"I was in a concentration camp, in Germany. Yes. Three years."

"You were!"

"Oh yes."

"And now you work for the secret police?"

"Someone must be punished."

"So why me?"

"Nothing personal," and he took out a tin box of cigarillos, each scissored in half. "Smoke?"

"No."

"You are a good-looking man. I was watching you."

"You were."

"Yes. It's my job, to watch. You have a nice sullen impassivity, if you don't mind my saying."

"You're sure?"

"Ah well, who can be sure of anything these days? But I'm sure women find it very attractive, that sullen mouth of yours."

"I wouldn't know."

"Ah, you are offended ... Well, you are also free, because the colonel is a scrupulous man. He's even ordered that your car be brought around for you. I would have shot you, you see. The fewer pictures the better, that's what I say."

"Verdi," Adam said and left the old professor looking puzzled.

* * *

There was a small room on top of the mansard roof of the old stone school, a room with windows on all sides and a widow's walk. Sometimes a priest would sit alone in the light-filled room, staring out over the water where the long tankers loaded with grain moved slowly past a spit of land, the Eastern Gap to the harbor. In the autumn, before the first snow, a boy was chosen to chisel and scrape the year's pigeon lime from the slate roof of the little room, his feet wedged into the rain-gutter, his head bobbing against the blue sky, and it was old Father Zale who said, "The bird is the symbol of the soul, the lime the stain we leave in time." The boys who wanted to be hockey players, who sat in class squeezing tennis balls to strengthen their grip, laughed, and one of them called out, "A bird in the hand is worth two in the bush, unless your hand is in her bush." Father Zale broke a ruler across the boy's shoulder, raising a welt. "Out of the mouths of brutes ..." he said, and began to write on the blackboard:

if $x = y = 1$
then $x^2 - y^2 = x^2 - xy$
$(x - y)(x + y) = x(x - y)$
$[x + y] = x$
$x + y = x$
$x + 1 = 1$
$2 = 1$

and he turned to the class and said, "There are some things in life that seem obviously right but are absolutely wrong, and until you understand that you understand nothing."

Sometimes men with pale blue eyes and closely cropped hair stopped Adam in the street near the school and told him the Church was a whore and the priests fucked the nuns in secret tunnels. Web, who was home again and treating Flo with an elaborate courtesy that unsettled her – as if it were some signal of pain to come – said only a fool could believe the city was full of nuns and priests in tunnels. "The terrible thing is, though, the world's full of fools who believe what they want to believe and they'll kill for it. Pay no attention to grim fools," he said. "Laughing fools are okay, but not grim fools." He patted Adam's head. "By the way," he said, "have you found out what fucking is?" Adam shrugged and said, "It's got to do with vacancy." They both laughed, but for years whenever Adam saw a vacancy sign in the window of one of the rooming-houses he liked to think the woman of the house was advertising for fucking. All his boyfriends talked about in the evenings was fucking and how they didn't dry-bone a girl any more, they fucked her, and Esther Klein, the week before she got married, showed them her vaginal cream. "That's because he's so big," she said laughing. "Not like you little peckers." Esther's father – Itzak – who drank clear tea in a glass and wore a black fedora at his supper table and ate chicken boiled so white it reminded Adam of the hands of the albino boy in the crèche – had grown sullen and silent, like all the men who wore the little round skull-caps, as if they were expecting the worst, and that year tough gangs cropped up all over town. Adam stood by an iron fence and watched a van-load of Albany Angels drive by looking for Jews ... chanting Bring Out Your Kikes, Bring Out Your Kikes ... and they had chains and baseball bats and their clubhouse was in the stone cellars of St. Alban's Church. One of the men with the pale blue eyes, who wore shorts and knee-socks and was a scout leader, drove the van, and one afternoon, to prove how tough he was to the van driver who delivered soda and seltzer water, he ate a raw sausage. "I bet you eat dick raw, too," one of the truckers said. "I eat the likes of you alive," the man with pale eyes said. The truckers laughed. "Eat shit," they said and when Adam laughed the scout leader chased him down the street, tripping at last over a tree root. "I'll cut your pecker off," he screamed, sprawled on Miss Skinner's front lawn. But then the gangs suddenly disappeared as inexplicably as they had appeared and the man with the pale eyes was appointed to the police commission, and Esther got divorced as soon as she came back from her honeymoon. Web went on the road again. "All men," Esther said, "are no-good pricks."

* * *

John Mayberry Waters
1897-1942
Qualis Vita,
finis ita

* * *

Women living and working alone sometimes ran screaming from the rooming-houses into the stillness of the night. The police patrolled in slow-moving cars and Adam and two boys were taken from Sibelius Park for no reason to No. 11 Station and back-handed across the face by a burly cop who had little sweat pimples all over his neck. His mother, however, said things seemed normal to her. Sometimes there were gunshots in the streets, but no one called the police. He hung around with an older boy, Arthur, whose father was a minister in the African missions, and there was a big photograph of the man over the mantelpiece. He wrote long letters home to his son: "Homesickness with the blacks is stronger than a fear of death ... many of them are indeed men who have become human animals, not merely savages, but creatures who have sunk below the level of savages ... I daresay we should have fewer difficulties if we could occasionally sit round the fire with them and show ourselves to them as men ... but there is no time for that, as they cannot comprehend our reverence for life." Adam and Arthur agreed they should like each other because their fathers weren't home very often. In all his photographs, the minister had a razor moustache and was dressed in white and was surrounded by black children. Arthur sat on an overstuffed sofa with dried equatorial wildflowers framed under glass on a table and they went through Adam's *National Geographic* magazines, ogling the bare breasts of black women, but then Arthur said, "That's kidstuff." He had a pile of *Playboy* magazines. "Now that's twat, man. How'd you like to be trashed by that twat?"

"But they've got no hair between their legs," Adam said. "Women have got hair between their legs."

"Hair's too sexy," Arthur said, "so they shave it or airbrush it out. My father says Eve didn't have any hair between her legs till she was booted out of Eden."

"She had a vacancy."

One day, alone in the back garden, Arthur showed Adam a .22 rifle. His father had given it to him. He and his father had gone down to the bluffs and fired round after round into the emptiness over the lake. "There was nothing to hit, not even a seagull. It was just a lot of stupid empty sky." Arthur was on his knees filling a dozen Sheik condoms with tap water. He knotted the balloons and then clothes-pegged them to his mother's wash line. They hung there like grey tears among the hollyhocks and he sat on the stoop and fired, letting out a little whoop with each explosion of water, and when he was done, he said, "It's too bad your father doesn't give you a gun, then we could play real cops and robbers."

"Jesus, we'd kill each other."

"So? It'd be real. I'm sick of make-believe."

Harry O'Leary said that he believed in his daughter because she really believed in the make-believe world of dancing. "That's it, plain and simple," he said. "She's going to go to New York as a dancer and with a little bit of luck she'll knock 'em dead." He rubbed his large hands together. "Some people don't believe in anything." He touched Adam's shoulder. "So they don't lose anything."

"My mother warned me I was going to lose my voice."

Harry held his cigarette in the cup of his hand. "That's how it is every year. A voice breaks. You got no choice. We got no choice in who we are, or how we do. You gotta grow up, and forgive those around you for making you grow up. But sometimes you come back with a bigger voice," and he opened his arms wide. "You come back when you're a man, you'll get your man's voice."

Then one day Harry told Web that there was going to be a big stakes race at Woodbine racetrack and the president of the Jockey Club, a cripple who came to mass in a wheelchair, had asked Harry if his wife and his beautiful daughter Gabrielle wouldn't like to present the silver cup after the race and have their picture in all the newspapers. "Oh, this is a big chance," Harry said. "A girl who wants to be in show business has got to get noticed and this is a big chance. That's what show business is, your notices."

On the afternoon of the race, he wore a grey silk tie and grey spats, and his wife, a puffy-faced silent woman with auburn hair in a snood, watched him and stood apart with a strange wariness, a bruised air. That was the look in the eyes of the older women on his street that Adam had seen, their faces suddenly at windows, full of loss and panic, trapped behind glass. But Gabrielle was calm and wore white high heels. "They'll eat out of your hand," Harry said, stroking her hair fondly. "Yes," Gabrielle said. "I know men." She wet her lips and looked at herself in her pocket mirror. Web shook her hand and said, "God bless the child that's got its own."

The next day, there was no picture of Gabrielle O'Leary in the newspapers. There had been a midnight fire in the barns and several horses had been burned alive and all the pictures were of the fire in the night. Flo bought all the editions and then forgot what she was looking for and began to scissor out recipes. "It's funny," Web said. "What Harry wanted was her picture in the paper. Some people don't think they exist unless they get their picture taken." She nodded and smiled. He said it again and wrote it down in a little notebook.

Adam went out and climbed onto the roof of a garage behind the house. He felt a terrible sadness, remembering the haughty look in Gabrielle's eyes, as if everyone was finally going to know how well she thought of herself, but now no one thought of her. He wished he could cover Gabrielle with seed pods, but only Marybeth Dignan was up on the roof, and as they snuggled into a hidden corner he taught her a song, surrounded by the leaves:

> *Two Irishmen, two Irishmen*
> *sitting in a ditch,*
> *one called the other*
> *a dirty son of a*
> *Peter Murphy had a dog,*
> *a dirty dog had he,*
> *sold it to a lady*
> *to keep her company.*

She fed it, she fed it,
she fed the little runt,
it slipped up her petticoat
and grabbed her by the
country boys, country boys,
sitting on a rock,
along came a bumblebee
and stung'em on the cock
tails, ginger-ales,
five cents a glass,
if you don't like it stick it up your
ask me no questions
tell me no lies,
if you get hit
with a bucket of shit
be sure to close your eyes.

Then they took off their clothes and she had delicate blonde hair between her legs but as he lay on top of her she said, "No, no ... I don't want to break it, I'm a virgin, I'll suck you." She pushed her long hair back from her face. "You have to promise though, no coming in my mouth. You can come on my tits." When he came, there was a small pool between her breasts that began to trickle down her rib cage, so he cupped his hands and scooped up the semen and was confused, wondering what to do with it, but she giggled and dipped her fingers into his cupped hands as if they were a font and said, "It's full of hormones, it's the best thing there is for a facial, at least that's what my older sister says," and she rubbed the semen into her forehead. They got dressed and climbed down from the roof by a rope ladder, going through a broken board fence so they could avoid Miss Skinner's garden because of a lightning-struck tree that was there, its limbs sawn off and the bark stripped, a lustrous dead-white tree with fungus shelves at the base and mushroom tents in the spongy earth. One of the boys had said, "It looks like my dad's dick." The tree had been known ever since as Dad's Dead Dick and since childhood they'd all been afraid of lightning.

But he stopped going up on the roofs. He usually sat alone reading in an empty shed between the garages. It was where families used to keep garbage cans, a little house with its own window and rat holes in the floor-boards, an overgrown doll's house. He had swept it clean and painted the walls pale blue and as he sat in the shed, playing solitaire or just moving his hand in and out of the floating dust in a shaft of sunlight, a man suddenly spoke to him. "What are you doing in there?"

"I don't know. Daydreaming."

"Dreaming. It's dirty dreaming in there. You'll get a disease."

He was Lester Wrong, a frail old man who was secretive and gentle. He had been one of the inventors of TNT and had worked for the government on the development of the atomic bomb. "You'll get sick. There's nothing worse than rats."

On Firecracker Day, he told everyone not to waste their money on burning schoolhouses and pinwheels and Roman candles because he was going to create a pinwheel of light on the lawn. "You'll see stars," he said. They all sat on the stairs as powders and chemicals were spread and then there was a quick intense flash of magnesium light, and when the smoke cleared the lawn was gone. The landlord, Mr. Myles, refused ever to seed the ground again. "It's like the mark of Cain," Web said, and soon after Adam and three other fellows hosed down the plot so that it was a lake of mud and then they had a tag-team mud wrestling match until Flo cried, "Get outa there, look at you, you're filthy." She cracked him across the back of the head and he was so surprised and sorry to have angered her that he couldn't help crying, but his tears had never upset his mother. "Tears are good for you," she said. "They wash everything away." When he was lonely he tried to cry but he couldn't, and there were times when he felt so lonely that he didn't think of crying. He stared into a hole in space, which was the way he stood one afternoon in Christie Pits where he played baseball, where the old drifters, unshaven and sipping cheap wine, spoke to him, telling him about rowing races on the lake and how the rowers were called scullers and the boats sculls. One of the old men died, falling down near second base, trying to scoop the base under his head like a pillow. He rolled over on his back, his eyes open, and began to shake and flop his arms, trying to wrench his bones free from his heart while the other old men shuffled in a loose circle until the dying man jack-knifed and lay still, a line of blood coming from the corner of his mouth. Another old man came close and covered his face with a newspaper. "Wait'll you see this." He opened the dead man's shirt. The dead man's smooth hairless body was tattooed all over with fish, fish arched in the air. "What d'you make of that, eh? He wouldn't eat a fish to save his soul." A red stain appeared on the newspaper.

*   *   *

Here lie the bodies
of GIBSON WATERS and ALICE his wife
She was temperate, chaste, and charitable,

BUT

She was proud,peevish and passionate.

She was an affectionate wife, and a tender mother

BUT

Her husband and her child whom she loved

Seldom saw her countenance without a disgusting frown.

Whilst she received visitors whom she despised with an endearing smile

Her behavior was discreet toward strangers

BUT

Independent to her family.

Abroad her conduct was influenced by good breeding

BUT

At home, by ill temper.

She was a professed enemy to flattery,

And was seldom known to praise or commend,

BUT

The talents in which she principally excelled

Were difference of opinion and discovering flaws and imperfections.

She was an admirable economist,

And, with prodigality,

Dispensed plenty to every person in her family

BUT

Would sacrifice their eyes to a candle.

She sometimes made her husband happy with her good qualities.

BUT

Much more frequently miserable with her

many failings
insomuch that in 30 years' cohabitation he often lamented
That in spite of all her virtues,
He had not in the whole enjoyed two years
of matrimonial comfort.
AT LENGTH
Finding that she had lost the affection of her
husband
As well as the regard of her neighbors,
Family disputes having been divulged by
servants,
She died of vexation, July 20, 1898,
Aged 48 years.
Her worn-out husband survived her four months
and eight days
And departed this life Nov. 28, 1898,
In the 54th year of his age.

WILLIAM WATERS, brother to the deceased, erected
this stone
As a weekly monitor, to the surviving wives of this
parish
That they may avoid the infamy
of having their memories handed to posterity
With a PATCH WORK Character.

*   *   *

On Holy Thursday night, he was in the choir stall. Across
the altar, a lone plain woman sat reading her missal. He
watched her. The priests seemed to sidle around her, drawing

close, and when she leaned near the rail they shied away and she rocked back, white-faced. She had the holy curse, the stigmata, the bleeding wounds of Christ. She came from a small town on the Black River. She opened her hands and then knotted them in prayer. He saw the red welts. All the choirboys had been warned that if she bled they were not to move, they were to keep on singing because she held the divine pain in her hands, and he waited for her to cry out but she was silent and took communion alone in her stall. He wondered what she did with her hands, whether she ever drank alone or knitted or chain-smoked and whether she had blonde hair between her legs and what she would think if he streaked her face with the dust of Itzak Klein's butterflies.

"Maybe some people," his father said, "are bleeders, just like some horses." He wrote that down in his book, but Adam said, "They looked like little red stars in the palms of her hands." Web laughed. "So does a spider's bite. Looks just like a little red star, the spider's kiss. Or maybe she's just starstruck."

Adam shook his head. "But maybe there's supposed to be no connection," Web said. "Maybe god just fired a blast of buckshot into the sky and that's it, stars, a buckshot wound in heaven and she had her hands up when the gun went off."

"It's like the tattoo man who died at second base," Adam said, standing in the doorway. "It's little dots, and if she's starstruck it's god who struck her."

"Ah, the gods," Web said. "The sky's full of them."

There were many men in the streets who had tattoos ... stippled blue daggers and dragons and names and anchors. They worked in the gardens or sat in the sun in their undershirts. A soldier who had just come home and had only one arm, covered with *shazzam* lightning bolts and harpoons, winked and said, "You've got a while yet but your father'll find a war for you. That's what fathers are for." Sometimes at lunch Adam bought himself fish-and-chips in a newspaper funnel and stood in the doorway of a tattoo shop on Dupont Street, watching the tattooist dart his needle into the skin of silent, passive men, leaving the little purple wounds, and one day he asked a fellow whose arms were blue with a lacework of animals and who had a camel tattooed on his neck if it didn't hurt, and he said, "No. No, it makes me feel good."

"So how come you did a camel?"

"A camel can go for ever without water," he said.

"I can't stand needles," Adam said. "Every time I go to the doctor I get sick."

"Yeah, well then, you're gonna have a painful life, kid."

*   *   *

Samuel Waters
was blind in one eye
and in a moment of confusion
he stepped out of the receiving
and discharging door
of a Front Street warehouse
into the ineffable glories
of the celestial
sphere
1898-1928

*   *   *

Then one day he and Gabrielle started going to the movies. She had dark almond eyes and wore white peasant blouses. Her breasts were large and full. As they sat in the dark with their arms around each other, she solemnly explained that she loved her father and could always smell his hair, but she let Adam touch her breasts. "My mother says men are very greedy." She kissed his fingers. One night, they went walking by a hedgerow and he stripped off a handful of red berries. "Don't eat those berries," she said, "you'll die." He laughed and told her how his grandfather had said the same thing and how he had thrown handfuls of hard little berries at windows in the night and she said, "My mother is always looking out the window." That night while her mother and Harry were at the hospital visiting Harry's sick brother, she took off her clothes and they huddled under the blankets in her bedroom and then, with a startled cry, she sat up in the lamplight. There was a line of dark blood down her thigh and the sheet was stained. He was afraid but she was excited by the blood. He had expected her to be pained or hysterical, to shudder with some great sense of loss, but instead she was at ease and satisfied, even a little smug, and so he laughed and shrugged, too. But he was disappointed. He masked his disappointment by sitting cross-legged and hunched forward on the bed, as if he were completely self-contained. She suddenly streaked his brow and cheeks with the blood on her fingers. "There, now you really look like a chief." He kissed her and pushed her onto her back and entered her again, this time into blood, aroused by the rank smell and the wet ease. "My mother will kill me," she said, and laughed. "She doesn't want me to grow up."

They made love in the shed behind Adam's house, lying on an old blanket that had belonged to his grandfather, their legs locked together, gently rocking as someone with a cane or a strange dry cough went down the alley. One night Miss Skinner came out into the darkness in a chemise, drunk and singing quietly, *"There's no business like show business."* She did a little pirouette and then sat down in the cinders and whispered, "Well Gerald, how do you like them hot licks?" He told Gabrielle that he had often waited alone in the dark as a child for lights to come on in the windows, bursts of light in which somebody was doing something private and un-suspecting ... just as no one suspected they were there making love.

"What do you think of when you come?" he asked.

"Nothing."

"You can't think of nothing."

"Sure, that's what's so wonderful. It's all light, it's like being flooded with painful light and you just want more pain ..."

"You're lucky, you can come while I'm in you."

"If you come in me I'll die," she said. "I'll die if I have a baby, though I'd love to have a child."

Then one night they heard the rustling of a rat under the floor-boards and they huddled together, afraid of being bitten, and after the rat had gone he licked her nipples and she fondled him but they ended up unmoved and only cradling each other and she said, "I'd cry if I could ... I don't like it out here in the dark any more."

"My mother and father sit in the dark," he said. "They light candles and she says they talk best in the dark because they can't see each other's eyes."

"Talking's for old people," she said. "You're tired when you're old so you sit and talk. My mother talks to herself."

"I sing to myself," he said.

"My mother says I only think about myself," and she laughed.

A month later, Adam stopped Harry by the weeping birch in the church yard and said, "I think I lost my voice, I'm just pretending when I sing." Harry smiled. "I know, but sometimes pretending is the best you can do and that's better than doing nothing." Adam quit the choir and his mother cried because she said a boy's voice was like a crystal glass set singing by the wind and his father, who was home again, said, "Oh, that's lovely, I like that," and he wrote it down in his little book. Adam said he felt like he was a stone. Web didn't know what he meant, so Adam said, "I lie awake listening for my voice inside myself but I don't hear anything so I feel scared and lonely and one night when you were both asleep I started singing, 'It's a Grand Night for Singing,' just like when I was a little kid except it wasn't my voice or anybody's voice."

On Christmas Eve, he went to mass with Gabrielle and there were steaming overshoes under the hot radiators and the air was heavy with candle smoke and incense. He knelt beside her and they prayed and held hands, listening to the choir. Adam felt a bitter yearning, yet he never wanted to be a boy again. He watched Harry leave the altar during the sermon. Then his face appeared in the glass, lean and drawn, and Harry stood all through the sermon against the glass as if he were a fugitive, and for the first time Adam saw a fugitive look in Harry's eye, but then Harry hurried out to the organ. Adam held on to Gabrielle and they went to communion together, the gold paten catching all the light under their chins as they drew into a gentleness and closeness and a sense of purity that was so sure, so confirmed by communion, that it was sensual, and as they strolled home through the cold snow-bound streets they cradled each other and walked slowly for blocks until they were tired and there were no lights in any of the windows.

They went into her dark still house, and with her mother and Harry asleep, they undressed and he knelt and kissed her cleft, breathing in her musk and salt dampness. She wet her fingers with her saliva and rubbed her nipples. "Why do you do that, what do you feel?" "It's like a direct line to my cunt, it makes me tingle more while you lick me." They made love in front of the fire in the fireplace, and after they muffled their cries, trying to keep quiet, they sat staring out the window at the stars. "This is terrible, sinning like this after swallowing Jesus."

"We aren't sinning, you can't sin if you're making love."

He gave her his silver watch. He didn't go to confession because he didn't believe he'd done anything wrong. He tried explaining himself to Father Zale under the old trees by the bluff, facing the water, but the priest shook his head and said, "A man might think of anything to avoid God." In the spring, Adam stopped going out with Gabrielle. For some reason she had withdrawn inside herself and lay watching him while they made love, her body still eager but her eyes clouded, unyielding. He said, "I love you," and she said, "I love you too," and they talked about the sadness of life and how true love always had to be tinged with the sadness of loss, and Adam felt older and stronger, as if he were suddenly capable of bearing the remorse-soaked sweetness of life. "I'll always love you," he said, savoring his sadness – so that he felt at last that he was a man – and she took off her clothes and said, "Just look at me, I want to think of you always seeing me." She kept the watch. "It was like an eye," he told his father, "and I never liked the way it looked at me."

"That's good," Web said. "You should write that down."

*　*　*

"Just write it down, that's good," the desk clerk said, as Adam stood at the counter in the crowded lobby of the hotel in San Juan where he'd gone because he liked to gamble, liked to shoot craps. A large enamelled Buddha holding a shiny brass lotus sat behind him mounted on a block of marble beside white wall sconces filled with silk flowers. Adam, leaning on the Buddha's knee, was dressed comfortably in a dark green silk shirt, a light linen jacket, a Liberty print tie, and soft leather loafers. Several years ago an old gambler had told him, "The Chinese understand ease of mind begins with the feet. If you ain't easy in your mind you don't win. Tired in the ankles and arches is no good if you're gonna go for broke."

Energetic and eager women milled in front of the elevators wearing braid and silver fringe, sequins and tassels, and many had electric-permed their hair into hives after a day in the sun and salt wind. "High and shellacked," a bellhop with his own bleached hair said to Adam. "They look like their clothes were designed by an architect."

Then, after a burst of applause, a bride in a swirl of lace and confetti rushed through the revolving doors and four women began to sing in harmony: *"Mr. Sandman, send me a dream ..."* The brushed-steel elevator doors slid open and the singers disappeared but the lobby was still crowded and another bride appeared, spinning through the revolving doors. "What have we got, a fire sale on weddings?" an old man called out. More confetti was thrown and another group of women began to sing:

Moon river ...

"What in the world is going on?" Adam asked.

"Oh, it's wonderful. They're Sweet Adelines," a woman with brown pouches under her eyes said.

"Who?"

"Barber shop quartets." She clapped her hands as four other women sang:

We ain't got a barrel of money,
Maybe we're ragged and funny
But we travel along,
Singing our song
Side by side.

All the women began to crowd into a big outdoor amphitheatre attached to the casino hotel. A pasty-faced St. John's Ambulance girl said, "They've been here for two days. They're so hearty, they never pass out, there's nothing to do." Adam stayed in the lobby, listening as the "Show of Champions" began: quartets called the Deb-N-Aires, the Singrays, the Whispering Dogwood Chapter – and they were introduced by a Marlene Peddle who said she was from Moscow, Idaho and she told jokes: "Even birds have a canaryable disease," she said, "Chirpies." Portly women smacked their knees and spread their legs and laughed.

"Why in hell would anyone come here for that?" Adam asked.

"It gets in your blood, I guess," the bellhop said.

Adam left the lobby and walked across Calle Cristo where some of the confetti was blowing in the street to a church of gleaming white plaster walls. The windows had been bricked in and someone had painted false windows onto the brick. Inside, under a vaulted ceiling, there was a carved cedar altar and little wooden columns gilded with gold, the spires and cornices so riddled with termites that only the gold leaf held the wood together. He genuflected before the flame in the red glass hanging by a chain from the ceiling. Then he went back out into the broad formal square with its dwarf trees and wrought-iron benches: on a high stone pedestal, with only a carved garland and wreath, Ponce de León stood in his iron suit, one hand on his hip, the other pointing off into the hills of his illusions, his body a bottle green, the statue made out of discarded cannon melted down. Adam walked around the pedestal, smiling, *and you see mother, this is what I saw, not your breasts but the naked yearning to keep coming back into the world, the naked yearning* the morning he'd walked into her bedroom just as she was lifting a chemise over her head, and instead of the strained, sometimes wary woman who smoked too much and played harmlessly with fire, he saw a taut bare body, the hollows of the knees, the quiet unsunned breasts, the wall of the rib cage and the tuft of black hair ... so much thick black hair, sluttish against the track of pure white skin ... so that he forgot her tired smile as she stood unmoving *looking so young ... so young with the life that is created within us, the inextinguishable light of a day shining, seeking the magic urine of the gods,* and later that afternoon Flo had stood dressed by the sink running tap water over a head of lettuce – her nakedness unspoken – and she'd said, "Adam, you peel me one of those big Spanish onions."

He'd begun to strip the brown brittle skins to the first wet whiteness.

"Take it down layer by layer," she said.

He made little slits with a paring knife and peeled away sections. His eyes began to water.

"How far?" he asked.

"All the way."

He took away a layer and then another, the ball of onion shrinking in his hand, tears streaming from his eyes, and he began to laugh.

"Get right down to the heart," she said.

He pried and peeled and then there was nothing in his hands, only flaps and broken layers of onion flesh on the counter. "See," she said. "You can know what you want, where you're going, but when you get down to the heart, there's nothing ... only all the left-over bits and pieces, and your tears ..." She turned off the tap. "Now, scoop them up and put them in the pan. We'll fry them up good."

part FOUR

After an ice storm in January, the black branches of the trees were sheathed in ice. In sunlight the air seemed filled with crystal veins of blackness. Web slowly eased a tube of ice from a twig and blew across its open mouth, making a faint high note. "Music melts away in your hand," he said. That evening, he took Flo and Adam to the Conqueroo club on Queen Street. Neon lights rippled around a sign: THIS WEEK ONLY – THE LEGENDARY WEB "SWEET" WATERS. The small intimate nightclub was owned by Johnnie Kufu, a fighter who had been billed for a few years as a "White hope" but he'd suffered a detached retina while sparring with Muhammed Ali. ("He laid his black hand on me and put out the light.") Johnnie led them down a narrow hall of mirrors, drumming his fingers along the mirrors, hand touching hand *looking to see if he's really there* as the hall opened onto a dimly lit room, a petal-shaped dance floor, and a small bandstand. Kufu, who stared at people with a lopsided grin because of his eye, was effusive. "Sweets, we don't do a week this good since I don't know when. Look around kid," he said, laying his heavy hand with its swollen knuckles on Adam's shoulder. "Packed ... the only trouble is I got a doorman who keeps wandering away for little walks ... he likes to look at antiques in the windows along the street for Christ sake ... and a girl working the bar who's so dumb her tits are in a trance." He held a chair for Flo at a table close to the small bandstand. "Champagne," he said, and hurried to the kitchen, coming back with a bottle in a silver bucket. "I got a convention of thieves in here tonight," he said, "and you know what's wrong with thieves? Thieves love to steal. No matter how successful. Before they go out with the wife, they got to steal a credit card from someone, or else they won't go. I got a roomful of stolen credit cards tonight." He poured the champagne into chilled fluted glasses and laid his hand on Adam's shoulder again. "Now what am I gonna do, Sweets? Your kid's a man already, a regular man *but a man sports a lady, that's what Dad said one night looking Mother up and down till she got up and said, Sit down, you're outa line, 'cause you're mine and that's that, and he said, Shut my mouth* pretty soon I'll have to let him in the joint alone."

The waiter tied big white bibs around their necks. They ate lobster dripping in butter. "Always order male lobsters, kid," Kufu said. "Don't ask me why but the male species steams up sweeter." They were joined by two blacks – Rufus Paillard, known as Rueful, and Slim Ottis. They were Web's sidemen. They were older men who sat like polite grey-haired school-boys with their brass horns laid across their knees. Adam stared at Rueful's hair, straightened and slicked into a combed cap close to his narrow skull, and he wondered why his father had always wanted to ride from town to town with such dark men, their black skins shining, bluish, like wet stones that had hidden indigos, copper, and mulberry, *and how'd he get his hair like that? shining like tinsel* staring, so that Rueful said, laughing, "They call that conking, boy ..."

"What?"

"Some black mens conks their hair, you get some lye and lard and if you can stand the burning on your scalp then you can stand the good womens." He let out a little *Whoooee* whoop and slapped his thigh and sang:

> *I got 500 women, I need 500 more*
> *Then I gonna snap a padlock on my door.*

"Kufu says the room's full of thieves," Flo said. "No lock's gonna lock your ladies up tonight, Rueful."

"That's why they call me Rueful," he said, wagging his head, "since I always know what's going down, but also what's going down be coming back up, least, that's what my momma told me. She says that's all Jesus done ... He gone down to come back up on the great getting up day" *and Mother told me, the earth is always pushing up a stone, every farmer knows that: you plough and plough and then go stone picking, like there's an unending supply that appears like stone birds, and when you die and put your bones back in the earth, they put a stone on your head, in place of your head, and carve a face in place of your face, which is you being remembered and if you're remembered then you're still alive ...*

Web wiped his mouth with his napkin. He closed his eyes and massaged his temples as if there were a deep soreness inside his skull, and Adam was suddenly afraid, but then Web and Rueful and Slim stepped up onto the platform to loud applause and for a moment Web sat at the piano staring into the spotlight, blinded, the lines around his mouth deeper

than Adam had ever seen them before, enclosing a mournful-
ness, and Web sat very still, unable to see in the light. Then he
crouched over the keyboard and sang:

> *Me and my baby we fuss and fight*
> *Jess the next morning everything's all right*
> *One of these days I'm going crazy*
> *Buy me a shotgun and kill my baby*
> *And it ain't nobody's business if I do.*

His hands loped along the keys, a solemn detachment in the
tilt of his chin and a disengaged stare, locked on a point of
light or fire in the air, intense yet aloof, lost so it seemed in the
stillness of remembrance, while Adam's mind wandered to
the stillness of the first time he'd danced naked with a girl,
*surprised at the lopsided heaviness of her breasts ("the left, over the
heart, always heavier") and the oval shape of her nipples ("drawn by
the weight, you dummy") as she pranced awkwardly, trying little
kicks, and I rocked back and forth, cock wagging until I said: "The
damn thing's stupid, stuck out in the air," and she said, "It's not
supposed to be stuck in the air," and then we tried to waltz, holding
each other at length, her hand cupped in mine, elbows bent, spinning
slowly and then leaping in wider and wider circles: "The goddamn
thing's going away, I'm losing my fucking hard-on," and she knelt
and held me in her mouth, her eyes closed, holding my buttocks,
pushing until I could feel myself against her throat, and then she fell
onto her back and easing into her I whispered, "It's the funniest
fucking thing in the world, a cock's goddamned loony," and she said,
"Just fuck, man, just fuck, it's sleepy time down south so turn out the
lights ..."* and one night Adam had been wakened by the
piano in the house, lying in the dark, seeing no crack of light

coming from anywhere, and so he'd gone down the long hall, feeling for the wall to the living room, staring into the shadows, the deeper shadows, hearing the *dunk dunk* of bent and flattened notes, *a loneliness in the silence between notes, the lip of the abyss, a kiss that led to strut,* and then he heard his mother's voice moaning low, half-whispering:

> *Tell me how long, how long*
> *That lonesome train's been gone*

and then *only the sound of breath, light breathing and no sound at all for a long, long time* and he'd felt a panic, as if a gap had sprung open in the dark and everyone he loved had fallen through, gone *a long time, gone though they were still there somewhere in the dark full of the promise of foreboding.* He'd flipped the light switch on the wall. Web was sitting with his arms folded and Flo, wearing scarlet high heels and a pink satin half-slip, was sitting bare-breasted on the piano top with her legs crossed, holding an unlit cigarette, staring out the dark windows. Neither moved. Web said: "Why don't you sit down, son ... kill the lights, with the lights on you can't see what's off in the dark, sit down because your mother's singing a song." He turned off the light. "You see," Web said, "just because a man's getting some shut-eye doesn't mean his eye has to be shut," and they laughed, *a laughter in the dark that was the easiest assertion of the self I'd ever heard, full of mockery of the daylight hours, of the locksmiths of the heart* and Kufu, drawing a chair close to Adam, said, looking up at Web's face held in the wafer of light, "Nice, eh kid! He can tinkle them keys, Sweet. Ain't nobody plays better on the black. Put him on a roulette wheel and tell him to play the black." Adam said the single line of sweat down Web's cheek looked like scar tissue. Flo blinked and said, "Oh dear ..." but suddenly Web stood up, hammering the keys, his eyes wide open, letting out a high-pitched nasal moaning cry of pain *tell me how long, how long* and Flo touched her lips as he hit a last chord, threw his arms into the air, and sang:

> *I drink to keep from worrying,*
> *I smile to keep from crying,*
> *So's to keep my good woman*
> *From digging what's on my mind;*
> *Someday I'll be six feet in my grave ...*

As Web stepped down to applause, Rueful took the microphone: "Like the man says, he's Sweet, he's delectable, he's irrepressible, impeccable, sensational," and blew Web a kiss. The crowd laughed and applauded. "Afterwhile child, so stick around, the best is yet to come" *oh yes now, she cried, her ankles hooked behind my buttocks, her strong thighs scissoring, biting my lip, pleasured and wanting my seed ... Cum, Cum ... Momma telling me about old tribes along the Danube whirlpools who had built stone altars on the shore, the fire pits facing the river, and when the river flooded the seminal waters entered the pit and put out the fire, seeding the land, and then the water receded – and lying beside her still body, legs closed, my seed hers, I said: "There was a kid next door, Arnold Hunter, who used to get a hard-on and then he'd pack his cock in wet mud and clay and lie in the sun on the roof and let it dry and then he'd crack it open and he had a mould of himself ... and he always looked sad like he was going to cry with his little shrivelled-up white dick staring at that bigness of himself in the earth* and Web sat quietly for three or four minutes, a strange stillness in his body, holding Flo's hand as if they were sharing a very private consolation, and then he smiled, patting his hands together with pleasure, the lights dimming so that they were sitting in shadow.

"You feeling good?" Web asked.

"Okay," Adam said.

"No. Not okay. How you feeling?"

"I don't know. Relieved, maybe."

"Relieved of what?"

"I don't know. Just like suddenly there's a space, spaces where nothing needs to be said."

"That's good, I like that."

"I don't know whether it's good or not."

"Yeah, but I do. That's what music is, that's what art is, man."

"What?"

"The spaces, what's left out. But some guys, when you hear them play, they're filling every hole there is, like grave diggers filling in holes, but it's the silences between, what's left out between notes, that carries the music."

"Kufu says you play only on the black notes."

"Kufu's cock-eyed, he's hearing only the tone to the silences in between."

Adam folded his arms and closed his eyes. He could hear whispering behind him and shuffling feet on the dance floor; dancers, though there was no music. He did not turn around, afraid they might not be there.

"What are you doing?" Flo asked.

"Nothing," Adam said.

"Nothing?"

"Maybe I'm trying to find a silence. Somewhere inside a silence."

"Haw, that's great," Web said, just as Kufu sat down, and suddenly they were talking about baseball and spit-ball pitchers and whether or not a great athlete ever needed to cheat and how terrible it was with politicians telling lies – not that they lied – but that the people, the pit bulls in the bleachers, now applauded their lies, promoted the lies ("It's like some Oreo cookies pretend Johnny Mathis sings soul when he ain't nothing but a black Tiny Tim," Rueful said), and there was so much laughter and clinking of ice cubes in glasses that Adam lost the sound of the dancers on the floor turning to their own inner music as he sat humming:

> John Brown's body lies
> A-mouldering in the grave,
> But his truth goes marching on ...

Just before the closing hour, taking Web and Flo by the arm, Kufu walked them to the long hallway of mirrors, effusive and filled with a need to be generous that left him helpless and confused. "Great, great," he kept saying over and over again, and then, desperate to make some gesture, he picked up a huge potted poinsettia and handed it to Web. "Here," he said, "a token, a token of appreciation."

Embarrassed, Kufu shuffled back toward couples still huddled over their drinks. Flo, laughing at Web's face buried in red leaves, followed him down the hall but then Kufu heard a crash and a cry from the front door: "I got him, Mr. Kufu. I got him." Kufu came running and then stood as if struck: the tall doorman had Web high in the air in a half-nelson, holding him in a lock so that his legs dangled, his arms stuck straight out, his head tucked forward down into his chest. "Jesus

Christ," Kufu cried. "Don't you know who he is?" The roots of the plant had broken apart at Web's feet, the pot smashed, and Flo – knocked down by the lunging doorman – sat crosslegged, staring up, bewildered. Kufu kept smacking the side of his head with his hands as the doorman cried, "I got him, Mr. Kufu, I got the dirty thief."

"Jesus, no."

They told Kufu, who stood rubbing his hands together, not to worry, said goodnight, and drove home in silence where they stood on the frozen mud of the front yard, staring up at the dark windows. Web said: "What're you gonna do with me, a guy who wants to stay at home where his roots are but lives his life in hotels?"

At the end of the week Flo was alone at the window. She said to Adam, "Better get that big old dot of yours back up on the wall, your dad is gone, he's a gone goose." She had a pair of long shears and went to Web's closet and took out his suits and sports jackets and scissored an arm from one and a leg from the other, and she scissored Grandfather Waters' long-john winter leggings. She hung them all up again in the closet, piling the tubes of sleeve and pantleg in the fireplace where she burned them, sitting on her haunches in front of the flames. "Rest in peace," she said. She lay down in bed for the afternoon. The shears were on the bedside table. After that, the shears were always on the bedside table.

A couple of months later Adam listened to a raging argument when Web came home and found all his clothes scissored, followed by a stern unforgiving silence. "You cut yourself loose, babe," Web said bitterly and went to the Barclay hotel and night after night Flo sat alone in the dark. She would suddenly snap on the light and find herself staring into the mirror. She lit a cigarette and said aloud, "See, I knew you were in there all the time. You can't fool me."

"Dad's not fair," Adam said to his mother.

"Who said life was fair?" she said. "And besides, what's between me and your dad is between me and your dad. The less you know, the longer you'll love us."

"I'll love you anyway."

"That's how it is with me and your dad. We love each other anyway."

Then, in a few days, Web, full of easy laughter, said, "Your left hand must never know what your right hand's doing." He and Adam went for a walk. It was early autumn, their coat collars were turned up against a chill wind and they kept their hands in their pockets. "A man should never stand still," Web said. "When you stand still you stop being amazed at yourself, and when you stop wondering at yourself you know you're dead on your feet. The real killers are practical men, penny-wise, who think they know what's what but what they know ain't worth knowing. But they'll kill for it, bored by it all. You should always be amazed at every moment you have alive. That way, you'll never kill anyone."

By the gates to the church, a policeman was fighting with a man who was swinging a black satchel, trying to club the policeman with it, and the satchel snapped open and silver chalices fell out. The man wheeled and lunged wild-eyed at the policeman, who shot him. The thief lay in the snow, blood seeping through his coat. Web knelt down and undid the laces on the thief's shoes and held the man's ankles, looking up at the man's moving fishmouth. "He could've killed me with one of them cups," the policeman said, half pleading as he watched the thief's blood drain into the snow, turning it pink, the color of candy floss. A young priest came running out of the church. He said the final prayers over the thief and crossed his forehead with oil. Then the dying man said, "Y'ain't nothing, cop, nothing. You're a fuckin' zero." He died. "Rest in peace," the priest said. "Nice shot," Web said to the cop and took Adam by the arm and walked him away.

They sat in silence in a café and then after a while Web said, "What a man wants in this life is a quick getaway or nice easy loose shoes."

*   *   *

Ruth Waters
Daughter of Gibson and Alice Waters.
Died June 11, 1888
aged 9 years, 4 months, and 11 days.
She was stolen from the grave
by Roderick R. Clow,
dissected at Dr. P. M. Armstrong's office
in Port Hope
from which place
her mutilated remains
were obtained and
deposited here.
Her body dissected
by
a fiendish man,
her bones anatomized,
her soul we trust has risen to God,
where few physicians rise.

*   *   *

As he drove away from the colonel's office and the cemetery and the burning swamp fires, the old professor waving to him in the rear-view mirror, he took the twisting logging road into the bush. The rented Mercedes 300 skidded on the slick grades of mud. After two hours he passed a flagpole with a tattered flag he didn't recognize (a country that didn't exist?) and clusters of huts and one-room hutches and shacks, the rust-colored plaster falling from the lathing, the ribwork open, obscene – like flayed bodies – and there were oblong family graves by the doors, concrete pads set above the ground to keep out the white ants. He felt swollen, bloated by water, swelling with languid anxiety in the reeking dampness, the clammy humid decay dense with growth. In the middle of nowhere, a black smiling soldier wearing fatigues, running shoes, and silver sunglasses stopped Adam's car at a checkpoint and said: "De wrong time dis place, man, smart mek turn back ..." He was wearing a Walkman headset under his khaki cap and the checkpoint was a disused one-room gas station with a single rusted pump *I knew a girl who changed her hair from blonde to blue in a Texaco shithouse*, Adam thought as he said, "What you listening to, man?"

"Michael Jackson," the soldier said. Adam sat back and stared blankly into the well of overhead green, the dust-speckled windshield blurred, while the soldier kicked all the tires, as if he were a hard-headed used car dealer in the bush ... *like a distracted child whom they drag by the hand through the world my eyes cling sadly to things* ... lines from somewhere inside his head that forced their own solitude, suddenly heard for no reason, or no reason that he wanted to know. He drove on, with the feeling that he was under water, pressured by water. He became terribly thirsty, trying to drive on but finally stopping to drink his bottled water, tepid and gummy, almost a weight on his tongue, looking around because he had never felt so abandoned, *being at a precise point here could be anywhere*, surrounded by lush green feeding on itself, voraciously perpetuating itself, and he could feel the pulse of this perpetuating, except there was also a pulse in the dead and rotting foliage. Death is alive here, he thought, as he got out of the car to stretch his legs, bemused by being free on the loose by the side of the road, charmed by his bemusement. He found it impossible to imagine his own end – since there'd been none of the signs he was sure would signal his death – and if he couldn't imagine it, if he couldn't believe in it, how could anyone else? He knew this was absolutely stupid, but even now he refused to think about his own death, sure that if he did, he would certainly die, perhaps right there. He walked into a clearing just off the road, intending to have a piss, wondering who he thought he was discreetly hiding from, when he saw a boy of about seventeen, a beautiful head and muscled torso down to his hips *a sculpted beaming face, the white-haired boy charred black here in the bush*. The boy sat on the ground with thin legs like hoses under his hips. His family appeared and laughed and slapped Adam on the shoulder and asked him to come along a sunless trail to another clearing deeper in the darkness, to sit with the elders and drink palm wine from a communal cup. He suddenly was wary of their eager friendliness: *"Ich will mit dem herrn kommandanten sprechen ..."* He looked back, and in the gloom of filtered afternoon light, half-heaving, half-sliding down the trail, a wild gaiety in his eyes, smiling like a deranged crippled spider, the boy came after them, laughing, his legs flailing over roots and through the long grass. When they got to the village of ten huts where the palm wine was kept in big glass jars buried in mud, he saw two old men curled up close together holding each other's hands, locked into a detached serenity. "Waiting," the villagers assured him, *waiting* Gabrielle had said *you don't know how much waiting, stuck in this place, this narrow little world with its two-storey dreams so ingrown ... you don't know how ingrown, feeding off itself, feeding, sucking the lifeblood ... sucking ... singing their little local songs ... how I wait to get out of here, and some never sing, I've never heard my mother sing and my father never sings ... a choirmaster who never sings, that's a scream ... and yet he sits with my Uncle Jackie talking peace of mind, how to keep calm, "You ain't nothing unless you can keep calm, calm squatting in all this crap," and my uncle is a boss, Tonton Jackie they call him, a big man in all the back rooms ... brutal, a hood who sings, he sings all the time, his arms wide open as if he loved the world, St. Francis of Assisi in a zoot suit, and I know he's broken arms and legs and the heart of anyone who ever owed him anything, except Harry, he loves Harry because Harry wouldn't have any part of the rackets, like, somehow Harry made it all okay since he played no part in the strong-arm shit, no violence, except he slaps my mother, how do you like that, he slaps my mother and looks at me so forlornly as if I should understand, but understand what? ... why a woman should be slapped by a choirmaster who never sings while my uncle makes like his wife is the Virgin of Perpetual Light ... never touches her, never, though to be fair I think Harry never touches my mother either, not like a lover, at least that's what I see when he sits playing with my hair and strokes my wrist, and certainly no one has ever touched him, not in the heart ... but then, I don't know where my own heart is and how to touch it except I know I want out of here, I don't want to swell up and smother and die here with him handling me before I've even been young* and he drank from the jar. They all stood smiling at each other. A woman cleared her throat and spat. She drank and handed him the jar again. He shuddered, suddenly aware of disease, but he drank and smiled and then walked back to his car. "Maybe this is what it's like waiting to die." He drove away from the villagers, down out of the bush and high hills into a small plain of fields divided by a wide river and the road. The rutted road had wearied his arms and the endless green had left his mind blank yet his nerves were taut; he felt strangely aroused, as if boredom had left only the humid heat he felt through his loins. He thought of stopping to deal out his cards on the seat and play a little solitaire, as if that could be a sane, still, ordered moment, a promise of a future, and he could see again her shut-eyed, sensual serenity, his substitute for the black queen. But he kept on driving, and suddenly there were single files of children and old people moving along the shoulder of the road, the children leading the old people by short leashes tied to their wrists. He stopped and got out of the car, realizing the old people were blind, river blindness, and their children were leading them out into the maize fields as flocks of black big-winged birds rose and swarmed into the sky. The children left their mothers and fathers standing alone in the sections of the fields, at their work, human scarecrows. The children ran back to the road and as some leapt into the river, splashing and squealing, their bodies shimmering in the spray in the strong sunlight, Adam suddenly yelled, "No. No," waving at the motionless black figures in the fields, knowing there was nothing to be done, screaming, "No, it's all wrong," until the children crowded around him, laughing and giggling and prancing, as if he were a mad man.

* * *

It was late afternoon. Web phoned, saying he'd been in the city for several days, staying at the Barclay – he often stayed alone, unknown – he laughed, "You're old enough, Adam, to handle these things, the comfort a man can feel in his own aloneness, when maybe he's truest to himself, but it's hard being alone when you're sick," and he was sick and worried though there was no quaver in his voice, not that Adam could hear, "but the blood, you wouldn't believe the blood, it's like a great big yellow and red stain spreading all over my stomach and abdomen and it's like a stain in the wallpaper pushing through, all around my side." Adam went for him in a taxi, suddenly afraid that if his father died, his blood, his tap root, everything would drain out of his life and he alone would be left, the root *but of what? and who were you when your father died? a remnant, a repository, someone at last let free, especially after fending for him, for years yielding to the waywardness that comes from his life's long habit of doing what he wants, so a son ends up being the coddling forgiving father to a lifetime's acquired childishness* and as his father undressed in the cubicle in the hospital's emergency room he thought *I don't want to see him stripped down, defenceless: years ago I wanted him dead but now I don't want him defenceless.* His father stood barefoot on the grey marble floor, naked, talking about baseball as if nothing were the matter, as if they were in neutral space, all emotion neutered, and neither spoke of a silent unseen tumor, somehow spawned, nor said the dread word, cancer, the big C, but only stared at the yellow, purple, pink, sepia blood in rippled layers, a relief map under the translucent skin, *all the places he's been, the altitudes.* But the doctor, a young man wearing steel-rimmed glasses, shrugged and smiled as Web sat up on the brown rubber sheet of the examining table, his slightly bowed legs dangling *and his penis is so small*, remembering when he was a child in the bathroom, his father standing over the toilet, his penis between two fingers, thick, so big, so heavy, and now it looked like his memory of his own childhood penis, small, hooded, *shrivelled by fear, his only sign of fear, and why am I looking at his penis? when it is actually his bony feet, the long bony yellow toes and toenails that appal me, the hard yellow nails and the thin shins and crinkled blue veins and the flesh hanging loose under his arms like a woman's, the little womanly tits with tufts of hair around the small nipples (why do men have nipples? what taunting sign of ineffectuality, lost powers, sign of the lost rib, surrendered out of loneliness)* and laughing lightly, Adam said, "Goddamn, you sure look like the resurrection of the dead to me." The doctor laughed too and said, "Don't be so dramatic. You can thank your lucky stars, it's only a ruptured artery. Like everything that's easy it looks terrible. What's always terrible is what you never see."

* * *

After a two-hour drive along the ridge of hump-backed hills, through checkpoints that were only rusted Shell oil drums filled with sand, he shifted into second gear around several half-tracks and armored cars on the outskirts of the jungle city, their motors idling. The early evening sun was a red opal, the city house walls seemed all maroon and sepia, comforting, the color of dead leaves (*and Mom and I used to drive out of the city, into the Caledon Hills, to see the autumn leaves: "Beautiful, our most beautiful home season ..." always anxious to get into the hills before it was too late, the moment lost, before the winds blew the trees bare, black bones*) and at the central traffic circle where there was a bronze statue of a nineteenth-century French general with his head blown off, he waved jauntily to soldiers on the back of a jeep mounted with a 50-calibre machine gun. The gun was aimed at a row of stone houses. Two motorcycles drove past, men glittering with medals in the sidecars, beefy men with shiny brutal faces. A long white empty Mercedes followed the motorcycles, empty except for the liveried driver who waved back at Adam. The wide river through the centre of the city was yellow and filled with sandbars, swamps, eddies, and pocket ponds. Adam parked the car in front of a vacated shop in a small plaza by the shore, the windows and the yellow and black Budget sign shot out. *Cheap fucks everywhere.* The hotel was on an island in the middle of the river, and in the falling light the hotel seemed adrift on a knoll of luxurious leaves and vines. It was still hot, the heat was heavy, sticky, a glue against the temples. He crossed in a pirogue, a canoe hollowed out of a grey and salmon log. Fat old women were gathered on the other shore by the dock, beheading fish. All the heads were kept in a wide basket. *The head, the eyes, are best in soup*, Itzak Klein had said. The hotel lobby was unlit and he could barely see heaps of luggage and bundles in the brown shadows. There was dust on the luggage, as if it had been there for days. He could taste parching salt and the iron of blood in his mouth as he wandered from room to room. The empty barroom was also a tiny disco, the walls lined with grey-blue cardboard egg cartons stapled to the walls as sound insulation. Then suddenly, from behind the front desk, a wiry man who wore polished brown boots, shorts, and a white T-shirt lettered with M'BEGOV NIGHTCLUB said, "I am Henri. *Vas-y, poupée.*" He carried Adam's bags and black leather camera cases up the circular cement staircase to a room on the fourth floor. "There is air up here," he said. *"L'air absorbant l'absence dans la lumière ..."*

Adam slept for two hours and then went down for a supper of baked whitefish in a small enclosed balcony dining room facing the river. A lean woman with grey eyes *a strange still grey the color of dusk*, who owned the hotel, said, "Yes, we are in the middle of nowhere but we make amusement many ways, yes, we have a baby gorilla, very amusing, it laughs just like a human, like a man. Sometimes it laughs just like my Henri." She said that her name was Esmelda Waites and that she was the daughter of merchants who had died of black-water fever before the revolution, leaving her the hotel. She had one withered finger on her left hand. She went out to a thatched cage under the house and came back, wobbling slightly on her high heels, carrying a small gorilla about three feet high. The animal bolted out of her arms and bounded around the dining room from chair to chair, and then clutched Adam's leg, reached for his arm, and took hold of his wrist and tried to gnaw his fingers.

Adam held him high in the air by the hands and spun around as if he were on a carousel dancing with a dwarf, and then the gorilla swung his legs around Adam's waist, lips drawn back in a wild cheerless smile, and Adam held him under the arm-pits and began to tickle him and he giggled, a broken tenor laughter: then he wrenched free and leapt away, circling behind a chair, peering warily at Adam.

"He is a very strange gorilla," Esmelda said with distracted sadness. "You can see in his eyes, he knows he's going to die."

"You're always dreaming of dying," Henri said.

"No. I never dream. Do you?" she asked, turning to Adam. "Do you dream?"

"Not that much. Just the same single dream sometimes."

"What do you dream about?"

"That I've killed a man, and then I wake up and start counting and they're all there, no one's missing."

"I dream," Henri said, picking the gorilla up in his arms. "I dreamed last night of emptying bags of quicklime on anthills so I'd stay alive for ever and then a soldier said to me, 'The best friend a person has is someone who has just died.' I want no one to die, so perhaps I will have no close friends."

"Do you think there'll be real fighting?" Esmelda asked.

"Hard to say," Adam said.

"Everyone says something but no one says what's going to happen."

"Talk's cheap."

"Praise the lord and pass the ammunition," Henri said.

"But you took the road in, you must have seen something."

"Just trees and trees and checkpoints and jumpy bug-eyed soldiers. Some mortar positions down by the river ... I don't know, after all, it's your town."

"No, it's not," she said, "it's no one's."

"These bush battles," Henri said, "they are really just gang wars."

"Holy Christ," Adam cried, pointing to the ridge road on the other side of the river, a road that slanted down out of the hills. There, in the dusk ... a truck and flat-bed trailer, and seated on the trailer, the polka band, the five bulky white men in lederhosen and alpine hats were playing, broadcast over a portable loudspeaker system mounted on the back of the trailer, with a big blue and white banner – BAVARIAN BEER – fluttering over their heads, the bass drum and braying voices and *phfump* of the tuba echoing through the valley. The trailer truck pulled in behind a cluster of trees and stacks of rusting bedsprings close to a loading dock. The sound system was shut down: a loud echoing *pop*.

"Sounded like a shot," Esmelda said.

"What the hell are they doing here?"

"What a question," she laughed. "What are any of us doing here?"

"It is what Conrad taught us," Henri said. "At the heart of darkness there is always a German."

"I'd like to photograph you," Adam said.

"But why?" Henri asked, genuinely surprised.

"So I could study your eyes, why a guy like you is here."

"*Mais c'est très simple.* Love."

They sat watching each bandsman come across the river in a separate pirogue, brass instruments gleaming in the last light.

An hour later, Adam stretched out on a narrow hard cot. He was drunk. The floor was bare concrete, painted sky blue. *So which fucking end is up?* He shut the louvered window by propping a chair under the handle. Sweltering in the humid heat, listening to the bird ruckus in the trees, he lay in the dark wondering how he had come so far and would Gabrielle actually be there *and did she ever in this place where decay and monotony pervade, the green drab decay in everything, dream of sitting on our haunches naked in the hot water, facing … washing my sweat from your breasts … those looks we exchanged … so full of yearning, hesitation, pride, uncertainty, almost an inability to believe that we meant so much to each other … those looks, those pockets of silence as we waited, strangling with silence and the helplessness … your slender fingers, and before the mirror, that huge mirror, the pain of pleasure drawing deep lines in your face and your wonder that your face should be so drawn at the moment you felt such a rush of pleasure … such joy and unbelief that we had found each other …"give me your mouth" you said … "give me your mouth" … and I said all love seeds its own dying, its own decay and felt stupid for saying so because I loved you, tormented by ever losing your love, tormented because of the play of your fingers in the palm of my hand, lines of life and the names of hotels we will never see, the taste of salt and sweat, the run of your tongue along my lips and your low laugh when you nestled in against my belly and cock … I hear that laugh all the time, so throaty and warm, filled with pleasure* and he rolled onto his side, aching to find at last, perhaps in a day or two, her face … and he turned on the bedside lamp and stood up and went to the window: there were two dried and withered pieces of soap on the window sill; a sudden burst of gunfire, and then the silence that was never still but filled with cries and whistling frogs. He took a book from his small suitcase and lay down to read:

> *The morning glory of my life*
> *Is a tear. And as long as it grazes*
> *From flower to flower and forgets,*
> *My tears shall be turned to music.*

Long, tubular, wide-winged brown insects seeking the light came in through the loose, warped casement, wobbling out of the shadows, landing on his bare skin. He shuddered and shut the light.

* * *

The casino walls were covered with a plum moiré silk. There were chrome slot machines inside the heavy glass doors, several roulette wheels, twin rows of blackjack tables, and six craps tables. In the occluding light, the green baize of the tables had a seductive sinister sheen *the color of slime-covered stones in clear water*, and Adam went to a craps table, the croupiers in matching maroon suits, the stick man and pit bosses in black with an air of well-groomed disdain, efficient, bemused among the lunging betters. An elderly man, opening and closing a silver pocket watch, said to Adam, "I was in the Great War, before we gave them numbers."

"That's what comedians do to each other with jokes," Adam said.

"What?"

"They give them numbers. They don't tell the jokes, they just call out the numbers."

A woman in her sixties signed a marker for chips. She had a blade nose and was accompanied by a young man wearing a cream suit who carried a riding crop, wore rings on each finger, and had oddly flared, flattened nostrils. He was blind and held the woman's elbow. She took four stacks of $100 chips and set them in the wooden runnel along the table rail. The stick man scooped the dice toward her. She picked them up, holding the red cubes in her fingertips. The blind boy opened his eyes, an underbelly fish color, and said, "*Sol'eri in terra.*" She rolled a seven. The blind boy said, "*Se'nel ciel felice.*" She rolled a five and made several side bets; the field numbers, the hard-eight and hard-six. Her hand dangled, dice loose in her fingertips; the men around the table were unsure of her. The blind boy called, "*Sol'eri in terra,*" and she rolled, and then rolled again, and made her five, and this time she said, "*Se'nel ciel felice,* thank you Jesus." She scooped up handfuls of $100 chips.

"Praise the fucking Lord is right," a plump man with big fleshy ears said. Others reached over the table, bulging arms and thick necks, bodies bent, suddenly sure the old woman had the touch, except for a man Adam had seen the night before – a lean, imposing man he'd shied away from at the tables, a small-boned man, olive skin shining on his skull, with bird-quick cold eyes, his left hand encased in a taut, shiny black leather glove. Adam called him the Dead Hand man ... the kind of carrion bird, the lean bone-picker he'd often seen sidling through the crowd at Paradise Island, always betting against the winners in casinos, looking for the cold table, the sour faces of losers, his left hand a little black mould for the roll of $100 blacks he carried. He only played the DON'T COME line ... always betting against the shooter, always hunching his shoulders before each roll, counting on crap-outs, as the croupier cried *Saliendo*, the dice caroming around the curve of the table. "Crap," and the shooter muttered, "Shit," but this evening the old lady kept winning and the bone-picker was losing, looking into the face of the blind boy who had light dead on his eyes. (Web singing:

The blind man got a letter
while he sat in jail.
The blind man got a letter
in the daily mail.
The blind man burned the letter
said love can never fail
so long as love's unspoken
in the daily mail.)

Arms flailed, hunch-betters, their fists full of chips, tried to get bets down, and the croupiers chanted: "All bets down, big shooter coming out." The old woman smiled. The Dead Hand man backed off, his lips bunched, a drawn purse. She waited, and then she said quietly to the blind boy, "Is it a no-go, Nelson?" He nodded. She set down the dice and said, "Cash me in." The players howled. "What kinda Mickey Mouse routine is this, lady, you're red hot, lady, you're hot ..." The croupier shrugged and a man in a western hat said as they stacked her chips, "You gotta give a blind hog an acorn every now and then." The dice passed to a portly, pink-faced man. "New shooter coming out ... fine new shooter ..." He blew on them in his closed fist. "Baby needs new shoes ... Ten, ten ... the Big Dick from Boston took out his balls and wash'd em ..." The Dead Hand man bet $500 on the DON'T COME line. "Ace-deuce, crap." Everybody lost, including the Dead Hand, with only the house collecting on snake eyes. "Four thousand six hundred," the croupier said to the old lady, having finished stacking her chips. Adam followed her out to the lobby, into the humid night, the humidity relieved by light air coming in off the ocean.

The rose rug glittered from fallen gold and silver sequins, pink and white confetti littered in among the little discs of fallen light. The brushed-steel elevator doors opened and the old woman leading the blind boy stepped in as four women in blue chiffon stepped out and stood at attention facing the empty lobby. They linked arms and sang, *"Boom boom boom boom, somewhere there's music, how high the moon"* and went into the night. Adam said to the desk clerk, "Have you ever seen anything like this?"

"Are you kidding?" the clerk said, lifting his hand with amused disdain. "This is the real thing. Last week it was a Tupperware convention, hundreds of the little darlings, and they all showed up dressed as either the Yellow Brick Road or the Tin Man."

The heavy glass casino doors slid open. Two burly men in dark suits and mauve silk ties stepped through the doors. "There must be an undertakers' convention, too," Adam said to the clerk and laughed. Then, the Dead Hand man helped a long-legged and beautiful woman, braless and wearing a white silk blouse covered with small red stars, through the door. She had big almond-shaped eyes.

"My god," Adam said. The two men eyed him and shrugged. They all went quickly down the hotel steps to the crowded night street. Adam stood in the lobby, unbelieving. *Gabrielle.* He ran to the steps of the hotel just as a silver-grey stretch limousine pulled away from the curb.

He went upstairs and spread a sheet over a balcony lounge chair. He lay naked, the wind making a tearing silk sound as it swept around the hotel tower, and he listened to the breaking of the sea, the urge of the sea. Though it was two in the morning, grim men and women were down below playing tennis on floodlit fluorescent green courts, a constant *plock plock* of tennis balls, a hollow sound against the fall of the breaking waves, and he lay watching for the lights of cruise ships beyond the beach littered with empty deck chairs. The waves broke on two reefs, a white spray hovering over the dark water, silver hair combs in the moonlight, and he remembered the silver racing cup, the picture of Harry O'Leary's wife and Gabrielle standing beside a horse, smiling and holding a silver cup, the picture that had not appeared the morning after the race but only after Mrs. O'Leary had checked into the Park Plaza hotel, sitting down later and having a drink with two curators from the Royal Ontario Museum, men she had never known before, and then she had jumped off the rooftop patio and fallen seventeen floors and killed herself.

"Astonishing," one of the curators said.

"She seemed like such an orderly woman, she was so sensibly dressed, and what's more, she knew all about our very fine Chinese collection."

Gabrielle had left home for New York earlier in the week and could not be found. "This'll be the end of Harry," Flo said. "Those women were his whole fucking life." It was the only time Adam had heard her curse. They went to the funeral and three small boys in red soutanes sang at the grave. Harry slumped into Father Zale's arms and the priest said, "There's a lesson in this," but he didn't say what it was as he strode off into the tall trees on the edge of the burial yard. Adam let two grey speckled stones that he loved because he thought he could hear voices in them fall into the hole. They bounced off the box with a loud *clunk*. "Don't wake the dead," his mother said. "She might come back and tell you things you don't want to hear."

part FIVE

Adam woke with the first light. Cocks crowed. Esmelda knocked on his door. She had hot coffee and fruit. A milky steam rose out of the earth, a steam that turned acrid yellow in the sunlight and spread like rags over the swirling dun water. He peered through the shutters, waiting, listening to the rippling call of little birds and whistling parrots. The sun, a blurred hazy ball suspended low in the sky, was clearing the brush, turning the river into a sepia flutter of mirrors. It was light filled with a dead-weight silence, a light lacking joy. Then, with a sudden wind, dogs began to howl and the cocks crowed again. Across from the hotel, six men, their heads wrapped in white cloths, slipped between the pillars on the second floor of the concrete shell of an unfinished building, the structural steel rods standing erect in the air like antennae. They crouched and waited. There was machine-gun fire across the river in the brush, the island basin was an echo chamber. Suddenly, a muezzin made his nasal call to prayer over the loudspeaker in a small minaret, sun-bleached blue shutters were pushed open, and someone – as if deaf – threw a red and black rug over a wrought-iron balcony railing, airing the room. Between bursts of more machine-gun fire there was a distant, faint wailing, like hundreds of keening women, but it was the hysterical screeching of thousands of yard hens. Adam had heard the screeching of hens before in the streets of Beirut, hens caught in cross-fire between snipers. He'd lost the tip of his left little finger to a shrapnel explosion, but he did not flinch at gunfire: he'd been afraid before but he'd never felt the woozy detachment that comes with panic ... a hapless sapping of energy. He'd always quickened with fear, so that he saw things with clarity, a depth ... "My eye just gets in the groove and I see what's there like ballplayers say they sometimes see the ball, big as a cantaloupe ..." and he had won awards for his photographs, framing each moment, cropped so that a face or a hand held in the air always seemed full of as much intensity as it possessed, apparitions emerging out of layers of darkness, a strange silken sable light in his prints that was never grim or determined but tonal, like laughter heard across dark water, or the black notes that Kufu heard when Web played, and this effect seemed natural, as if light always fell that way ... but now, when a guerrilla in the building across the road fired a single shot into a clump of trees, he felt a blurring ... as if, for a moment, he wasn't sure he was there, as if he'd lost contact – not with the world but himself ... *unhinged Miss Purdy, we're all coming unstrung* and he hurried down the dark hotel stairwell to the first floor, past two women washing dishes in a kitchen alcove, and out into the glass-enclosed dining room. The light startled him. One of the long windows, cracked from top to bottom, had not been washed for weeks. There was a line of dirt in the crack like a geological shift in the air. The heavy bulbous men of the polka band, wearing blue shirts and white shorts and striped knee-socks, sat around a table pointing across the road to two men with rifles running from house to house. Their tuba and the trombones were on the floor, in the sunlight.

"*Und morgen die ganze Welt ...*"

"Sorry, I don't speak German."

"Come see the crazy nigger show."

* * *

In the morning he walked the beach behind the casino. The retreating waves left little air holes in the sand, buried clams. *Wisps of clouds white like an old woman's soft white hair: what would Flo have looked like with white hair?* Adam was looking for Gabrielle among the women sunning on cedar-slat chairs. He walked between two airline pilots who were playing shuffle-board on a concrete pad beside the chairs. The pilots were wearing matching powder-blue leather clogs. They giggled and shoved little wooden discs along the pad and clopped back and forth calling their scores.

He found her by the pool. She was facing the sun. The lids of her eyes seemed heavier, her lips fuller. He saw she had the habit of lifting her chin as if reassuring herself that she was aloof ... "Well," she said as he sat down on the cedar bench beside her, "I knew it was you last night, I caught you out of the corner of my eye ..."

"This is wonderful," he said. "After all these years, I don't know where to begin."

"Here we are, that's all."

Two women in bikinis were sailing a frisbee across the pool, the still water lying like a turquoise lozenge in the red sun. The frisbee fell into the pool and lay on the water. The women stared at it and went back to their chairs.

"Do you want a drink?"

"It's still morning."

"It's nearly noon."

"I never drink in the morning, it's no good."

"Neither do I. But it's been a long time. You never came back home."

"Not for good."

"Not at all."

"No, not true. I did come back once. To see my uncle Jackie."

"You didn't see Harry?"

"I saw Harry but he didn't see me. And I saw you. After I did what I had to do with Jackie I went to where I knew I could watch him, I went to mass on a Sunday and there he was just like the old days, up on the altar playing the organ with one hand and wagging the other at his choirboys. It was very nice, it almost made me want to cry, and then there you were too, standing very straight just a couple of pews away with that air of yours, so separate no matter how shoulder to shoulder you are with anybody *And a father watches his son grow," Web said, "he can't help doing that, and there are loners and there are loners, like some guys are mad with a kind of stubbornness, and then there are guys who seem able to rise up over their wounds, and you can tell*

*those guys feel something taking root, relaxing and letting it flower
in the sunlight. Flowers don't try, they just are, whether there's
sunlight or rain, and that's what gives me a lift about you, because
it's always a joy to discover back near the fence a spot you've been
paying no attention to at all, and let's face it, with my being away so
much I was hardly paying much attention, but there's a flower
suddenly blooming, all on its own, without attention, just being
itself, and surprised, I look at it more and say to myself, 'I wonder
how you happened there,' and that's the way it's got with you"* and
that gives a woman pleasure, at least it gives me pleasure, and
I followed you out of the church, sometimes getting up close
behind you, and I knew you wouldn't look back, so self-
enclosed, so self-absorbed, so I could get close, except you're
not self-enclosed like my uncle Jackie is because, outside of
me, he hurts people and I don't think you hurt people, so at a
stoplight when you turned and crossed the other way I blew
you a kiss and felt my head spinning a little, like I should have
gone after you ..."

"And Harry never went after you," he said.

"He never knew where I was."

She folded her arms and smiled, and then said in a
distracted way, "All my childhood Harry gave me big
spinning tops ... you know how you pushed them down and
then the tops whirled and hummed. All the way to my tenth
birthday he gave them to me. I've still got those tops, the
clown faces and flowers like magnolias, some in boxes, and
on the shelf in my bedroom ... and some nights the spotlights
in the mirror behind me when I'm dancing, they look like big
flowers and sometimes I shut my eyes and feel filled with
flowers spinning in the eyes of all the men ..."

"You never stopped dancing ..."

"Why should I?"

"Harry would be happy."

She touched his hand. "I don't think you knew Harry," she said. "It all started with you, you know."

"What?"

"The thing is," she said, taking off her sunglasses and stretching back into the chair, "when I was a little girl and when my mother went away playing bingo or something, my father used to sit with me while I washed in the tub and then he'd braid my hair into two pigtails, and sometimes he'd circle them into a crown on top of my head, and sometimes he'd drop them down over my chest and my breasts were just beginning. You don't know how strangely painful it is, your breasts beginning, like your bones are being moved, and one night he cut my braids and suddenly my hair was cropped real close. And he used to wash me at night and dry me with a great big towel, and then another night when he was drying me he handed me the towel and said dry yourself between your legs and though I was a girl I somehow knew I was a woman with the way he watched me. I mean, then and there I made up my mind I was a woman, and I felt very sad about that quiet thing lost between me and my father, but I felt all full too, you know, so I was ready for you, the night you made me bleed" *the butcher, Mom's butcher, saying: Okay, who wants to be a man, step right up – who wants to be a man ... hold out your hands in a cup, cup your hands ... pouring out of a can a steady stream of beef blood ... "Cattle beasts, boys" ... thick, gooey ... "You got the blood of the beef you eat on your hands," smacking his aproned thighs with glee, until I screamed, "You're outa your fucking skull,*

Mr. Battaglia," and raging, he threw the rest of the can of blood into my face. "You get some goddamn respect for people who's older than you, you little prick," and he started winding string around me standing there blinded by blood, giggling, like he was trussing up a rib roast ... and his son began to chant: BLOOD, BLOOD.

"I still dream about you," he said. "Sometimes you pop up in the strangest places, places you've never been."

"Maybe I've dreamed the same places. I believe in dreams. I think I'd like to disappear in other people's dreams. Maybe that's what love is."

"I loved Harry, he was tops when I was a kid ..."

"Life was for top guys," she said coldly, "that's the way he talked."

"You didn't like the way he talked?"

"I didn't like the way he whispered."

"But you used to sit in the church blowing him kisses."

She laughed. "I like it down here," she said, wrapping a beach jacket around her shoulders to shield herself from the sun. "It's kind of my secret life out of New York down here, and Harry has his own secret life, too." She stood up and looked at him. "You've become a very elegant man," she said. "There's something very elegant in you."

"Really."

"I think it is silence," she said, picking up her towel and walking toward the hotel, and then she turned. "You share that with Mio ..."

"The man last night?"

"Yes, except he can also be very cruel."

* * *

A squat armored car, flying a small flag with a black star on a yellow field, moved down the hotel street, a 50-calibre machine gun mounted on the back. Henri, who drank pernod with water in the morning, said he had heard the counter-revolutionary guerrillas were in control of two hills to the south-west. "There's been big trouble, *mon ami*," he said. "Men of sacrifice, so they say of themselves, many tied explosives to their bodies and threw themselves into the tanks and others lay down in the paths of the tanks. *J'en viens à être ce que je fais.*" He was lean and had long delicate fingers. Sitting in a canvas chair, he spread his legs and his legs began to flap apart like the wings of an awkward, half-alive bird. His right arm hung limp to the floor, his fingers working yellow worry beads. He leaned back, detached, preoccupied ... "*Assis drapé dans son manteau il comme un moine déchu.*"

The guerrillas across from the hotel had fired on a small troop carrier. The troops raked the concrete walls and the stone houses beside the unfinished building, orange sparks showering the air, a wooden awning cut to pieces, left hanging tattered from its hinges in a pocket of silence, *pockets full of plenty three bags full since plenty is in the silences*, Web had said, but bombardment had begun in the south-west, a steady engine-chugging sound, the pumping of a plunger in heavy humid air. Puffs of smoke appeared above the trees, blown away by the wind. The guerrillas scattered out of the house across the road.

The government troops mounted a mortar position beside the hotel. Five small tanks pelted the dense bush on the southern hill. The shells made a sucking, draining sound. Houses broke open, letting out balls of white smoke, *like milkweed seed pods*, and then a yellow smear settled over the hillside. The troops, all running as if their boots were too big, moved in a 105 howitzer rocket rifle on a Jeep truck, the long thin insect-like barrel casting recoil as a concussion through all the houses and the hotel, the windows in the dining room suddenly shattering, and a beefy man in the band cried, *"Mein Gott, diese wahnsinnigen Dschungelkaninchen werden unsermorden!"* Henri hardly flinched: *"Répandez leur sang ... qu'ils dorment ..."* But the musicians, clutching their horns and the tuba, barged into the hallway, trotting to their rooms. The light crackling sterile clatter of rapid fire continued, the howitzer and mortars sounded like dry thunder thuds, the thundering broken by the dry whistling of old infantry rifles. *Somehow*, Adam thought, *the air is pushing out through the walls ...*

"I brought you a revolver," Esmelda murmured to Henri.

"I want to marry her, you know," Henri said.

"Our children would rut in the mud."

"But that's what they are dying for, so they can have children who rut in the mud," he said and laughed. *"Il captait la longue file de lui-même ..."*

Adam went to his room, to his unpainted plaster walls, a lamp on a hook by the bed, and an old stained sepia photograph of Victoria Falls over a wash stand. *Livingstone was here ...* He pulled the tilted chair from under the handle of the louvered window: the sun bounced off the corrugated tin roofs of shacks. White stone houses shone through the yellow smoke, chips of bone. With each break in the firing, he heard the hysterical hens, but no human voice – only a stagnant calmness, *the sound of a humming child's toy top ... the note of manic calmness ... the whole of time hanging by a rope of sand over a trap door to wherever Livingstone went* ... The sprawling shack city to the south-west was on fire, and he could see down an incline under dwarf palms a curled body, an ember of flesh surrounded by a litter of brass shell casings. He took out his cameras. Henri appeared at the door: "The army says there is a guerrilla spotter in the hotel, a maid or someone ... they will shoot anyone they see in the windows."

Four infantry trucks pulled up beside a stone retaining wall, part of the unfinished building. Within a few minutes, incoming mortars from the south blew out the wall and two trucks, bodies catapulting into the air. A gunner wheeled and pumped jack-hammer rounds into the hotel, tearing a foot-wide hole through Adam's bathroom wall. He sprawled on the concrete and waited for the night so he could drag his mattress into the hallway.

* * *

The casino was crowded again. A teenage boy wearing heavy glasses picked up the dice. He had a loose smile and hundreds of dollars in the runnel of the rail. His tanned father urged him on, wanting a bond to be sealed between them, blessed by a win. Other players bet against the boy. "Goddamn virgin dice," one sneered. Adam bet with the boy and the boy won, gleeful, and suddenly baiting the croupiers, his father beaming, and they kept winning *because the least likely are the elect, the chosen*, Father Zale had said. A man in a lapelless jacket stood staring down at the baize. He'd bet against the boy, doubling up after each loss, and as the father and son left with their arms around each other, he let

out a low gasping wheeze beside Adam: "God ... my god."
Then, above the noise, Adam heard the chanting: "Here come
the man, here come the man ..."

Gabrielle, in a long black sequin dress, carried a silver ice
bucket from the restaurant attached to the casino, and Mio
was beside her wearing a tweed hunting jacket and an ascot
tie, his forehead shining and his hair mussed, his gloved hand
in his pocket and his right hand wrapped in a large white
napkin, his wrapped hand down in the bucket. "Here come
the man ..." Before the startled croupiers could stop them,
Mio had slipped in beside Adam at the table, with Gabrielle
laughing. "Sir ..." the pit boss said sternly, but a bosomy,
good-looking woman in her forties wearing a scoop-necked
dress called across in a drawl, "Leave that man be, he's gonna
make the rooster strut, you just hold on an' roll them bones
boy."

Mio, his cold eyes darting, waited in his own silence for the
dice. The stick man whipped them to him as he unwrapped
his good hand and said to Gabrielle, "You make all the bets, I
roll, you bet." Then he said, *"Was hab' ich getan, dass ich so
leiden muss?"* He clamped his ice-cold hand on Adam's arm
and whispered, "But you don't bet ... not on me." Adam felt
the weight of two men behind him. Mio threw the dice back-
handed ... eleven ... and came back with a seven, and one of
the burly men cried, "The man, the man is here ..."

In the crush around the table, with bets and back-up bets
being called, Adam stood silently, unnerved, but Gabrielle
winked at him. "She's drunk," he thought, "she's crazy as a
loon." They stood waiting for the croupiers to get the bets
down after each of Mio's winning rolls. He seemed immune

to caution, or the crack in conviction that comes with caution, *alive, he's got the clarity, that inner lightness heavy with what you know will happen, an inner note in tune with outside music* and he let Gabrielle double the bets, slowly wrapping and unwrapping his hand in the ice-cold towel ... but, as he was about to roll for his fifth straight pass, a man with little black hairs in his pocked cheeks smacked a stack of chips down on the DON'T COME line, snarling into the moment of silence, "He's wrong, he's coming out wrong." Mio hesitated: the snarl had its own force, but he let out a little whoop of laughter and said, "Don't be ridiculous." He rolled a seven, whispering, "The man is on you ..." The woman in the scooped-neck dress leaned toward Mio, "Touch me boy, touch my tits for luck, you got it all," and Mio looked bemused, and then brazen. He drew his ice-cold forefinger down between her breasts, deep into the cleavage so that she shuddered, and then he picked up the dice and rolled boxcars, a loss, and then he rolled a seven, craps, another loss.

"Whyn't you keep your tits outa this," a man yelled.

Mio turned to Adam and said quietly, "You'll excuse me. Coming to play with you tonight was only a whim." He walked through the crowd, leaving his two men to go to the cage and cash his chips, and Gabrielle, holding the silver bucket filled with sloshing ice, laughed as he went out the door.

"What was that all about?" Adam asked.

"You saw it," she said.

"Yeah, but what was it all about?"

"Really, I thought you were smarter than that."

"You mean he was just doing a number on me!"

"What did you feel when he put his hand on you?"

"I wondered what you felt."

"When?"

"When he puts his hand on you."

"Safe," she said and took his arm and they walked up a short flight of stairs to a patio facing a swimming pool with only underwater eye-lamps in the walls giving off any light. At poolside, the man with the lapelless jacket was walking in a tight circle, mumbling and muttering to himself, and when he saw Adam and Gabrielle, he rushed forward and took her by both arms, crying, "Jesus H. Christ, I came back, my whole bloody life was down the drain and I made it back on that crazy guy's roll, just like I came back from the dead ..." He whirled and with a whoop of joy, luminescent in the strange underwater light, he took off fully clothed into the water and after the explosion of spray he bobbed in the water, dog-paddling, giggling.

"Poor man," she said, "he'll probably live in someone's life like that a long time."

"Will I?"

"You worried about Mio?"

"Maybe. Is he your man?"

"Not the way you think. Otherwise he might kill you."

"So who is he?"

"A man who loves me and wants no one ... or, maybe it's the other way around. He wants me and loves no one."

"Do you love him?"

"We've never been alone in the dark."

"You've never been alone?"

"Only when there's lots of light. He makes me think of my

father, in ways you wouldn't know about. He was a child
during the war, he was buried alive. I told him that you were
my first love. He's impressed by love, he respects it, is even a
little afraid of it, and I told him that my childhood blood was
on your hands." She laughed. The man was swimming on his
back, still giggling. "Shall we throw him a rope?" she asked.

"No. Leave him be. It's where we come from, the water ..."

They walked through a white filigreed iron gate, onto the
ocean beach, the waves breaking in the full moonlight. They
lay down on chairs close to the water line, the screen of lights
from all the hotels on the strip hanging in the air behind them,
and they lay looking up, listening to the roll of waves. "You
want to know why," he said, "all the ancient wise men looked
so long at the stars? They were the only damn thing they had
in their whole lives that was fixed, that was their clockwork,
the stars they could count on, and trace little figures and
stories in, but even so, in their heart of hearts they knew all
the arranging of the stars was an illusion and all the little
stories were only lies covering up the dark empty truth," and
he took her hand, "and that's why shooting stars were so
special, stars that shot chaos through the system, and magic
men followed those stars, ending up unknown rivers, delirious in a dream ..."

As they lay on the beach, salt spray on their lips, he looked
out over the dark water and saw lights, suspended rows of
lights moving in the air, cleaving the night sky. He said,
"Look," pointing at a liner on the moonlit ocean: *he's out there
on the poop deck, sitting crosslegged in his old iron suit, searching the
scouting maps spread on his knees, following his star, my old plunger
man, Ponce.*

* * *

Albert Waters
1901 – 1951
A Sailor on an Outrigger
He Had Wanted
To Be
But Steamships
Made Sail
Arbitrary
So
As Tailor and Outfitter
He Went Down to
The Sea

* * *

In early December, his father came home from the west coast. It rained all week. The storm sewers flooded and there were pools of wet light on the road. He and Web sat on the back porch wearing heavy sweaters. They were silent for a long time. Web had always hugged Adam and held him when he came home, but now they were the same height and Web, trying to hold him, had to press his strong fingers into Adam's back and shoulders, and only a woman had held Adam like that. There was a grey streak in Web's hair and his eyes were hooded by loose flesh. Adam felt suddenly afraid for his father's life, and a surge of irrevocable loss settled over him. "I never knew what to say to a child," Web said. "But now you're a man, a young man, and I assume I have something to say, but not necessarily." He smiled shyly.

A raccoon had come into the driveway, snout down, scurrying toward the garbage cans on the other side of the house. "Look at him, he knows we're here," Web said, "yet he's absolutely indifferent, that hunch in his back ..." He struck a match and the coon disappeared. He had taken to smoking a pipe, but the stem had snapped earlier in the week and now it was held together with a piece of copper wire left over from some plumbing work done years ago.

"I had a friend back about ten years," he said, "a sculptor, and one night he told me all the looting in ancient ruins was no more than garbage picking and it was good pickings because if you really wanted to know how men lived, who they were, then you just needed to look in their garbage, and I suppose he was right, if you think men are kind of like coons, which I don't. It seemed somehow right to me that he did all his sculpting in stainless steel."

Web had been down at the courthouse all week, at Osgoode Hall, because a friend had been arrested at the border for possession of cocaine, and then, after his friend – FRANKIE DAPPLE AND HIS DUAL TRUMPETS – a horn player who blew two trumpets at once and led a band with a black transvestite singer – had been freed on bail, he stayed around the courthouse, intrigued by an inquest, a story that had caught his eye in the newspapers: a Yugoslavian boy who had been shot by a cop down a back alley. He was fascinated, he said, because everyone in the old oak-panelled courtroom wanted to avoid any trouble for the police. "Even the boy's mother wanted no more trouble and she was looking for a way out. She just wanted to get on with her life, and this getting on with life was bigger for her than any idea of vengeance, let alone justice. She just wanted to keep her snout down, close to the ground. She'd sized up the situation and turned into a coon. Maybe there's some coon in all of us."

"You got some coon?" Adam asked.

"Well, when I was the only white man around this town playing what your good decent folk called nigger music, they used to call me a coon lover, but that's a different story. I just kept my head down and sang the song."

"Has Momma got some coon?"

"Your mother has bare-faced audacity. The last time I left she said as solemn as a saint, 'Web, you're a good man,' and I tried to laugh. But to tell you the truth, I didn't like her for saying that. It was the first lie she'd told me in years."

It began to pour rain again. There was a strong wind and the rain blew in on the porch.

"Unless you want to soak yourself, we'd better go in," he said, "but don't wake your mother."

They sat in the kitchen.

"You know what old Itzak Klein asked me the other day?" He handed Adam a glass of armagnac. "He wanted to know if I didn't have a view of myself, and I said god no, and I don't want one."

There was a loud clatter of cans in the alley.

"Damn coons, they've knocked over the garbage again."

"What ever happened to your friend?"

"Who? Frankie Dapple?"

"No, the sculptor."

"I don't know. The last I heard he gave it up and went off into the desert."

"And you've got no view of yourself?"

"Nope."

"You wouldn't lie to me."

"Not necessarily."

*   *   *

Night came, with no electricity or water. Adam stretched out on the cold concrete floor and listened to the pumping shell fire and snipers. No candles could be lit in the rooms. The guerrillas and the army had fired into the hotel. Adam spread his bedding out at the end of the corridor and then pulled himself along on his belly to the small balcony. An animal was screaming in the trees. There were fire clusters in the bush on the hill. Red tracers streaked across the sky. "Burned out shooting stars," he said. A phosphorous shell exploded on a rooftop, a cloud of searing white light and then a ball of luminous smoke, as if lit from within. Heavy machine guns still raked houses in the dark – or fired blindly into the bush. Suddenly, a house came alive, like a twisted white face, the dark windows ... hollowed eyes, the doorway ... a gaping mouth. He turned and crawled back through the room, thudding mortar fire rattling the french doors, into the dark hotel corridor crammed with mattresses. The bandsmen and a consultant for a pharmaceutical firm were lying awake. Short-wave radios lost connection. A voice spluttered and then drifted away. The guerrilla station played Victorian martial music. One of the bandsmen, a little drunk and scared, began to march up and down the dark stairwell making a child's drumming noise in his cheeks. The guerrilla radio announced that all their positions were secure, that they had destroyed twenty-one tanks along the N'Chala road.

"Where's that?" the consultant asked.

"Who knows?"

"North, zer is the desert ..."

"There's oil in the desert."

"Zer is nothing in ze desert."

"God's in the desert," the consultant said.

"What zis is all about is oil."

"No it's not. It's global."

"Global my ass," Adam said.

"I'd like a piece of ass, and a scotch-and-soda," the consultant said.

"You lederhosen guys have got a whole flat-bed trailer full of beer kegs out there."

"Ze army machine-gunned zose zis morning."

"They shot the fucking beer."

"Zey shoot ze sky, birds, zis is no joke."

The army radio station announced the guerrillas had been driven out of the city, back into the bush, and that all the traffic circles were under control.

"Jesus fucking Christ," the consultant cried, "what're they talking about? The goddamn bush is only five hundred yards away."

Incoming shells shook the hotel. Henri appeared at the head of the stairs, elbowing past the marching German who was making an abrupt right turn on the stair. "Gentlemen," he said, "I have just informed the colonel that everything is normal in here. We will forget him if he will forget us. He has agreed, but points out that he cannot forget us if he sees us. It has a logic, *oui*? *Qui demande pourquoi se figure qu'il a un futur* ..." Someone began to sing, " *Strangers in the night*," and then said, "This war ain't going nowhere ... you watch, this ain't going nowhere and we're stuck." Adam lay on his mattress, his eyes closed even though it was pitch-dark, thinking of trees, lilac trees and weeping birch, red berries on the bushes, and a soldier he'd seen on the road sitting under an umbrella surrounded by piles of clothing and shoes, and the sandals and bare feet and breast of a woman he'd loved and the pointed breast of a woman he did not love and one day when he was a child he'd fallen off the end of a dock into the water and lying there in the dark he could see the face of his father on the floor of the lake and photographs he'd taken of that face, gathering and shifting in the sand in the light, a strange absence in the light that said nothing, it was only absence, the clarity of absence, the zero ring of a lens, but when he looked through his lens it was like a ring that could snare a moon, a flat moon like the flat round reading glasses of Miss Skinner, her wry drunken laughter in the dark and the languorous wry laughter of Gabrielle as she lay naked in the dark day-dreaming of hummingbirds saying it was going to rain, that she could feel it on the wind, *and why in the middle of sleep, why her sudden reaching out as if I had never been there, or was gone, or maybe to comfort me, like I was about to disappear, and then her clutching, as if she could only be sure of me after she was exhausted, drained, half-asleep, thankful,* with him trapped as a memory in her blood and the memory of her in him, and they had gone to sleep enclosed in each other's arms, a ring around the moon, promise of rain ...

*   *   *

Adam went down the grey marble steps to the church basement, to the choral room. It seemed much smaller. The ceiling had been painted glossy battleship grey and it glared in tubular fluorescent light. The newspaper picture of Gabrielle hung on a stone wall in a pewter frame. She was holding the silver racing cup. There were Palm Sunday fronds behind the frame. "I've converted," Harry said. "I'm a dogan at last. I've come into the Church, and when I look at her picture I don't think anyone's dead at all and I still have hope for Gabrielle wherever she is." He lit a cigarette. His hand shook. "We've a new pastor," he said. "He's a Scot, and the new night watchman is a Scot. They don't understand me. Their dreams are all flat. Ever notice that? The Scots all dream flat, that's why they're all bankers or watchmen ..."

He shuffled choral sheets into a pile and then he walked around a cluster of wire music stands to set them down near the photograph of Gabrielle, but he did not look at it. "They told the watchman to keep an eye out for me," he chuckled, "or what's a watchman for, on the look-out for what's wrong." He pulled at his chin, a mocking little smile on his lips. "They tell me I'm wrong because I don't want any forgiveness, but I don't want to think about myself at all. I don't want anything. I think that's fair."

"Well, I want something."

"Like what?"

"I want my voice back."

"Haw, we'd all like to get something back. That's what it's all about, coming back," Harry said. But then he shrugged. "Maybe it'll come back, maybe your voice will come back, you never know. Basso profundo ..."

"Then I can sing the *Miserere* ..."

"That's right, none of that castrati *Regina Coeli* stuff. Verdi, the *Dies Irae*, there's nothing like Verdi, the *Missa Solemnis* ...

Libera me, Domine, de morte aeterna, in die illa tremenda ..." He laughed and lit another cigarette. "Do you remember the little white-haired kid years ago, the kid we put in the manger?"

"Sure, Whitey," Adam said, "and you made me stand in the snow till I thought I'd die."

"Because you laughed at him."

"Well, I was only laughing because he got everything backwards."

"And that's why he couldn't come into our choir," Harry said, his hand covering a dark stain in one of the wall stones. "But you never know who's got what backwards, you wouldn't know what I've done backwards. You were lucky. We were all together for a while, and you'll come back to us."

"I wouldn't bet on it."

"Well, it's all luck, or no luck at all, *tremens factus sum ego et timeo*," and suddenly Adam saw Harry slumped like an old suit, or his grandfather's long-johns in the wind, and he loved him deeply and wanted to cry because his grandfather's long-johns had one leg scissored and they were hanging in a closet and he felt Harry's life was somehow hanging mutilated in a closet.

"Are you still playing the organ at the hockey games?"

"Oh yes, yes. Music's more and more to me, it's all I've got, I love Verdi and marching music."

"Well, be good," Adam said.

"What's good?"

"Who knows?"

"What's good in the fifth, that's all the watchman wants to know. Flat dreams."

part SIX

Themere was sulphur and ash on
the early morning air as Adam and Gabrielle drove through
the rolling central hills of Puerto Rico to the other side of the
island. They stopped at a beach café, only a few feet from
turquoise water lapping the roots of dwarf palm trees. The
earth around the café patio was spongy, and behind the café
there were wild orange trees, the leaves speckled white. A
long rickety dock led over the water to three pink rowboats,
the water so clear the sun cast the shadows of floating leaves
onto the rippled sand under the water *where I saw his face on the
floor*. There were clouds behind Caja de Muertos, a breadloaf
island of stone, sliding like a burial box into the sea.

"I've been in the inland hills," she said, "but I've never
been here. I can't believe the stillness, the water."

"This is the secret side of the island, the city side's for the
gonifs and grafters, the guys with the stretch limos."

She kissed him on both cheeks, said, "Naughty boy," and
walked alone to the end of the dock, to the rocking pink boats.

"You see the tips of those tall trees," she called back, pointing, "that's where my dreams are flying."

He went down to the end of the dock, quickening with the urge to hold her, to smell the sun in her hair.

"It's strange," she said, taking his hand. "Being here is so beautiful, it makes me want to go everywhere even though I just got here."

"I'd like to see Russia," he said with a sweep of his arm.

"I'd like to see the onion domes, but Russia's such an enormous thing."

"How about a safari? You got a tent?"

"No," and she nestled against him. "I don't go anywhere unless I can take my hair dryer."

He lifted her long hair and kissed the nape of her neck, tasting the heat and salt of her skin. "You've got to have a place to plug in a hair dryer," he said.

"Take me to the zoo, any zoo ..."

"The Bronx ..."

"Why should I go there, to the Bronx, when I've never been to the Empire State Building?"

"I've never been to California."

"I've never been to Atlantic City either. It's famous. All corny things are famous."

"Would you like to be famous?"

"No, you've got to be corny."

They walked along the dock, back to the café. A tall man with straight black hair and wrap-around sunglasses brought them thimble cups of coffee. In the shade of the café wall, a black woman slept with a yellow flower in her hand. Adam whispered:

I plucked your petals as if you were a rose
So I could see your soul
And did not see it.

"You'll drive me crazy," she said.

"Why?"

"You've got all these words within words."

"Sorry."

"You're like Chinese boxes, it'll drive me crazy."

"Tell me about Mio ..."

"What's to tell?"

"Do you love him?"

"Life's not like that."

"What's he do?"

"He's a salesman."

"Pots and pans?"

"Guns."

"Fucking guns! And he reminds you of Harry?"

"Sometimes. Like when he sings, he can't sing to save his life."

"He's not in the life-saving business."

"Don't be nasty."

"I'm not."

"And don't be jealous."

"So, you do love him?"

"Are you in love every time you make love?"

"A little. Sometimes it's a secret."

"You know what I always wanted to be, secretly?"

"No."

"A figure skater, slowly spinning on the ice, that's the way I saw it. The way they bend back like flowers, it was always the way I wanted to be, and I used to practise in the mirror because I had my long legs except the trouble was I had weak ankles. I couldn't skate to save my life so that's why I dance the way I do sometimes, slow spins on the stage just like it was ice ..."

He lifted her hand and kissed her fingertips.

"You've got no secrets?" she asked.

"Sure, but that's why they're what they are."

"What?"

"Secrets. They've never been told."

"So tell me."

"What?"

"A secret."

"Well, my father burned all the little notebooks he'd promised to keep for me."

"Where's your father?"

"Copenhagen, the last I heard."

"I heard him play one night. He played on the organ for Harry and Harry did a shuffle step up and down the altar steps. I think they were both a little drunk and they carried on like a couple of clowns."

"He burned them all, except he missed one little book ... five or six notes in it, that's all."

"Oh, Harry loved him, or envied him. Harry always wanted to be someone else, or was someone else."

"Really?"

"Sure. He did things no one knew about."

Her mouth tightened, she looked grim, but then she smiled.

"Like what?"

"Like you wouldn't believe," and she leaned against him, kissing him again on the cheek, "my sweet innocent man, among other things he was a sandlot umpire."

"A what?"

"An umpire. Way out in the east end where no one knew him, season after season, and it wasn't even baseball, it was the fast-ball leagues, but he looked so terrific because he bought the whole get-up, the black coat and the little black cap and the black steel-toe shoes."

The woman holding the yellow flower began to snore.

"He loved it, getting all red in the face. I mean, if he could have got up on stage every night and called balls and strikes, he would have been in heaven, a real performer, shooting his fist up into the air like he was the big cop at home plate, and the league loved him, and sometimes he'd take off his mask to whisk away the dust on home plate so he'd always be able to make no mistakes, except you know, he made mistakes." She put on her tinted glasses, opened her compact and licked her lips, touching her lipstick at the corner of her mouth. "You see, something would always happen, some kind of confusion, and I'd see the little hunch-up of his shoulders. I knew what that meant, just like he did if I ever talked to him about my mother..."

"You never seemed like your mother..."

"We had things in common..."

"Not that I could see."

"Yeah, but you didn't see everything, you never saw Harry hunch up like when he didn't know what was going on. It's how he really was, and he'd make the call as if he'd seen the ball real clear-eyed but all hell would break loose, the players screaming around him, and he'd listen and then knowing he'd maybe been wrong but there was nothing else to do, he'd wheel around and pump his arm like he was pointing at the end of the world and he'd yell, 'You're outa here,' and he'd throw guys out of the game because he was the boss and it was the only way he could save himself."

The black woman sputtered, suddenly awake, gaping into the sun at the sound of Gabrielle's cry, *You're outa here*, the flower dropping between her broad feet, and the tall man with the straight black hair came out and said, "You desire someting, señora?"

"No ... no, sorry."

"You have come from a long way off."

"Yes, yes."

"Just so," and he picked up the flower and gave it to the woman and went back into the shuttered café.

They took off their shoes and walked barefoot along the sand, skirting the scrawny tufts of blue and grey roots clotted with pine needles. The wind had dropped. Across the open water, the stone coffin island had lifted off the horizon line and it sat suspended in the sky, a tinsel line of light under the island, water and air easing apart.

"You see," she said, "a terrible thing happened. Before Mother died, for his own reasons ..." and her grip on his hand tightened, "he stopped eating. He ate himself up, worrying. He got thin as a rail, but in a funny way he had even more energy. He was in charge of all the umpires and he had a meeting in our house, called them around for lunch and served them bowls of Wheaties. 'The Breakfast of Champions,' he said, except it was lunch. That was his own joke on them, this mush, and they all sat there spooning in this mush, dead sure he was dying or something, but he sat there smiling, everything under control. And one guy, he still had his spoon and bowl in his hand, he says to me, 'I'm a champion, you can bet on that.' And I said real fast, 'I wouldn't bet on you to save my life.' And Harry broke out laughing, red-faced and pleased, and he says, 'Mister, you're sucking wind,' and this guy sits stirring his champion breakfast like a fool and I really think that was the best thing my father ever said, setting that wind-sucker straight so I always knew that sappy guys like that, all those breakfast champions, had no place in my life ..."

The sky descended, the sea rose, the tinsel line of light disappeared.

"I love the sunlight, it's so warm and fresh, I feel like I'm fresh bread," she said.

"I like the nighttime," he said.

"It's no time at all," she said, standing barefoot in the clear water, "the wrong things happen in the night."

"Even so, I love the dark."

"You're a damn fool."

"I like the way the chill air always feels fresh."

"If you stay too long in the dark it gets in your eyes. Don't you know that? They found that out with prisoners, men locked away in the hole. You don't want to look like you've been down in the hole."

"How could I be in the hole when I'm here with you?" he said.

"You know the freshest smell in the world? Fresher than

this? It's cut grass, the sweetness of cut grass, and then you leave it in the hot sun and it dries out brown, drying grass and baked bread, those are the two best smells in the world. That's what I remember from when I was a child ..."

"I remember dust."

"Dust?"

"Sure, when I was a kid I used to lie on the floor playing with my soldiers, watching the dust dancing in a shaft of sunlight from the window, and I could smell the dust in my mother's rug on the living-room floor, but my mother told me dust was bad for me, bad for my breathing, my lungs would turn into dustbags and so, since I could never see dust in the shadows or in the dark, I figured the dark was good for me because the sunlight was always filled with dust."

*   *   *

Father Zale carried a furled black umbrella tucked under his arm, even on hot dry days. He had a high forehead, a long thin nose, and smelled of talcum powder. He loved birds and had built a cluster of wooden birdhouses close to the school on the edge of the bluff. In the mornings, he went out with a knapsack full of crusts hanging from his shoulder and he spread crusts on the ground and filled the feeders.

"Sometimes," he said, "in my black skirts I must look like a scarecrow."

One afternoon, while he was spreading crusts across the lawn with great sweeps of his arm, he said, "I was from the farm, you know. See, I've got farmers' hands," and he held out a big fist, thick through the thumb and the heel. "There are puzzles on the farm," he said. "My mother used to spread out a crossword puzzle as big as the kitchen table and work on it for a week, but there are bigger puzzles than that, like why pigs gang up and kill one another? Nobody knows," and he dug his fist into the sack of crusts.

"You always seem to like it when there are things nobody knows," Adam said.

"And why," he said, throwing out another handful of stale crusts, "do whales beach themselves and commit suicide? Tell me that."

"I don't know."

"Nobody does."

"But they will, they'll find out," Adam said.

"They'll find out," the priest said, "that the answer is only a bigger question."

He rubbed his hands as they walked under tall cedars along the bluff, seagulls swooping and crying behind them.

"Life's divided into two kinds of people," he said, "and it's all a matter of temperament. Those who find questions more interesting than answers, and practical men who want good sensible answers at any cost."

"So?"

"So, the new deal in physics," he said, "is chaos. Trying to figure out how whatever we thought was order turns into disorder, like when you're watching someone's cigarette burn down in an ashtray, did you ever do that?"

"Yeah, my mother. She's got her eye on the smoke the whole time."

"I figure we're just like that smoke. We unravel into a million particles in a moment of chaos, and chaos is in the core of the human condition, like someone flicked us on fire and up we went in smoke, it's what they call the inchoate. Maybe that's what evil is, in us, it's in the universe."

They were standing above the bluff of eelgrass and shale worn by the wind.

"Maybe things aren't evil," Adam said. "Maybe they just get tired, get weak."

"Maybe. My father used to say, walk around long enough and you get a hole in your shoe and a hole in your heart." He leaned forward on his furled umbrella, the steel tip digging into the earth. A maple tree clung to the edge of the bluffs and half its roots fanned into the air, the earth eroded under it. Other trees had fallen down the slope, the bark stripped and the trunks bleached by the sun, balls of up-ended roots full of seagulls.

"You know," he said, "you're going to leave us this year, and though you may never come back you'll be close to us, in the memory I mean." It had grown chilly and he tucked his umbrella under his arm and slipped his hands inside the sleeves of his black soutane. "One of the delights of life," he said, "is discovering our memories as we grow older, since it is in our memories that we discover ourselves."

He turned and looked back over the cedar hedge to his bird-feeding houses. "Only seagulls around here and seagulls don't really count as birds at all. They're like bone-pickers. Anyway, memory's got its own mind, and sometimes what we remember most is what we'd like to forget."

"Sometimes," Adam said, "I forget my father."

"You don't favor your father?"

"He was always off when I was a child."

"I'm sure he shares your sadness."

"I'm not sad, Father," Adam said. "I don't think he's sad either."

"No, but you're always alone with yourself, kind of cornering yourself. An animal in a corner finally just dies."

"Well, sometimes I do wonder why someone I love has to die."

"We never do," the priest said.

"What?"

"Die."

"My grandfather's dead as a doornail."

"Not at all. He's alive in God."

"I'm not sure I believe in god, Father."

"You don't?" he said. "You're sure of that?"

"No, I just don't beat my brains in thinking about it."

"Well, He'll burrow back into your brain, you'll see, popping up like a memory you'd forgotten you had. We come from God and always remember Him. I believe that."

"I'm glad you do, Father."

"Why?"

"It'd be awful if no one did."

"Ah well, when all's said and done, so will you."

"Never say die?"

"No, never say die, though we do die, but never say so. That's what my father told me. Never say the word. It's bad luck."

* * *

In the morning, several small oval armored cars sped down a side-street, fired into stone villas west of a traffic circle, and then sped back, parking in front of the hotel. Adam saw three men hunker down and dash out the back door of one of the villas. Rockets blew open the white walls. Silence. Then, three single shots, a dry clacking sound, and the army scatter-blasted the walls and windows and then dropped mortars. The guerrillas crept back into the villa and fired five more rounds. The tanks and a howitzer opened up: *thumpfthumpfthumpfthumpfthumpf*. Adam had had no sleep and kept breaking out into cold sweats, but he sat almost rigid with calm as he listened to the clattering racket of gunfire, as if giant children were loose in the bush with huge wooden noise-makers in each fist, and he sat very still, letting the sound seep into him so that it became normal; the silence seemed arbitrary, taunting. Looking out of Henri's office window, he could see that the army was also shelling a three-storey block to the east. "It is the insane asylum," Henri said, waving his hand.

"What in the world will they think is going on?"

"Who?"

"The crazies in the asylum?"

"I think," Henri said, "they are probably calm and talking peacefully about their childhood for the first time in years."

"Cut it out ..."

"*Mais oui*, for the first time the thunder of the world is like the thunder in their heads. They know now they are sane." He laughed and Adam, crouching by the window curtains, kept taking photographs: *click click click click* until he said, "This is stupid."

"You must stop," Henri said. "If the sun catches the lens, if the army sees the light, they will fire with abandon ... At last they will know why they are shooting at something."

Except for a circle of armored cars by the traffic circle, no one was in the streets or along the river, yet incessant firing and shelling seemed to warp the air. On the ridge of the far hill, beautiful black blossoms of smoke spread and opened against the blue sky, thin petal layers of smoke peeled apart. Cocks crowed as if the afternoon were the dawn. He heard the loud keening of a woman, a white woman circling bare-headed and bare-breasted in the bushes and long grass, holding her high heels in her hands, stumbling in wider and wider circles until she walked into a tree trunk and, stunned, fell down. She rolled over onto her back, staring, and began to wave with both hands at the sky, but he couldn't see her face for the long grass and the floor-length curtains bellying and floating in the wind, and there were shards of glass in the window frame and the white lace curtains did not float freely, flapping and hooking on the glass. A small black man opened the door and came into Henri's office. He had a hunch in his left shoulder and a jutting hip. He carried a galvanized tub, with two inches of water in the tub. Henri slumped into a chair under oval photographs of nameless stockholders in the old colonial company. He took off his shoes and socks and rolled up his tan trouser cuffs. "You do the same," he said to Adam. The black man set the tub down on the floor.

"But we've no drinking water," Adam said. "I haven't had a drink of water for three days."

"We've whisky, pernod ..."

"Where's the water from?"

"The roof. Over this room. A cistern on the roof ..."

The black man dragged a wooden chair to the other side of the tub. Henri eased his bony feet into the water and spread his legs; his knees began to flap. He sighed heavily. Adam slipped off his sandals, sat down, and put his feet into the water. He felt instantly soothed. The hunchback gave him a whisky and then lit the front burner of a propane stove, slid a chipped enamel pot over the flame, and put two dirty glasses on a packing-case table. He served hot syrupy tea, and then crouched beside Henry, who closed his eyes and rested his big hand on the man's hump. The whisky and hot tea drew the blood to Adam's empty stomach. Drained by sleeplessness and the relentless reverberation of gunfire, he went to sleep in the chair, his head lolling onto his chest, dreaming of a huge glider with wing spars exposed on the underside and he was hanging onto a spar in the air, stunt man in a silent movie, but suddenly the pilot threw the stick shift, like a truck driver in a tractor-trailer cab, and hidden motors drove the glider forward into a loop, trying to shake him down, and he heard a voice, "This is a shakedown, this is a shakedown," and the pilot was his son, yet he had no son, and he heard whistling outside a window, and when he opened a door in the sky, a man down a hall stared at him and then fled out an emergency exit into a street to the loud keening woman who was circling again from corner to corner, now completely naked but still carrying her high heels and waving at the sky, and men who stood every night in the doorways sleeping standing up, wearing wool hats pulled down to their eyes, began to sing the *Kyrie* and opened their flies and showed they were sexless, a vacancy, as the woman fled from them, still crying, and he felt a slow seepage of his will, of the sky, of all color, the widening cracks in the dry sky filling with dust drifting out of dead bodies on the wind, and he could taste dust, the dust streaming down the woman's body, over him on his knees, down her belly and into his mouth, and he cried – *I do not dance, but only by myself in the dark, the way some people sing in the shower, and I have no shower so I never sing* – until there was only the blessing of her eyes as she looked down at him, content, his mouth full of dust, as if at long last a man had come home to her ...

* * *

The blinds had been drawn for days, newspapers piled up on the front porch. There were no footsteps down from the door in the deep snow. The housekeeper had retired two years earlier. A policeman broke a basement window, went through the cellar, and found Miss Skinner upstairs, naked in her empty clawfoot bathtub, holding the plug in her fist, dead from a heart attack. "None too pretty," a cop said.

"Nope," his partner said. "None too pretty. And her great big house was full of junk food, hundreds of boxes of junk food."

A small service was held in Rosar's funeral home. She had paid in advance. A balding evangelical preacher who wore beige hearing aids in both ears read the Testament verse she had written for her service on schoolbook scribbler paper:

Ah, could my anguish but be measured
and my calamity laid with it in the scales,

they would now outweigh the sands of the sea.
Because of this I speak without restraint
For the arrows of the Almighty pierce me,
and my spirit drinks in their poison;
the terrors of God are arrayed against me.
Does the wild ass bray when he has grass?
Does the ox low over his fodder?
Can a thing insipid be eaten without salt?
Is there flavor in the white of an egg?
I refuse to touch them;
they are loathsome food to me.
What strength have I that I should endure?
Have I the strength of stones?
A friend owes kindness to one in despair,
though she has forsaken the fear
of the Almighty.

There were four neighbors at the service: Adam and his mother, Itzak Klein, and Lester Wrong. The preacher chanted verse over the closed coffin and then they sat together with the preacher in a long grey limousine as it went through slushy streets to the new cemetery on the outskirts of the city.

"Ain't it a life," the preacher said.

"I wonder if the Jays will win the pennant this year?" Lester Wrong asked.

"It's still winter, it's not even time for spring training," Itzak Klein said.

"Never too late, never too early to worry about these things."

"How come you came to the funeral, Mr. Klein?" Flo asked.

"Me, she never hurt," he said, shrugging.

"She used to complain about you all the time."

"We call it *kvetching*, and *kvetching* does not kill. Besides, I made her a promise."

"You should be a politician," Lester Wrong said, "only politicians make promises."

"This is not such a bad idea," Itzak said.

"I wish Web were here," she said. "He sometimes used to talk to her. She'd been in show business years ago when she was a girl, worked with a knife thrower or something like that..."

"I saw her dancing in the back alley by herself once," Adam said.

"Ain't it a life," the preacher said.

The new cemetery was beyond the suburbs. For the first time, Adam was a pall bearer. He tried not to stumble in the slushy snow. "Now I know," Lester Wrong laughed, "why I go to the Y ... the older you get the more coffins you carry." As Adam stood beside the aluminum tubular casing that held the coffin over the open hole, the tubes gleaming in the grey light, he realized that there were no headstones across the field. It was a new cemetery where no headstones were allowed – because they were too expensive the Church said; it was all a flatness of snow, of ugly fluorescent plastic wreaths and plastic flowers shining in a white emptiness, *devoid, devoid, just dead little moon stones laid flat under the snow, no monumental sense of small lives lived big or even remembered by lovers or haters but only neon glaring colored plastic wreaths, no assertion of herself* or anybody's self, flat, sensible, shoddy economic fields empty of everything except the overwhelming emptiness, but then Itzak Klein said: "I have a last word, a promise –

Yitgadal veyitkadach shmé rahbaw ...

* * *

In his darkroom, Adam opened a box filled with negatives and held one up to the light; shadow figures caught in a stillness, a transparent tissue of time, like a cell tissue, held in the air to the light, a moment reminding him that he'd actually been somewhere, a transparency that confirmed the fact ... but what is a fact, what is transparency? when you have to go back ten years to begin to understand two years ... and the boxes of prints stacked against a wall, were they the moments that had his stamp of approval? ... this I will remember: this will be found by someone ... perhaps forgotten or thrown away, but it will be found, and he spread six or seven prints on the table and constructed a scene the way it was or maybe all that matters is that somehow I came out of this with a detail, a glimpse and maybe a glimpse is the best we get, except for the shaping ... of how it was for me, and what else is there, except the way others want it for themselves? "The way others want it for themselves," he said, and shut the light that pin-hole of encircled emptiness, the lens, more alive the deeper I go into the darkroom, akin to lust, pleasure along the inside of my thighs, under my chin, a reverberation in my throat, heartbeat of a small animal trapped inside, in the fingertips, flesh pads so susceptible to pain, CLICK, like plucking petals, cruel yet sensual, consummated and discarded, lust, as faces emerge, the private

exhibition of the self as if life were a public peep show, each solitary
shadow a wound under the skin, unseen, and what if what appears is
always the reality under the skin, each shadow an image of what's to
come, a real life, a prophecy made and shucked aside in a drawer, all
the drawers I have now, drawers and drawers of evidence, but against
whom? For what? To prove something out there actually exists ...?
He often sat in the dark in the darkroom with new prints
hanging on a wire line, listening to the silences between
memories *which is where photographs hang out, in still spaces,*
memories of a windless hour with no birds in Jerusalem with a
writer who had no family, all lost in the death camps, who
told him, "You collapse, yet everything is normal. We've had
to change our attitude so many times that now our problems
are empty." He'd photographed him in the desert light,
standing in the rubble of stones and taut yellow thorn
branches, a dark shadow against dark shimmering waste, and
then in the light of dusk outside Dung Gate, his round face
flattened like a dead moon, deep lines bracketing his mouth
and the little sacks like prayer bags under his eyes. The next
day, he'd said: "See, there you are yourself, both of you, and
you'd hardly know who you are, except they're both you for
sure." They'd laughed and embraced, *stasis, stopped time,*
that's what we want, moments held, as if they were facts for ever even
if forgotten, or always there if needed, the face, a consolation in a
drawer between layers of silk as life dissolves and for the rest of the
week he'd walked with his camera through the lean stone
alleys, the stones at the top of the walls white, and in the
shadow of the wall, men seeking refuge, and a young soldier
with a red beard slumped on a roof above a rain gutter,
cradling his Uzi as pilgrims genuflected below him, kissing a

stone; and at the old temple wall, as evening darkness fell, rows of soft-faced paratroopers stood at attention in battle dress, young boys being inducted, while on a platform, under the huge paratrooper insignia set on fire in the night sky, a man let out a whining nasal cry, a prayer ...

Adam had sent that transparency, those rapt faces, their rifle barrels beside their cheeks, staring at a lone bearded man in khaki reaching into the darkness under the arc of fire, to his magazine with a note: "You collapse, yet everything is normal. *Man kann sich totsiegen!*" It was never printed, *these planes of light, as if some tension held the whole thing together, held the landscape with invisible wires, joists and crossbeams no one can see, at ease with the sea folding, held together in my eye as if there were an underlying meaning but who is holding me, my face that's never the same face in the glass, yet there I am, serious, puzzled, manic, pitying, detached, all true, none of it true* and back home several months later he had an argument about those rapt faces with his editor, a stern woman with broad shoulders and small breasts:

"Why not?"

"We'd get crucified, and besides, it's biased."

"What the hell are you talking about?"

"You wouldn't want to take a picture like that unless you were biased."

"It was right there in front of my eyes."

"The whole world's in front of your eyes. You're gonna give me soldiers and burning letters in the sky in the holy land and not expect me to get the point?"

"I didn't light up the sky."

"And I don't light up your life. So what else is new?"

"Nothing's new. It's an old story."

"The trouble with guys like you," she said, "is you don't love. Not with passion. You just look, and that lets you off the hook, because you think you can be cynical about people who deserve to be loved."

"So now I'm a lousy lover. Next thing you'll tell me is I've got no balls."

"You've got more balls than brains. And," she said picking up the photograph, "what is this *man kann sich totsiegen* shit?"

"It's true…"

"Don't fuck my head, I had it translated. "*Drive yourself victoriously into the grave*," and she laughed and said, scowling, "Look, you're one of the best in the world, you know the name of the game, gimme a paratrooper helping a refugee girl across the road, maybe we'll run them both. Balance. There's got to be balance, you know that."

"Balance is a lie."

"We got responsibilities, responsibilities to more than what you spy with your little eye."

They stood apart, Adam staring out the window through metallic slat blinds. Then he turned, smiling, as if nothing were the matter.

"I hear you've got all kinds of shoes, racks of them, fifty pairs of shoes."

"I got a lot of shoes," she said. "I like shoes, it's not a crime."

"I hear every Saturday morning, you vacuum inside your shoes."

"So, maybe I do," she said, drawing back as he put his hands on her shoulders, and kissed her lightly on the cheek.

"I'd like to photograph you vacuuming your shoes. I would. I once did a whole series on shoes. It's how I'd like to remember you."

*   *   *

In their small out-country hotel room overlooking the sea, Gabrielle set two stones she had picked up on the beach on the window sill, and then she stood facing the open window. There was a banana tree outside the window, the broad leaves chopped back, the trunk scarred, and the pulp of a banana exposed in a green cluster. A hummingbird hovered in the air, its needle beak darting into the white meat.

"That is so beautiful," she said. "To be able to fly so fast you can stand still in the air."

"We're lucky to find this place."

"I don't believe in luck," she said. "People who look for luck never get it. They get bad luck, or no luck at all."

She opened her expensive black leather travelling bag and hung several silk and cotton sun dresses in the closet, along with silk blouses and a black skirt. At ease, as if she were alone as he sprawled on the bed, she began to unbutton her shirt, and then she said, "Do you remember what I look like?"

"You've a mole on your right breast and a little scar from scalding on your hip, when your mother spilt a pot of water on you."

"Do you remember what I said to you the last time?"

"No."

"I always wanted to remember you seeing me!"

"I lived with a woman once for two years," he said, "and I

can't remember her body at all. Can't even smell her. Just the sound of her voice, a high-pitched nasal edge. I don't know how I stood it."

"Oh, American women," she said with a shrug, bare-breasted and undoing the belt to her skirt. "They have voices that could cut glass."

"She wasn't American. She was French."

"Worse. They all sound as if their sinuses are shot."

In her high heels, she let her skirt fall, turned the ankle of her long leg, and said, "It's not the leg that really does it ... it's the dip in the small of the back," and she touched the little hollow in her back. "Without the dip you really don't have it for a dancer," and she stepped out of her white panties and laid them over the two stones on the window sill. "So, now you see me again. It's not luck. I somehow knew you would," and she turned slowly in the late afternoon light. "Now I'm going to take a shower." She kicked off her shoes and he heard the drumming of water on the walls of the glass shower stall.

There was a swan craning its neck, as if caught in a trap, stencilled in the glass of the shower door. He stepped into the shower and she seemed startled – her eyes widening, filled with wonder, and that had always been the mystery of her beautiful eyes: no matter how self-assured, how knowing, she always seemed struck by the freshness of a moment, staring at him as if she'd never seen him before, slowly soaping her breasts, glistening with an oil sheen, the water pouring down her shoulders, and then she reached out and soaped his chest, as if to make sure he was actually there in the steam as he took her in his arms, cradling her, and then they kissed, water running into their mouths, and they tried to keep their eyes open in the rush of water but they blinked and laughed and he kissed her breasts and her nipples and then slid down her body, holding her waist and then her buttocks, his head in the hollow of her thighs, shower water tumbling down her belly and into his mouth, streams of water rushing in his ears as if he were suspended in stillness until she began to shudder, rising up on her toes, and then she sank down into the shower well with him where they held each other, water pouring against them as they lay there, coursing over their faces so that they hid in each other's necks, soothed under the force of water.

part SEVEN

Their small hotel was on the outskirts of the country town, past a squat white church with a tin roof and SOFT DRINK shack along the side of a road that went down a slope of pigeon-grey stone to the sea. Through their bedroom window, beyond the banana tree and palms and candlewood and satinwood trees that covered the slope, they could see the sea and taste salt on the humid air in the morning. They showered and drank coffee from small porcelain bowls in the warm shade of the branches of pink and yellow *poiu* trees in a courtyard of red clay walls covered by yellow climbing alamanda vines.

"Did you hear the *coqui* last night?"

"The night birds?"

"They're not birds."

"It sounded like trees full of chirping birds to me."

"They're frogs, tiny little frogs."

"They sound like birds."

"Well, they're not."

"You hear the cicadas now, with the cicadas going on like that it's going to rain."

"No it's not, the sky's cloudless."

"It doesn't matter, the clouds'll come."

"What'll we do today?"

"We'll swim naked in the sea."

"No, we won't."

"Why?"

"Because we're going into town. We should see where we are."

"I don't want to know where I am."

"What do you want?"

"To swim on your body."

"You see this," she said, running her hands through her long hair so that her hair fell over her face, then touching a tendril of slightly withered buds that was clinging to a stone. "It's very beautiful at night. It's like blooming drops of water and it only blooms at night, and it dies with the daylight."

"You know something," he said. "I don't think you're nearly as dark as you like to think you are."

"I'm not dark," she said, "I've got beautiful porcelain skin."

"I mean inside."

"Inside," she said, "we play hide and seek."

The owner of the hotel, a man with a clipped brush moustache and white wrinkles at the corners of his mouth and wearing a black band on his shirt sleeve, came through the lattice doorway into the courtyard.

"What would you drink?" he asked.

"It's awfully hot," Adam said.

"Let's drink white wine," Gabrielle said.

"Cold white wine."

"Or beer. Big cold beers. Two big glasses of dark beer."

The owner brought two glasses of brown beer and put the glasses of beer and two hemp pads on the table.

"I am sorry," Adam said.

"What for?" the owner asked.

"You are in mourning."

"No, no, it is over," the owner said, slapping his hands to his chest and laughing. "It is over now, the nine nights of *floron* are over and I know the child who died last week is truly dead and there will be playing by the other children on the little hill."

"What hill?"

"The hill you drove down. You must have your drink and then come back up the hill."

A bell struck ten in the church tower in the town. They walked along a narrow sandy road and the brown grass beside the steep road was ankle deep. Shadows seemed stencilled into the grass, still shadows under a pale blue sky, with a poised gull in the sky. They passed half-cleared fields and cactus farmers and a row of dead trees. There were clusters of birds in the dead trees. They heard voices from over the rise of the hill, and then on a small flatland facing out to the sea they saw twenty boys and girls dressed in white blouses scampering in circles, flying kites into the wind off the cliff and holding fistfuls of colored balloons by long strings *and they walked around the bodies of young boys and girls stretched out and slumped against the buildings, grey and tattered children, and someone had propped up a sign: REDEMPTION IS LOVE and* two girls with long black braids curtsied to each other and began to dance, laughing, in the long grass *and then a pale girl with black eyes stuck up her head and saw Adam coming and said, "Say man, snap your picture with my pussy for five bucks …" a long string tied to her toes and at the end of it a white balloon floating in the air, a distress signal, and the white balloon got lost in a night filled with rippling electric stars* and Gabrielle said, "It's like a dream. They look like dream children."

"No, they are our village children," the owner of the hotel said.

"What's your name?" Adam asked.

"Trigueño."

"Adam."

"Gabrielle."

"How do you do?"

"Very well."

"The weather is good for you. It is always good at this time of year."

"But the cicadas."

"The cicadas are wrong. There is no reason why cicadas should always be right."

A boy carrying an armload of scarlet *flamboyan* was giving a flower to each child. He handed flowers to Gabrielle and Adam.

"Would you like to go first?" Trigueño asked.

"Where?"

"What for?"

"To throw flowers."

The children had crowded close to the cliff. A strong breeze had come up, pulling the kites and balloons, so that some children while trying to hold on to their balloons dropped their flowers and then as they knelt to pick up the flowers they lost their grip on the strings and the balloons, yellow and blue and green, were caught on the wind and carried out over the sea, disappearing into the sun as Trigueño, his hand on a child's shoulder, chanted:

Y Dios sobresaltado, nos oprime
el pulso, grave, mudo,
y como padre a su pequeña,
apenas,
pero apenas, entreabre los sangrientos flamboyans
y entre sus dedos toma a la esperanza

and the children all threw their flowers into the wind and watched as the flowers like gaping blood-filled mouths fell to the sea but two boys who had lost their balloons began to cry and point at the balloons and then they wrestled with the children beside them, trying to take their balloons, and the balloons broke: *pop pop pop* ... a little girl ran to a tree and threw her arms around the trunk as if she were reaching for her mother's apron strings. As the other children suddenly scattered over the hill, going home, running between other cactus farmers, Trigueño shrugged at the bawling children and said, "Tears, tears, the cicadas were right," and he pointed out across the water to the balloons that were specks in the far light: "They are like souls gone away for ever." He stood in his own silence, shielding his eyes from the sun. Adam laughed and took Gabrielle's hand. "Maybe," he said, "but that's not what old Itzak Klein said."

"Itzak Klein?"

"Yeah."

"How come you remember him?"

"I always remember him."

"So what did he say about what?"

"He told me once that balloons breaking, in the language of balloons, was their laughter. Maybe those balloons were laughing at the ones who thought they got away."

* * *

Here lies
John Plewes Waters
Who came to this city
and died
for the benefit
of his health.
1898–1932

* * *

"I like to sing at funerals," Father Zale said. He was not wearing a soutane but a tailored black suit and a black shirt. He did not wear his soutane any more. He was always dressed very carefully in black, except sometimes he wore a white panama hat against the sun. "I think graveyards are lost places of play. We should picnic on the heads of the dead, let them know we're not afraid. Do you know what's strange about growing old? Not just the smell, because age has its own smell, a strange, almost acrid marigold smell that eases out of the pores, but for the first time I can feel the weight of my hand as it hangs at the end of my wrist, the weight of my lower lip. We grow older and get more fragile, yet all I feel is weight, everything gets heavier."

"How about your heart?"

He was sitting on a white wooden lawn bench under the bird feeders with a thermos by his feet, the silver cup-top in his hand filled with chilled white wine. His skin was pink and he was flushed because he hadn't seen Adam for four years and he fussed with a fistful of notes in his pocket and then he handed the cup to Adam and opened a book that had been beside him on the bench. "What do you think of this?" he asked, reading aloud: "Nearly everything great comes into being in spite of something – in spite of sorrow or suffering, poverty, destitution, physical weakness, depravity, passion or a thousand other handicaps ... met by a haughty masculinity which stands motionless, ashamed, with jaw set, while swords and spear points beset the body ... and to be poised against fatality, to meet adverse conditions gracefully, is more than simple endurance; it is an act of aggression, a positive triumph – this is enough to make one question whether there really is any heroism other than weakness. And in any case, what heroism could be more in keeping with the times?" Father Zale rubbed his big hand across the white stubble of his unshaven cheek and said, "What do you think of that in these times?"

"They're wild times," Adam said.

"More woolly than wild."

"How so?"

"I'm old, I just sit watching TV after supper. That's what old folks do."

"That's what kids do."

"Then they're old before their time. Anyway, sometimes it all seems like one great big talk show. Never had so many snappers and snarlers pumping information at me in my life but nobody seems to know anything."

"We know their names."

"Who?"

"Everybody doing the talking."

"Well, that's just it. It's all name dropping."

He poured white wine into the silver cup. They both drank, looking up and listening to the drone of an old passing single-prop plane. The tall pine trees were full of starlings.

"I know all about droppings," Father Zale said, laughing. "First it was seagulls and now it's starlings, scavengers and noisy twirps," and he took hold of Adam's forearm. "You've been all over the world since you left here, so what's the most moving thing you've seen?"

"Moving?"

"What touched you, what left you motionless, and ashamed ... ?"

Adam hunched forward, his elbows on his knees.

"A shoe," he said.

"A shoe?"

"Yes."

"What do you mean, a shoe?"

"An empty shoe by the side of the road."

"Where?"

"Doesn't matter. Somewhere near Sidon. It was a canvas shoe, maybe a small woman's shoe, like it was just stepped out of by the side of the road, and I stood there staring into the empty shoe, right out in the middle of nowhere, and I thought of all the shoes that ended up nowhere, just stepped out of by somebody on the road to nowhere. It suddenly seemed to me that the whole of life was in the empty shoe, like it was a wound along the way to where we all want to go, to wherever we're going, but we don't get there, we just leave our shoes behind."

"Yes," the old priest said. "Yes, I can see that."

"I began to see it all over the place. Shoes. Wounds left by the side of the road, filled with the emptiness of pain, filled with a light ..."

"Pain is a light for you?"

"Empty shoes are a light, like the light in faces, worn out or down at the heels, polished till there's nothing left to polish, too paper-thin to last ... They're everything we are." They both turned toward the *scree scree* of seagulls settling on the mansard roof. "And why not, because the nerves to every place in our bodies are in our feet. A woman taught me that. There are little spots on your feet, there's a map to your feet, and you can rub and massage those spots to ease your liver, your spleen, your heart. That's why when they burn the soles of a man's feet he can feel it everywhere, fire inside the whole of his body. The worst thing was a huge pile of children's shoes. Somehow it was worse than seeing stacked bodies, it was like all those lives had been sucked out of the world, vacuumed out ..."

"Clean wounds?"

"Something like that."

"Full of their own light?"

"For me anyway."

"You'd better be careful," the old priest said. Though the ground was covered with crusts, he took a fistful from his knapsack and cast more broken bread across the lawn.

"Why's that?"

The seagulls lifted off the roof and circled and then settled around the bench, spearing crusts with their beaks.

"I'm just saying pain's something a priest knows about, that what a priest carries inside himself is all the possibilities of pain, the five wounds."

"Is that where you think god's living?"

"Yes, in his wounds."

"Maybe," Adam said, "god is really old Mother Hubbard, living in a shoe."

"Why would he want to live in a shoe?"

"So he can put the boots to us."

"You know," Father Zale said, laughing, "Shakespeare had it all wrong."

"What?"

"Saying whoever jests at scars has never felt a wound."

"So?"

"It's those who've been wounded who jest at wounds."

"You mean god's sitting in his shoe laughing."

"Yes."

"Why?"

"That's the only defence a victim has."

"And he's a victim."

"Sure. Of all our sins. I heard a man the other night on TV who said he'd lost his whole family in concentration camps, and now he's a minister of defence or minister of public order or something like that and he was standing beside a tank explaining that the world had to understand that there's a new and terrible terrorism loose, and guys like you, Adam, taking pictures of kids throwing stones at soldiers who shoot the kids, guys like you showing the soldiers in a bad light, you are part of it, part of the new terrorism of the victim, that's what he said, the terrorism of the victim, and just behind him there was this kid with a stone in his hand, smiling, and I thought to myself, there is God in that smile."

* * *

There were three green balloons on their bed. The shutters were closed, the room was dark and the floor tiles were cold. They could smell jasmine on the humid air.

"I don't want to sleep," he said. "I don't like to sleep in the afternoon."

"Neither do I."

"Do you want a cold beer?"

"No."

"Neither do I," he said.

"It's funny you should remember Itzak Klein."

"Why's it funny?"

"I knew him."

"We all knew him."

"No, later, in New York," she said, sitting down in a white wicker chair, closing her eyes and slipping off her shoes.

"When was he ever in New York?"

"Right after I got to New York."

"You mean after your mother died?"

"Right after she jumped. I knew she would."

"You knew that?"

"Sure."

"You couldn't stop her?"

"How could I stop her?"

"I don't know."

She opened her eyes a little, holding very still, her stillness suggesting a half-awake resentful defiance as she seemed to look past him, past everything.

"So when did you see Itzak?" he asked.

"He came to a nightclub, I was a kid in the chorus line."

"And Itzak just dropped in and said hello."

"No. He didn't see me at all."

"You saw him?"

"Yes. He was with his brother."

"His brother?"

"Yes."

"I didn't know he had a brother."

"Neither did I. So I sat down and said who I was and he stood up and we shook hands and said we're friends so his brother said if you're friends then I guess we're all friends."

"I can't believe it," he said, lying down so that the green balloons bounced and rolled off the bed onto the tile floor. They watched them rock to a stop.

"Neither could I," she said.

"He was a wonderful man."

"You sound like he's dead."

"I don't know. I don't think so. I haven't been home for a while."

"He and his brother owned a hotel."

"In New York?"

"No. Nowhere you've ever been."

"I've been a lot of places."

"You been to Gabon?"

"Where?"

"Gabon."

"Cut it out," he said.

"I'm not kidding," she said, laughing. "I worked there, Libreville."

"Libreville?"

"Sure. I worked for his brother, Danilo, in the casino."

"You're telling me little old Itzak Klein shuffling along our sidewalk in his slippers owned a casino hotel in Libreville?"

"Itzak and his brother. His brother was a hard man."

"And you worked there?"

"Right."

"And he never told anyone, not even Harry, that he'd seen you in New York?"

"Right."

"Right. How the hell can all this be right?"

"Because that's the way it was. I was just as astonished as you are when he told me all about himself and his brother and how they'd made their money during the war." She crossed and uncrossed her legs. "He was very sentimental in New York, seeing his brother. He said he hadn't seen him for three years."

"Yeah."

"Yeah what?"

"How'd they make their money? Itzak never had any money. He went around collecting butterflies and mumbling about revolution and getting beaten up."

"He and his brother got out of Vienna when they were boys."

"The war?"

"They got to Tangiers where there were these Orthodox families dealing in currencies, anybody's money, even Vichy francs, and they got in on that and made a lot but what they really made their money on was chocolate."

"Chocolate!"

"They said it was like gold during the war, better than gold. You could trade it with the Krauts for prisoners, if you can believe that. And when the war was over, his brother looked on a map for where to go and he went with all the money to Libreville and they built a hotel and got richer and richer and met every three years in New York."

"And you just took off with them?"

"With Danilo."

"You were Danilo's little girl?"

"I was a croupier."

"I thought you were a dancer."

"Not there. You sign a contract for a year, and they're mostly English girls with wonky accents working to get money to buy into a boutique back home and slip through the class system but they give the bush hotels by the ocean a little tone because they seem so stern and thin-lipped and they're not supposed to mingle with the blacks but that's no problem because they're all pretty prejudiced anyway and stick to themselves since they can't stand black men but they like being cooed at like little duchesses and then when their year's over most of them go home except I met Mio and I didn't go home."

"What about Harry?"

"Harry's where he is and I'm where I am."

"And you were with Mio?"

"Yes."

"What was he doing?"

"Managing the casino."

"A couple of high rollers."

"He and Itzak's brother got into the arms business. They're the only straightshooters in casinos, the guys with the guns. And after that I took off into the bush for a while, I worked at a hospital."

"Shooting craps ..."

"Don't be smart. You're smarter than that."

"So what were you doing?"

"A leper camp hospital. One of the girls came down with leprosy so I took her there and I went to look after her."

"And Harry knows nothing?"

"No."

"Why not?"

"Because I don't want him to."

"Why not?"

"Because I don't."

"How can you be so hard on Harry?"

"I'm not hard on Harry. He was hard on me."

"You treat him like he's dead."

"In his own way, he did die in me, but he's alive and in me all the time."

* * *

It was raining. A shell burst near the river bank. Soldiers in grey helmets and grey uniforms carrying grenades clipped to their belts and machine pistols slid down a red mud embankment and climbed up into the back of a troop truck, the canvas flapping in the rain and wind. The truck ground its gears, drove onto a short bridge, and blew up. Wounded men crawled out into the long grass. One had his hands in the air, waving a map. He was shot dead by a sniper. The map fell into a rut full of slimy water. "Sneak attack, sneak attack," a soldier yelled and fired flares, silver-red blooms in the dark rain, flares that suddenly went out, and Henri stepped out of the tub of water, swept up a worn blanket from an old worn horsehair settee, and hung it across the window. He unchained the baby gorilla and held him in his arms as another shell exploded close to the hotel. The stench seeped into the room.

"They have hit the garbage dump," Henri said.

The gorilla whimpered.

"Seems like it's goddamn dead on," Adam said.

"I wonder where Esmelda is."

"You worried?"

"No, except she has no resilience any more, the heat here draws all your nerves to their ends ..."

The gorilla curled his lips back from his big yellow teeth.

"Why do you think we met?" Henri asked, putting his bare feet back into the tub of water.

"I don't know."

"No one knows, but even if we do not know we should try to say why."

"Why?"

Henri rested his head against the gorilla's neck. His eyes were hooded, absorbed, serious, his legs trembling.

"I wish we had cigars," he said.

"You want a cigar?"

"*Mais oui. Le chemin par où je suis venu je l'ai oublié.* So I close my eyes and dream I'm on a beach in Cuba."

"You ever been to Cuba?"

"*Non. Mes lèvres bégayent un je ne sais quoi.*"

"Why do you want to know why we met?"

"Because this is *une existence sans contour ni désir, stupide.*"

"Who said life had to have a shape?"

"Our only revenge is to laugh, and to insist that there was a point, *un peu de pudeur,* that we met for a reason," and Henri, with a sad smile, reached for his revolver and aimed it at the framed row of oval portraits. "Maybe the point is to kill them at last."

"The founding fathers?"

"Yes."

"If it gives you pleasure."

"It will not."

"Seven little pigeons."

"If it gives me no pleasure why should I kill them?"

"To give them pleasure."

"No, no. It is necessary to do better than that. It must be something more tantalizing ..."

"But who cares?"

"I do," Henri said fiercely, "I care. *Qu'à ton choix tu choisisses.* Do you think I care what is done by those morons out there, when they are shooting each other in the back?" Henri tossed his head, his hooded eyes half-open. Adam stared at him, feeling a stirring of kinship that lifted him out of his lassitude; he had the vague sense of disintegration, of danger in Henri's eyes.

"Have you drunk river water?" Henri asked.

"No."

"Maybe that is why we are here together. *La tantouze tient le fin bout*, to get the taste of slime, the river water."

"We may never get back down to the river."

Henri nestled against the gorilla's neck. The shelling had stopped and so had the rain and a strong breeze had come up, belling the blanket in the window. The man with the hunch took down the blanket and asked if they wanted more tea. Adam tried to get control of a sudden rage that astonished him, a blind desire to beat the hunchback, his nerves suddenly feeling on fire, and he sighed, shaking, almost as if he had a fever, full of his own exhaustion, and he slumped in his chair, overcome by the heavy acrid reek of sour rot and blossoms *in the room all through the night, the coqui drilling two notes into the dark scent of jasmine until in the morning light, holding me with her wide eyes, her half-averted head, full of that half-asleep resentful defiance as she seemed again to look past everything, seeing the shadows in sunshine, and in spite of all she saw she still was lost, lost with me hurrying after her afraid of the loss I felt in her, as if a hollow had taken root in her, a growing hollow, and the more happy, delirious we were, throwing her arms open in the night, the more she sank into herself, lying there half-asleep in her dreams, clutching*

— Do you know?

— What?

– ... how could you?
– Maybe I could.
– ... except in a way you already have
– And if I couldn't?
– ... replace him, the way he touched me so gently while Mother sat across the kitchen table from her favorite choir master as proper as could be and smiled as if she was happy to see him gentle, even if it was gentle with me, so she chose to think, mothers are strange,

and drenched in sweat she went back to sleep and maybe those morning half-sleeps sweating it out were why we met again ...

"What?"

"Nothing."

"You say we met to sweat it out," Henri said.

"No, no."

"That's what you said."

"I did?"

"Yes. We are sitting here to sweat it out."

"I guess we are," drenched in sweat except it began with blood, the stain on the sheet they used to fling out the window so that everything proper and sacred and necessary could begin and suddenly Harry was free, you'd set him free, and towels didn't matter, and I didn't want to resist though I was repelled and I didn't want to say no though I'd stepped like a shadow through a door like I'd left myself behind, appalled by my own pleasure, as if my soul was being drawn out of my body through my bones that were long hollow reeds and I heard the high droning note my soul made like cicadas as it fled through the hollow into an explosion of light

thumpf thumpf thumpf

"Jesus, I can't believe it ..."

Incoming shells seemed to be exploding just behind the hotel.

Henri leapt up, and the gorilla flailing in mid-air bounded to the hunchback huddled in a corner.

"You goddamn better believe," Henri cried. *"Que la tantouze tient le fin bout, et que c'est en quoi que nous sommes à la coule ..."*

Howitzer rocket rifles were firing *thumpf thumpf thumpf thumpf* followed by the heavy clacking of 50-calibre machine guns and the whine of shells. Explosions blew bits of branches through the window. They sat staring into smoke and fire-filled trees, each leaf on fire, and Henri handed Adam the revolver as they heard a trombone call from the floor below, a shot, and then running on the stairs. Henri reached under the settee for a machine pistol and as he stood up the door was stomped open by two guerrillas. Henri wheeled around but a guerrilla shot him, two short bursts, and Henri jack-knifed onto his back into the galvanized tub of water, the machine pistol still in his grip, pointing straight up as he stared, firing into the ceiling, tearing holes in the white plaster, and the baby gorilla swung away from the hunchback and around the tub, leaping onto the shoulder of the guerrilla who had shot Henri, sinking his yellow teeth into his throat, the man reeling back, his gurgling howl smothered in the arms of the gorilla, his jugular blood swooshing like a fan over Henri's head. The other guerrilla backed into the dark stairwell, giggling hysterically, and then spun around toward the stairs. Adam aimed, repelled, though unable to resist, and fired. The man slumped and rolled down the stairs to the landing between floors. Adam went down the stairwell, the blood-drenched gorilla leaping up and down behind him, hysterical with a happy crazed look in his eyes, curling his lips. The guerrilla's running shoes had holes in the soles. Adam couldn't stand the gorilla's happy screeching. He thought of shooting the gorilla. He went back upstairs. Dead Henri had emptied his machine pistol. Water was pouring through holes in the ceiling, silver streams of water drenching Henri's face and chest, washing the blood from his wounds into the tub.

"Fuck, you shot out the cistern," Adam said.

The hunchback was moaning and weeping in the corner. The gorilla sat on the dead guerrilla's face, beaming, blood still drooling from his jaws. Then he leapt across the room and crawled like a child into the hunchback's arms. Adam sat down facing the founding fathers, the pistol loose in his hand.

"Now," he said ruefully, "maybe we know why."

He waited. The reverberating *thumpf thumpf* from the hills stopped, the dry clattering of gunfire stopped. He felt worn out and raw as if his skin had been scraped from his bones. The sun had come out and a strong wind had come up, blowing away the haze and smoke. But the trees were still smouldering in this fresh silence. Tanks pulled away from the hotel and parked beyond the traffic circle. Someone turned on a radio, the music pulsing through the trees, and then, in a clipped accent, he heard the BBC news. He waited. He had never killed anyone, and in his mind he wanted to weep for himself because he was now defenceless, he could never again say, "Why me? What for?" He stared at Henri washed in his own blood, waiting for someone to charge up the stairs and arrest him, but there was no sound, no one came up the stairs, no one called. No one came and Adam got up, the water from the roof cistern overflowing the tub. Henri was half-afloat in the pink water, his head bobbing, eyes staring into the drip drip drip, the floor slimy with his blood. Adam stood up and saw the gorilla and the hunchback holding each other: "I'm sure you are innocent," he said and aimed at them, surprised by his own cackling laughter. But he didn't fire. He shoved the revolver down into his belt and went down the dark stairs, stepping over the dead guerrilla whose arms were bent back between the shoulder blades, reaching for his pain. Stopping at his room he listened but there was no noise down the hall. He picked up a small suitcase and his camera bag and went down to the dark elbow-shaped lobby. A bandsman lay dead, curled around his trombone. He was wearing leather short pants and blue and white striped knee-socks. The other bandsmen were sitting by their luggage crying. There were no soldiers in the street and Adam waited in the doorway, not moving, waiting for a sign. There were only lone bleary-eyed men in brown great-coats, wearing woollen caps, who stood in the doorways of blown-out stores. He realized what he had been missing: there had been no helicopters, no swarming air-sucking thwacking of the silence ... but beyond the hotel trees, the troop truck on the bridge was a charred steel frame and three men covered in mud and burned cloth lay on the slope of the embankment. Then, in the long grass under the charred trees, he saw the keening white woman, naked, crawling in circles. She still held her high heels in her hands. She stood up, her face smeared with mud, shaking her head: it was Esmelda, squinting at him, sparrow-breasted, little folds of flesh under her large nipples, and narrow-hipped, a thick blotch of black hair between her legs. He had never gotten used to the boldness of a blotch of black hair on a pale woman's body: it, more than anything else, made him turn away from all the old photographs of dead women stacked in mass graves, hair that kept growing after death, hair hiding the hollow of the womb:

"*Rien n'est perdu*," she cried.

"Oh yes, yes, it is," he said and made sure the revolver was firm under his belt. He hunched forward, running toward the river docks. Empty pirogues were tied together, the longest at one end, the shortest at the other: "Christ, they look like a fucking flute," *or coffins for all shapes and sizes, give me your long, your short, your tall*. He cut the end one loose and lay down in it, letting the current in the narrow channel carry him toward a hook in the opposite shore, and then he sat up, realizing there were no soldiers on the shore, and paddled as hard as he could, driving the pirogue into the mud. He leapt out and ran to his Mercedes that was still parked in front of the BUDGET sign. The hood was covered by the ash of burned leaves and the windows had been blown out and there was glittering powdered glass all over the front seat. He sat in the car, not moving. All the soldiers seemed to have moved south. One of the men in a brown great-coat began to snicker and move out of a doorway toward him. He was a hulking man. "That fucker's gonna eat me raw." He started the car and drove slowly to the other side of the traffic circle and across the canal bridge to the north. He pulled over to the side of the road and waited. "I got more nerve than Dick Tracy," he said aloud, began to shake, and then laughed. He wasn't sure why he was running now, but all his instincts told him this was the time, "and if you don't bet when you get the hunch," an old gambler had told him, "then you wear the hunch on your back." There were no tanks on the road as he leaned forward over the steering wheel into the empty window. There were birds, big black birds. He inadvertently ducked, afraid they might dive and pluck out his eyes, but when he quickly looked up going around a bend he saw a grey tank with a black star on the turret sitting by the side of the road between tall trees. He felt as if a fist had closed in his bowels and he was about to brake but instead accelerated, his forearms aching with the weakness of panic as he held the wheel on the rough road, watching the tank cannon swivel toward him, picking him up, following him ... as he pushed harder on the gas, charging into the exploding fireball if it was going to come. He passed the tank, refusing to look back, hunched up over the wheel, pressing against the wheel, unable to believe that he had actually gone around another turn, that he was out of cannon sight. He braked to a stop on the empty road, letting out a whining moan, pain tearing at his lungs. He closed his eyes and didn't move for a long time. At last, he opened his eyes and looked down the road, down the hollow through the relentless dense green, and then he heard birds and looked to the side and saw two barefoot soldiers in tattered fatigues hanging by the neck from a branch. After a moment's silence he began to sing quietly – more of a cry than singing:

> *Oh we ain't got a barrel of money,*
> *Maybe we're ragged and funny*
> *But we travel along,*
> *Singing our song,*
> *Side by side.*

part EIGHT

He found his mother at her dressing table. She had on an old felt cloche hat and though she was staring at herself in the mirror she was sitting so still she seemed asleep. Then she said to Adam in the mirror, "You left all the lights on last night."

"No I didn't," he said.

"Who did then?"

"You did, Mother."

"It couldn't have been me," she said.

"Why not?"

"I like to undress in the dark."

Sometimes he heard her pacing in the dark and got up and went to look for her. Sometimes she wept in her sleep, and then in the morning, as if she had been awake and listening to herself, she bit into her dry toast and said, "When I was a little girl I had a round glass ball. It was very heavy and full of falling snow if I turned it, and I turned it all the time. I thought I had hold of the world. Now everything gets whiter and whiter and I spin and spin inside my sleep."

One night in early April, after the last thaw, he found her out behind the house walking in slow circles, staring up at the stars in the clear sky.

"You always loved the stars," she said.

"Yes."

"They told me when I was a child that there were angels on all the stars and now the angels are all gone."

"Are you sure?"

"They were there when I was a child."

"But how do you know they're gone?"

"Because we went out and looked, and the moon's gone too."

"No it's not. It's right there."

"But there's nothing there. The moon's nothing. They walked all over it and I've got no angels any more. You can't be a little girl without angels."

"Sure you can."

"No you can't. The sky's full of stones. It's like a stone in your shoe. It hurts. I'm the old woman who lives in her shoe."

*   *   *

In a heavily treed park downtown, there was a plain yellow brick church tower, one of the oldest towers in the city; the gutted walls of the church had been pulled down after a fire that had started on a cold day in a wood stove but the lean tower had been left standing and chemically cleaned and now it was surrounded by rose gardens and weeping willows across the road from a small squat steam bath, The Grange Health Baths. Web and Adam sat in one of the white-tiled steam rooms beside each other on an upper cedar bench with white towels wrapped around their waists. The steam was dense and they were sweating heavily. There was a man across the room on another bench, a thick-set shadow in the steam except for his spindly calves and bony feet that seemed to hang out of the cloud of steam clinging to the ceiling.

"How's it going, gentlemen?" the man said. He had a quiet husky voice. He spoke slowly, deliberately clipping his words.

"Okay," Web said after a pause.

"Me, too."

"Good."

The man crossed his ankles and put his hands on his knees. "I see you sitting there, Web," he said.

"You do," Web said, surprised, squinting into the steam.

"Sure I do. I sit in a lot of steam in my time. You learn how to see."

"So what do you see?"

"You. What else? I see you and your son. It's some years since I seen him but he seems like your son. How you doing son?"

"Okay."

"That's good. We should all do okay."

"Who are you?"

"You can't see?"

"No, I can't see."

"You don't know me, my voice?"

"No, I don't know you."

"I could take offence."

"Maybe you could."

"Except I don't take cheap offence. That's for showboats and dumbheads," he said, stepping down to the next bench, and then to the floor where he stood before them, naked in the dim light, square-shouldered and smiling. Adam stared at his nakedness. The man was scratching his scrotum.

"Who needs a towel?" the man said, shrugging and laughing. "What's to hide, we're men among men. I got nothing to hide."

"Jesus, Jackie O'Leary," Web said.

"Right," the man said, holding out his pudgy hand. "Right, we've passed some time together, you and me."

"That's right," Web said, turning to Adam. "This is Harry's brother, Adam. Harry's little brother."

"Some little," Jackie said, smirking and folding his arms across his barrel chest.

"No, I suppose you're not little," Web said.

"We do some big things around town," Jackie said, nodding his head to Adam. "Some big things."

Adam wiped the running sweat from his face. Jackie's body was not pink and flushed from the steam. His skin, Adam thought, had the same grey-whitish sheen as the floor tiles.

"Heat doesn't bother me," Jackie said.

"Except when the heat's on," Web said.

"Haw. That's good. I like that. I never was quick with words. I like quick words. Among friends."

"How long's it been, Jackie?"

"How long's long? A long time."

"Not among friends."

"That's right. Friendship's short, too short."

"So's life."

"Yeah, but you can look after life a little. Take a steam, take a holiday. It prolongs."

"You can look after your friends, too, Jackie."

"It's easier to look after your enemies."

"How's Harry?"

"Harry's Harry. He looks after himself."

"I guess nothing changes."

"Harry's changed, but he's still Harry. He don't fool me, or what's a brother for?"

"How's he changed?" Adam asked.

"You see him, you'll think he's changed."

"How about you, Jackie?"

"Me? Could I change? I give change. I'm a businessman."

"So how's business?"

"Terrific. Can't complain, not about life."

He moved closer to them, leaning over the bottom bench. He had a round face, thinning hair, and pale blue eyes, so pale they seemed colorless.

"We should see each other more often. Keep up acquaintances."

"We both travel," Adam said, feeling menace in Jackie's tight little smile.

"You don't say. At your age Web, you're still at it?"

"Yeah."

"They say it broadens the mind."

"Yeah."

"I don't like to travel. I like to keep my eye on the ball," he said, putting out his hand again. "It was nice, a nice touch."

"What?" Web asked, shaking his hand.

"Meeting you, your son, like this."

"Sure."

"Nice to know some things never change," he said, shaking Adam's hand.

"Sure."

"Like you don't like me, Web, and I don't like you."

"If you say so, Jackie."

"I say so. I'm glad to say so. I'm a conservative guy, I get nervous when things aren't the way they were. So Harry makes me nervous, but with you, Web, I'm very easy. Very much at ease."

"That's nice."

"It's terrific. It's terrific to see you," he said, turning away and then stopping at the door. "I'll take a shower, it's very refreshing to take a cold shower after a steam." He closed the door behind him.

"Holy shit," Adam said.

"The guy's a complete shit," Web said.

"And he's Harry's brother?"

"He's a hood. He's Harry's brother and he's a hood, a hustler, a bad piece of business. He's always given Harry a little money, to help him out."

"Really."

"Sure, Harry's the family oddball, the whole family was always in the rackets. It was Jackie who probably gave Gabrielle the money to go to New York."

"You're kidding."

"Why should I kid? It was a strange family. Nothing gave Harry more pleasure than us getting drunk and playing a little boogie-woogie on the organ at midnight until the priests came running in and kicked us out."

"But his wife seemed so straight."

"Ah, his wife. There was a beauty."

"She didn't seem so good-looking to me."

"She wasn't. That's why she drove me crazy, this plain little skinny woman who collected things. That's what she did. Collected old glass, little antique tables ... and the damndest thing was she felt superior to everybody, inside her head she turned shopping into an art form, while what was fascinating about her was she had no charm, no charm at all. She had this smile that was somehow stern, like she was smiling in helpless disapproval, and it used to kill Harry, leave him absolutely limp."

"Why did Harry stay with her?"

"She never interfered. He was free as a bird. She'd just smile that smile at him until sometimes he hit her, and then she really had him."

"He hit her? Harry?"

"He beat her up a couple of times."

"That's awful."

"What was funny, Gabrielle always seemed closer to Harry than her mother, like she resented her mother, but then just before her mother jumped she took off leaving Harry all to himself."

"And he never heard from her."

"She sent him a postcard once from somewhere, I remember him showing it to me, this white jungle mask staring out at him and on the other side she'd just drawn a little round balloon head smiling. He said it was all some kind of joke, it had to be a prank. Maybe it was."

"You know what's strange?"

"What?"

"She was the first girl I ever loved."

"Really."

"Yeah. She still comes up in my dreams, in the strangest places."

"You slept with her?"

"Sure."

"You son of a gun."

"Just doing what comes naturally."

"I wonder if Harry knew?"

"One day I was in this camp, I was standing in Dachau of all places staring at this steel hook in the ceiling in front of the ovens where they used to hang men so they twisted in the air, staring into the ovens that look like great big bread ovens, and I suddenly had this strange feeling that she was there beside me, I could almost see her face except I don't know what she looks like now."

"What the hell were you doing in Dachau?"

"Taking pictures of shoes."

"Shoes. That's the damndest thing. You know I played in Munich, me and Fatha Hines were playing at the same time, and one day he said, Let's go see Dachau, so we went, but the mayor of the town heard about us going so we were invited to lunch and after the lunch the mayor gave us these beautiful old china plates telling us that what Dachau was famous for was their china, like we hadn't just come to lunch from the concentration camp, like it didn't exist."

"Where's the plate?"

"It got broken somewhere but I remember Fatha Hines, he was your mother's favorite player, saying men can forget anything if they want to, and it's true. I remember writing that all down in one of my little books."

"You still got those books?"

"Yeah, and I still got your mother, and I got you from time to time now. Maybe from time to time is the best anybody can do."

* * *

Gabrielle sat in the shuttered dark. He reached over the edge of the bed and picked up one of the balloons. Then she got up and left the room without a word. He was bewildered by his sudden sense of relief at being left alone, but as he breathed freely he felt her absence, a sudden irreparable sense of loss, and no sooner had he stretched out on the bed, letting his head sink into the soft down pillow while batting the balloon from hand to hand, than he leapt up and hurried after her, down toward the sea, passing a cluster of tall poles tied together, live land crabs hanging for sale from the poles. Three black women wearing sweat bands were seated on stools around a fire and an iron pot of *asapao*. They stared at him, each holding a long-handled wooden spoon over the thick soup of shrimps and lobster. He took a gravel path through burned-out brown grass, past palms and a spur of storm-piled black rocks, until he caught up with her. They were both out of breath. He held her, lifting her against his body, rocking in the fresh shore breeze. He held her a long time. Then she raised her face, tears and an elation and satisfaction in her eyes.

"Thank you for coming again," she said. He said nothing,

and then kissed her, her mouth open to his. They heard women's voices from beyond the spur of rocks and turned and walked along the water's edge, the green water clouded with sand churned by breaking waves, until they came to a cove of plane trees and satinwoods. A shelf of white sand fell away from a steep gravelly slope that was shaded by the trees. They lay on the sand, their faces petalled by light through the leaves, drowsed by the sun and the breaking waves. She said, "I spy with my little eye …"

"Still playing hide and seek."

She stood up and stepped out of her sun dress. She was wearing two delicate gold chains and a gold bracelet. Her nails were red, her breasts brown because, she said, she always sun-bathed naked. Sandpipers, white and small, skimmed the lace foam of the spent waves. She folded her dress across a low-hanging branch and ran down the sand, wading in, pushing her body into the heavy green waves. A breaker swamped her and she rose gasping, rubbing water from her eyes, snorting and pushing out farther beyond the breaking of the waves till her chin was at the level of the water. He felt a sudden panic. Her head seemed afloat on the swell, decapitated between waves, and leaving his trousers on a flat rock, he waded naked into the waves.

They fell toward each other through the water, blinded by salt, deafened and blowing water, seeing the sun like a glazed white wafer through the spray. Flocks of frigate birds criss-crossed overhead as they tried to lie, to float on the water on their backs, sliding between the sky and the sea into a gap of serenity, but they began to flounder, choking on the salt water, until clutching and hauling themselves up for air, spitting, they lunged toward the shore, dragging each other, the waves, heavy with sand and pebbles, breaking against the backs of their knees so that they stumbled onto the white sand in the cove, and as they stood naked and laughing, rubbing water out of their eyes, he looked up the steep gravelly slope, sure that he saw standing in the brush between two trees a tall wind-pocked man wrapped in stone wings, Mio, watching them, moving his lips, a warning or was it the light playing?

The next morning he woke and lifted himself up on his elbow and watched her sleep. He could not hear the sea but he could feel the sea on the wind through the open window. She slept soundly in the breaking light without a blanket or sheet. He lifted her short nightgown, drawing it above her breasts. She had one arm hooked behind her head and the other was flung to the side, her hand falling over the edge of the bed. Her legs were slightly parted. He brushed his open palm over her tuft of delicate hair and then eased his finger along the inside of her thigh into the hollow, lightly, so that she did not waken but stirred and shifted and folded her loose arm back across her waist. He put his mouth on hers and when she opened her lips and murmured he then touched her nipple with his mouth and nestled against her belly, drawing his tongue into the crook of her thigh and then back across her belly, resting his head against her breasts. She held his head. She seemed hardly to breathe as she pulled her knees up and opened her legs. He touched her, touched her wetness. Then, still with her eyes closed, she rolled over so that he was on his back and she straddled him, taking hold of him with two fingers, easing down so that he was up in her, her head against his, her long hair falling across his face as she moved her buttocks slowly. She sat up straight upon him, eyes wide open, smiling impishly as she swept her hair back from her face, her breasts lifting, and he licked his fingers and reached and touched her nipples with the wetness, seeing her sitting framed in the window, the banana tree behind her shoulder, and he said, "The hummingbird is back," so that she turned and looked, blocking the window from him. She stayed turned away for so long that he asked her if anything was wrong, but falling forward on him again, she said, "Oh no, no. It is all too wonderful. It's unbearably wonderful," her mouth, he thought, like the mouth of her sex, her tongue, the tip, and he took hold of the hair on her neck, and held her hard against him, her hair heavy and musky, and as she moved over him she kept a languid stillness to herself, sweating, the wet skin of her breasts translucent with turquoise-blue veins, her thigh muscles contracting as she came, the arteries sinking into the skin as if the blood had stopped, stopped time, stasis: "Each time I come I feel like I've been hanged, a burning light just jams up in me, in my throat."

"Is that why you laugh?"

"... like sucking ice when you've got a fever, cold stinging pain in all my veins ... I can't help laughing, it's the only way to cut the pain ..."

"I wish I could make you laugh for ever."

"That'd hurt too much," she said and kissed his eyes.

"So maybe we'll all get hurt."

"What're you talking about?"

"What about Mio?"

"Never mind him," she said.

"I've got to mind him."

"There's nothing you can do. What's done's done, and he'll do whatever he'll do."

"You don't know?"

"No."

"Don't you care?"

"If he does anything you'll never know, he's too anonymous."

"Any guy with a black hand who struts into a casino with his good hand in an ice bucket is not trying to hide himself."

"He's anonymous and he's got his hand in a glove for good reason and he doesn't want anyone to ever know how he feels about anything."

"You lived with him."

"I was with him but I didn't live with him and I don't really know what he'll do."

"He looked like he was capable of anything."

"But you'll never know and it'll be years from now if he does anything so no one will ever guess, and by then maybe it won't matter."

"It'll fucking well matter to me."

"I mean to him."

"You worried about him?"

"Look, he was a man who fascinated me. It was like there was a ghost in him. He was the keeper of his own ghost, his own childhood, I guess. But he never had any self-pity, and I liked that. I liked it a lot. And it's what I like about you. You're not looking for excuses or running scared though there's something in you on the run, that's for sure."

"Maybe I'm just looking for a moontan."

"What's that?"

"It's what my father used to call love."

"Maybe I'm the moon, maybe I'm a hole in the sky."

"Maybe I got a hole in my sock, maybe I got loose shoes."

"You got a screw loose."

"You're the one with a screw loose," he said, gripping her arm, "living with a guy like Mio."

"What d'you mean – like Mio?"

"A gun-runner."

"An arms dealer. The most pious guys in the world are arms dealers. They're the best, the pious guys."

"So now he's pious, too."

"I really think you're jealous."

"Why should I be jealous? You've run off with me. He's the one who should be jealous."

"Never."

"No?"

"Not a chance. He might be aggrieved, even aggravated, but never jealous. Besides, I haven't run off. When I run, you'll know."

They lay very still. Somewhere, children were calling to each other, and to hide how grim he felt, he whispered, "What does matter?"

"You didn't come," she said. "You held back, you didn't come."

"Well, that's what happens," he said, smacking her buttock hard, "when you flatten me out on my back."

"I want to make love again."

She took him in her mouth, the light ripening, and then

rolled over so that he made love to her, her ankles hooked on the small of his back as he rode her higher and higher till she was up on her shoulders, arms spread, clutching the sheet as if she were tearing up roots, pulling him down into her with her legs until he pitched forward, reaching for her hands, locking his fingers into hers as they strained and then slumped and separated, splayed on their backs, breathing heavily, eyes closed, the light wind from the open window drying their sweat.

"I'm covered with your hair," she said. "Your chest, you shed like a dog." She laughed and lay very still. He saw a single thread of spider web hanging from the ceiling.

"Do you see that," he said, pointing. "Do you think the spider just gave up, decided it was going nowhere and quit and he went somewhere else?"

"Maybe it was just a passing thought."

"Like pissing in the wind."

"I envy men being able to piss into the wind, anywhere, it's so free. We've got to squat, get our feet wet in our own piss."

"Maybe that's why I always liked watching spiders, watching them with my grandfather in the garden when I was a kid, the way they just shot silk out into the air, out into nowhere and then ran up their own threads, swimming weightless in the sunlight ..."

"Hanging their traps ..."

"Come on, it's just the way they dream ..."

"That's what men do. Piss in the wind and dream and then someone dies in their dreams."

"Hell," he said, kissing her fingers, "for a girl who just got her way with me you sound awful bitter."

"I'm not bitter, I'm hungry."

"You want something to eat?"

"No."

"Maybe we should get some coffee."

"I like it fine just the way we are."

"Good."

"It is good. It's wonderful. I haven't felt so wonderful for years."

"I always dreamed a little of you, you know. I can still remember the first time I touched your breast, at last you let me touch you."

"Touching meant something then. I remember one night you took my shoes off and kissed my feet."

"I did?"

"Sure. You kissed my feet and told me I would be a great dancer. I'm a good dancer but I'm not a great dancer."

"I didn't kiss you hard enough."

"Hard had nothing to do with it," she said, bending over him so that he could feel the weight of her breasts on his chest as she looked into his eyes. "I think I should tell you about Harry," she said.

"What about Harry?"

"About Harry and me."

He closed his eyes and drew his fingers down her backbone *and planets wheeled around and I discovered I could squeeze my eyes so hard that I saw little dots of light and songsters doomed from here to eternity* but she waited for him to open his eyes.

"It's really very simple," she said.

"Sure."

"Not that anyone ever knew Harry."

"My father thought he did."

"Your father didn't know anything, just two guys playing the piano, except Harry liked to play all that marching music on the organ at the hockey games."

They heard the shuffle of footsteps in the hall, and silence and a light cough, and then the footsteps went away.

"Who was that?"

"Who knows?" he said.

"Harry used to touch me before you touched me when we were kids and then he stopped."

"Jesus, you mean Harry molested you?"

"He didn't molest me. He touched me, he'd always touched me and washed and bathed me and, like I told you, he braided my hair, and then one night when he was soaping me and I already had breasts he told me to dry myself."

"He stopped?"

"Yes."

"Well, thank god."

"And then my mother showed him the blood on the sheet, she showed him that after you, I wasn't a virgin."

"So?"

"He started again. He did more than touch me."

"Did your mother know?"

"Yes."

"Why didn't she stop him?"

"She wasn't like that."

"Like what?"

"She never stopped him from doing anything."

"And did you?"

"No."

"You mean you liked it?"

"No."

"What did you do?"

"I don't remember."

"How could you forget?"

"I didn't forget. I just don't remember what I did, what we did. I remember his smell, the smell of his hair, the smell of his semen, and he got me pregnant ... that's why he stopped eating, that's why my mother killed herself, when she found out that I was pregnant ..."

"Holy fuck, she should have killed him ..."

"I killed the child, in New York ..."

She kissed his cheek and stroked his hair as if he needed comforting, and then she whispered, "Don't worry ... there's nothing to be done. What's done is done."

She kissed him on the mouth, and then on the neck.

"There's a dead child and a white face in everything and then everything whitens ... sometimes all the birds and the sun and the leaves all whiten and I just disappear ... that's what I want, that's what I hunger for ... I don't want to die, I want to disappear ..."

She dug her nails into his neck, kissing him till she began to bite, and aroused, he tumbled her onto her back. As if afraid of sinking, she clung to his back so that when he raised himself up on his hands and knees, she lifted off the sheet, her legs around his thighs. "Lick me," she said. "I'll disappear ..."

"There's nowhere to go."

"Lick me ..."

He knelt, putting his mouth to her, and as she slowly closed her thighs around his head, he was afraid suddenly of the power of the grip on his neck. He swallowed the musky sweetness. She let out a guttural wavering cry, and then a wail, arcing into the air, wrenching his head, his blood pounding in his ears as if an enormous swelling had entered his skull behind his eyes, and then she collapsed and spread her legs and he lay curled by her thigh, his upper lip swollen. They lay still, breathing hard, their bodies rigid.

"It terrifies me," she whispered.

"What?"

"I've never come that way before. I've tried but I've never ... it was like my soul was ripping out of me by the roots ... you swallowed my soul."

"You think I got your soul?"

"I hope not," she said, and touched his hair, "but I was absolutely nowhere, all white. Did it taste like ashes?"

"No, you taste sweet."

"No, I mean my soul."

* * *

The big parade passed the memorial to the dead airmen of all the wars, crimson dragon heads hoisted on poles, Shetland ponies, and Chinese boys wearing butterfly wings on stilts, hoe-down dancers and seven prancing dwarfs, Snow White in an ice cave, a corps of the Salvation Army marching crisply, and a small stage on wheels covered by spangled blue notes, a portly brown woman singing:

> Man's got his woman
> To take his seed.
> He's got the power,
> She's got the need.
> Only women bleed, only women bleed ...

but she went out of hearing, followed by a Shriners drill team on miniature motorbikes and male Hellenic soldiers in white knee-socks and white pleated skirts, and then there was a piercing trumpet blast as two boys carrying a banner – De La Salle Trumpet and Drum Corps – led a big marching band of fifty silver trumpets and drummers close to the memorial, trim in their black uniforms and silver capes, and Adam stood on the curb and raised his hand but then put it in his pocket, unbelieving, as he realized that Harry would never see him in the crowd, Harry at the head of the boys' marching band, stern-faced and stiff, dressed all in black with beautiful black braiding around his shoulders, carrying a silver-headed staff, jamming it up and down in the air to the drum beat, staring straight ahead, and then snapping his head to the left in a salute to the dead, a look of complete confirmation on his face.

* * *

Driving all day deeper and deeper into the dense enclosing bush, the wind scalding his face through the empty windshield, he sometimes heard gunfire from a long way off, a sharp dry clacking. He hunched over the wheel with tears of exhaustion in his eyes. Then, the narrow road flared into a slope of trees that had been burned grey by a flash fire, the slope stippled by thin bare trunks. He drove down to the river and docks and sheds, and at the foot of the wide mud road he found pirogues pulled up on shore. He tucked the gun into his belt under his jacket and stepped out of the car and stood at a tilt, as if he were going to topple. Two leper boatmen, one wearing a bowler hat, were sitting on their haunches on a concrete jetty. There were light sandbank patches in the water and drifting deadwood, and trees standing in the high water: mahogany, palms, breadfruit and tall okoumes with pearl-grey bark and wing roots above water, and papyrus groves and reeds. He got into a dugout canoe sitting very straight and still, turning only when the boatmen pointed to a peaked blue roof through the trees but he didn't hear what they said. In the clammy air of the late afternoon light he could see across the broad slate-blue water a cleared space on the other shore, a sand beach under tall okoumes, and along the gentle rise of the shore, long narrow sheds with peaked roofs of corrugated iron, raised on piles to let rain water run downhill freely, built from east to west so that the sun would not beat down on the roofs directly except at noon. The boatman wearing a bowler hat asked: "You mek mercenary?"

"No."

"No mek mercenary here?"

"No, not here."

"No fighting ever come here. Only drunk soldiers."

The boatman wet his lips from his water bottle.

"What are the sheds?" Adam asked.

"Old hospital."

"Old?"

"Empty. All mek rotten. White ants."

A humpback hill angled up behind the sheds, like it's been skinned alive, he thought, the taut underside sections of animal pelts sewn together, gristle-brown with flat white stripes, blade marks from the skinning and ridges, dried black veins and tendons and patches of flesh left on the skin, and little ponds, brilliant eggshell blue with porcelain-white rims.

"What happened there?" Adam asked, pointing.

"Farms."

"Farms?"

"Doctors mek farms. Now nothing."

The other boatman smiled and gaped. He had yellow eyes. He had been cracking small nuts between his teeth and spitting out the shells.

"I born there, bass," he said.

A heron with long yellow legs lifted off the water. It flew in a swooping circle, dragging its legs in the air, and then settled in a papyrus grove as Adam shifted his bags on his shoulders and got out of the pirogue and started walking up the grassy road, alert because the trees and the long grass were so still. When he looked back at the two leper boatmen they were sitting on a concrete abutment, their legs dangling over the water, staring after him. One tipped his bowler hat as Adam crossed in front of the ruined hospital sheds, the siding rotted or torn away by the winds. Rows of wooden bunk beds stood empty in the falling light, giant seed boxes suspended in time, *time for song so short and each letter I write is a song* though he didn't know if she'd got any of the letters he'd written over the last two months because he'd received no replies, *and each time I tell you I love you is a song, a song against sorrow of the heart, a song amongst the withering. It is the way I keep my mouth from going dumb with loneliness, with the darkness that lurks* and then as he got to a bend in the road, to a stretch of broken paving, he heard a bell, the same four notes over and over again ... CDEF ... EDCF ... CDEF ... EDCF ... no resonance, a dead clanging, as if some mad child were unable to get his fingers unlocked, but then once, there was only DDDDDDDDDD ...

followed by minutes of silence, and as he walked on, it all began again. He passed two squat concrete-block buildings. There were ornate burglar bars in the windows. Security men wearing mushroom-colored trenchcoats, khaki short pants, and patent leather shin guards laced to their boots were standing in the doorways. Farther along, there was a cement sidewalk, but it came to an end where a square-shouldered woman wrapped in a cape with a silver comb in her hair suddenly hurried from a long low ochre brick building. Fallen roof tiles lay in the rough grass. The woman passed him. She looked grim and angry. She was wearing a corsage of wilted red flowers on a plastic wrist-band. He went to speak to her but a tall white man with flat cheekbones hurried after her. He glanced at Adam. He was carrying a gun. "Nice night," the man said. "Don't forget the bowling tomorrow."

There were high barbed-wire fences along the street, fences that went back into the bush behind houses, each house set back from the street and surrounded by flowering bushes in a barbed-wire compound, and there were little white wooden frame doorways in the fencing. No lights were on in the houses. Adam looked for the woman with the corsage. She and the man with the gun were gone but an elderly black man and boy had come out of the shadows between compounds, the man carrying a big canvas suitcase and the boy wearing a cardboard sailor's hat.

"Where can I find somewhere to rest?" Adam asked.

The boy ran ahead, pointed past a corner tobacco shop and turned and waited, touching his hand to his lips. Adam looked down a short street. The boy was holding out his cardboard sailor's hat, still touching his lips. He moved his lips, soundless, mute. Adam dropped a handful of coins into the hat and walked toward a low grey building under spreading trees. The building had a small bell tower, a clock, and a tilted cross. It was a mission dispensary. Black women were seated on benches, waiting on the veranda of the dispensary, and as Adam came up the stairs a white nursing sister, her eyes alive with laughter, hurried into a front room maternity ward, a room of six or seven camp cots. Young mothers were nursing in the occluded light. In the far corner, where a mother was settled under heavy blankets against the dampness, the sister reached into the conical tent of white mosquito netting and lifted out a tiny reddish-black child, the head smaller than her hand, and she held it aloft and said, "See, only fifteen minutes old – look, life, isn't it wonderful?"

Adam leaned into a small front office, the windows also protected by rococo wrought-iron burglar bars. An older white man, wearing a freshly washed but worn white soutane, frayed at the throat and too short at the ankles, stood up and faced him. He folded his hands. He was reserved, yet there was something studied about his reserve, his long deliberate silence as he held the bridge of his nose between his thumb and forefinger, as if he were in pain waiting for Adam to speak.

"Could I talk to you?" Adam asked.

"Yes, of course I must talk to you," the old priest said. "You have obviously come a long way. Charity is the first virtue."

He looked tired and drawn with a bristle of white whiskers on his cheeks, his eyes back in their hollows, almost hidden when closed under grey eyebrows, and as he sat down in his corner chair with his eyes closed, he said, "You are looking at an old priest, because that's all I am now, an old priest, and I think at this time in my life, what is most important is to think about my fidelity. Fidelity," he said, unlinking his hands and then locking the fingers again, "is for me the heart of virtue, keeping my eyes on what God asked of me." His hands rested in his lap, like two people together a long time, as he sat back in the shadows so that Adam could not see his eyes.

"I just wanted some advice," Adam said.

"Yes, yes, of course."

"Before the sun goes down."

"Yes."

"Where can I go where I won't get killed?"

"Ah ..."

"Do you have any idea?"

"Would you like a glass of water?"

"Yes, I suppose I would," Adam said, trying to see more clearly the old man's face in the shadows.

"The glass of water freely given is still the most convincing proof for the existence of God, who is always present in the fevered face of the poor man," the priest said, pouring water from a jug into a glass and handing it to Adam. "What is your name?"

"Adam."

"Ah ..."

"And yours?"

"Father Chamane."

"It is very quiet here," Adam said.

"Yes. Almost serene."

He sat silently, as if alone, and yet obviously very aware of Adam being there in the sparseness of his office – a desk, a chair and a small bookshelf ... shuffling his feet in the stillness. "Yes, yes, this serenity. We have an old woman here, a widow. She entered two or three weeks ago to die. She is still living, the old lady. For an African," and for the first time he raised his voice above a whisper, "life is, I should say, the only reality. They don't believe in death. Death's not natural for them. That's why they can accept so much pain, to live. There is in them a biological joy that we don't have. Death is a great tragedy for them because life is the reality. But through faith they keep their dead present. You see, they bury their people near the house. There is no cemetery here. They go on living with their dead, still talking with them."

"But I was wondering where I might go ..."

"So you won't die," the priest said, laughing quietly.

"Something like that."

"Well, surely there's the town hotel."

"I didn't know there was a hotel."

"But I'd stay away from the skating rink."

"The what?"

"The rink."

"Where?"

"You'll see."

The sun had gone down. The priest held out his hand but still stayed back in the shadows. "Just go to the centre, you'll see the light," he said. Adam, as he left, thought he heard the old priest's muffled laughter. The women on the veranda bench were very quiet. No one was on the street and three streetlamps were broken, but he found the small three-storey hotel and the lobby was brightly lit by two chandeliers, two clusters of dewdrop crystal, and the whitewashed walls were reflected in the polished gumwood floors. The front desk had tiny niches, roll-top drawers, and folding shelves. There were two signs on the counter: one, elegantly etched in black glass – VALET PARKING IN THE REAR; and the other, on pulpy cardboard – MAKE MONEY – over grainy photographs of landmines, machine guns, grenades, and pistols, promising that cash would be paid to anyone who found weapons and turned them in. There was no clerk behind the desk and no one answered the bell. Adam, putting his bags in a small closet under the desk, went back into the dark and walked to the end of the street. He heard music coming from a big gabled building, white paint peeling off the gables, and over the door: SKATING RINK.

"Jesus Murphy ..."

Two young black soldiers wearing knee-socks were at the door, smoking and laughing at cartoons printed on the inside of two bubble gum wrappers. They were both a little drunk. "What the hell is this?" Adam asked, looking up at the big sign.

"Rink, bass," a soldier said sullenly.

"You mean they're skating, here?"

"No, no. Not since rich farmers mek away ..."

The two soldiers began to slap each other on the shoulder.

Adam went into the rink. It was big and wide and long. The floor was concrete painted grey but the surface had begun to peel, the concrete to crumble, revealing rows of rusty pipes set in the concrete. Huge rusted generators stood silently against one wall. Only four of the conical over-hanging lights worked. There were crowded tables in the corners of the hall. A man with a trimmed golden moustache and rust hair parted

severely on the right and combed straight across the forehead
stood in front of a small bar taking drink chits from black
waiters dressed in maroon tracksuits and white running
shoes. The waiters trotted from table to table, passing a single
squat old amplifier. The beat of the music from the amplifier
sounded as if it were passing over a rasp. Mixed couples were
dancing in the gloom and along the far wall there were
clusters of young black hookers dressed in long work shirts or
slit satin dresses, denim or printed skirts, bare feet or worn
platform shoes, while one baby-faced yellow-skinned girl had
draped herself in a poncho that looked like a nubbly chenille
bed coverlet. Standing back in the shadows with a whisky in a
greasy glass, Adam tried to get the feel of who was around
him, who might be dangerous, but then he shook his head in
disbelief and laughed out loud, staring through the smoke at
dark blue water and stone islands and snow painted on the
long plaster wall behind the hookers, and as he took another
swallow of whisky the hookers seemed to drift back in among
the islands, faded and stained by the dampness of his home
country – dark northern waters and crippled jack pines
floating in the dinge as one of the hookers turned away from a
client and leaned against a snow-filled cove. He went over, a
little giddy with the drink, and asked one of the girls to dance,
aroused by her hard young breasts pressed against him as he
spun with her, eyes fixed on a far stone island, a safe haven
lost in a blur of sweat running down into his eyes until he
gasped, worn out, his nerves frayed, and she had to hold him
steady. He gave her money and said, "You skate beautifully,"
and walked slowly out through the iron door, the hinges
grinding in the night. There was animal dung on the air, the
soldiers were squatting drunkenly in the grass, laughing and

hugging each other. The dispensary bell began to ring again but then stopped abruptly, as if someone had got the time wrong, or the right time didn't matter.

At the hotel, he signed the register for a blowsy old woman who wore a cameo carved in jet at her throat, *a death's head*, he thought, surprised by his own calm. "Anyone looking for you?" she asked.

"No," he said. "Why?"

"No reason. I just always ask. I worry about a man no one's looking for. That's a man all alone."

"I am," he said, leaning across the counter, "the *adelantando*."

"You don't say now," she said, drawing close. "And what might that be?"

"A man at home on the front porch of the dead," he whispered. "But no one's looking for me, I'm looking for someone."

"Yeah, who?"

"A woman."

"What else?" she said, sniffing as if she'd lost all interest.

He went up the stairs with his two bags and sat down on his bed and closed his eyes in silence for a long time and then he opened the drawer to the bedside table. He lifted out a small black leather-bound book, a bible, and inside, pasted to the flyleaf, there was an old yellow strip of folded newsprint, which, as he lay down, drained and thinking *I'm so tired I could die*, he read: WORDS FROM DOCTOR LIEBIG – WORDS TO ALL IN DESPAIR: "The reason thousands cannot get cured is easily explained. There are so many causes of Seminal Weakness, Impotency, Loss of Vitality, Memory, Sight, Hearing, Feelings, Imbecility, etc. Onanism, self-abuse, may cause the above diseases and symptoms which require a certain treatment; men whose strength is gradually wasting away, before all hope of restoration, should examine their urine: if any ropy sediment or brickdust appears, that is the warning stage of Seminal Weakness. Be of Stout Heart. Do not indulge yourself. We guarantee permanent cures in curable cases. No miracles performed."

* * *

Gone Home

MOHR

Adopted

WATERS

Henrietta   Susanna

```
S V W E T B S A 15 S T M O R E
E I R T E 2 Y D & H N S 10 H E
M A A D 17 & S H T N O A R M T
N A Y D H D R O F S M Y E H E
E N S O W M H M E O 2 D 26 T T
E V & E I R O M I F S G E E E
H R S 27 D I I E T W R 7 A O M
D A U H T A N M I S A 8 9 M T
H T S E S M E R E T E L I E S
Y E A 1 P H N I T A Y R I P M
E W N 8 9 5 A G E D 23 A P E L
E R N H S N W F W O I D T D H
I G A I 2 D I E H D E 27 H G O
T F R M O A D R N W N E V N A
F S O G D N A E O I H A E M Y
```

Readers Meet Us in Heaven

* * *

The weather changed. It was late winter with deep snow on the ground, but hot dry winds swept across Lake Ontario breaking branches and shutters, blowing powdered ice off the crusted snow into the eyes. It was hard to breathe, hard to sleep. People sat at tables outside the cafés in the slush. They smiled, soaking wet. Snow houses, the children's dark tunnelled hallways, collapsed. Old socks and shoes suddenly appeared afloat in the street gutters. Where the snow melted down to the flower beds, the earth reeked, giving off an acrid smell of decaying life. Adam came home from high school and found his mother standing in the bathroom doorway. She was wearing only her panties and bra and was in her bare feet. Her thighs were white and loose, ruined. "Sometimes it hurts, sitting inside your own head. When I was a girl," she said, "they brushed my hair and taught me to sing and arrange flowers ..." A week later, after the winds had died down, after the cold air had come back and the draining water had hardened into icicles hanging from eavestroughing and there had been a heavy soft wet snow, she said accusingly, "You look more and more like your father."

"I do?"

"Yes," she said.

Pale and thin and with her hair cropped, she locked herself in her bedroom. He stayed home from school and knocked for three days. She refused to speak. When she came out, she spent hour after hour washing the leaded front windows, breathing on the glass, polishing the panes. "So that the whole world," she said, "will seem shining." One evening he came home from school and found her slumped against the window, her eyes wide open, dead. "Her heart just seems to have stopped," the doctor said.

The snow was deep on the day of the funeral. Web could not be found in Munich. After the funeral mass, Father Zale and Harry O'Leary went with Adam to the graveyard. Flo had written a note saying she wanted to be cremated. "Dad will be angry about this," Adam said. "I think she did it to fix him, to spite him."

"How's she spiting him?"

"Dad loves his graves."

The crematorium was in the centre of the burial yard, sheltered by weeping willows. It was chilly and damp and grey inside the windowless domed building and the pews in the central chapel were cold. The chapel was surrounded by narrow passageways, the walls slotted with small sealed stone boxes holding urns, the ashes. There was continual recorded music, sweet lugubrious music. "Awful, her having to listen to that saccharine stuff," Harry said. "They'd never think of the *Missa Solemnis*, they'd never think of Verdi." Father Zale shrugged and said a silent prayer. "Let's say a prayer for Web, too," Harry said, "let's say a prayer for all of us," and they bowed their heads.

Father Zale went home with Adam, who made the priest a cup of tea with lemon and then sat alone on his mother's bed, wondering how a cluttered room could seem so hollow. He opened her dresser drawers, looking for his childhood drawing books, and books about the stars. They were not there. He found dozens of colorful matchbooks from bars and clubs where Web had played, and amid her underwear, a chrome-plated handgun. He folded back a black slip and a garter belt. It lay gleaming in the half-light. He picked it up and turned and saw himself in the big oval mirror. "You're more and more like your father," she'd said. He pointed the gun and pulled the trigger. A cap popped open at the heel of the barrel. There was a small flame, it was a fancy old cigarette lighter, and he stared for a long time into the eye of the flame and then said, "Well, goddamn," and laughed and went out and told the waiting priest, "Believe it or not, I just saw the end of the world."

In the summer of that year, there were high winds and no rain. Long hanging veils of white dust rose off the bluffs along the lakeshore, whitening the sun. It was hot and Father Zale was dressed in his good black slacks and a black linen short-sleeved shirt. He and Adam had intended to go downtown, to stroll through a music store, but instead they went down to the base of the bluffs. It was so quiet they could hear the rustle of dry leaves in the white birches. The sky had a mother-of-pearl sheen, as if it were going to rain, but it was not going to rain. "It's a mock storm sky," Father Zale said. "God patiently mocks us. My mother always said that and these days I hear the words of my mother and father more and more. I wonder why they're talking to me after all these years, butting into the middle of my prayers." Lying in bed late at night, he said, he'd lose track of who was saying what to whom when he was reading a novel and he'd turn out the light and hear, "you discover the light in darkness, that's what the darkness is for." Standing on the scrub sand along the shore, he squinted in the strange glaring white sunlight and wiped the dust from his cheeks and mouth and turned his back to the wind, clearing his throat and tasting dust, spitting with the wind: "You should always pray toward where the cattle beasts are turned in the morning because that's pure air coming in on the light, my father told me that." But he hadn't seen a cattle beast in the morning in twenty years, so what did that mean? "That I've put the beast behind me? Though what the light reveals is danger and what it demands is faith. That wasn't my father, that was an old parish priest friend of mine who died as an alcoholic, stiff in the service of the Lord," he said, laughing quietly as he sat on a flat rock between two white birches, staring at the water and seagulls riding a swell. Adam felt strangely separated from his teacher by the very fact that the older priest was confiding in him personally in a way he had never done before.

He walked down to the water's edge, leaving him sitting on the flat rock, calling out to Adam, "I remember my old parish pal drunk one night in a shed behind the church house, insisting he had never felt so close to God, laughing and chanting

> The sexual life of the camel
> Is stranger than anyone thinks.
> One moonlit night on the desert
> He attempted to bugger The Sphinx,
> But The Sphinx's posterior entry
> Was clogged with the sands of the Nile
> Which accounts for the hump on the camel
> And The Sphinx's inscrutable smile.

And then Father Zale took a searing blow through his throat as if his brain had been bolted shut, the air slamming up into his eyes so that he thought his skull had shattered, and when he tried to howl he felt he had swallowed the iron bolt. The sky folded over his head and began to seep blood because he had been shot through the throat with an arrow, by a boy out on the beach with a bow hunting birds on the bluffs. Adam ran and tackled him, though the boy had not tried to run away, and later the boy insisted to the police that he'd seen a crow in the birch trees and that he had not seen any man wearing a black shirt and black slacks crouched at the base of the white bluffs.

"It is a highly professional stainless steel bow the boy had borrowed from his father's basement workshop, the father using the bow only in survival war games he played with other professional men, his friends," the detective said at the inquiry, where it was concluded that there had been no intent to kill (the boy explained there had been a strange light that day and that he had intended to walk the other way on the beach and he couldn't explain why he was where he was except he hoped this wouldn't be held against him because his secret dream was to represent the country on the national archery team) and the inquiry recommended that bows and arrows be banned for bird hunting within twenty miles of the city limits.

Father Zale recovered at a nunnery north of the city. "I can still pray," he wrote on a mass card for one of the nuns, "I can't speak, but it doesn't matter. I've nothing more to say except what my mother said – God patiently mocks us." The nun became upset and told Adam, "No, no, he mustn't believe that." So Father Zale wrote: "Don't worry, I am full of a light that demands a faith in darkness." After six months he stopped shaking and clutching his throat. Adam took him home by taxi to his room at the school, to his bird feeders, and when he didn't sit in silence on the bench casting crusts from his knapsack he sat for hours in the small look-out room on the mansard roof or stood outside on the widow's walk staring out over the water.

* * *

As he left the hotel, telling the woman behind the desk that he was going to the village of light, she rested her elbow on the Valet Parking sign and said with a sly laugh, "Off you go now, sonny. Off you go."

He walked to the centre of town where there were tall trees in a small park and instead of grass under the trees, there was finely raked gravel and several men were playing games of *boules* on the gravel, the old priest in his frayed white soutane standing among them.

"Well now," the old priest said, palming the brushed steel ball in his surprisingly big hand. He looped it toward a small white ball, hitting and driving the white ball between two bare tree roots.

"No damn good," a white man muttered, the man with the gun who had told Adam not to forget the bowling. "Leek's my name," he said, "Captain Leek."

"Hello," Adam said.

"Fresh blood in the game," the priest said. Two other men crossed between them carrying their own steel balls, playing their own game.

"It all gets a little confusing, eh?" Adam said.

"Not at all. Not at all. It's just a question of how you look at things, how you look at anything."

"Well, I don't know," Adam said.

"What you don't know won't hurt you," Leek said, pitching his steel ball between the two trees.

"I'm working on a story about bowling in Africa," Adam said with a deadpan.

"You don't say," Leek said, staring at him intently, and then laughing out loud. "You hear that boys, bowling in Africa, breakfast at Tiffany's." Leek drew his gun and shot the white ball. The priest stomped off angrily.

"Now what if he took that attitude toward God," one of the players said and snickered.

The captain drew Adam away by the arm. "Come now," he said. "Come away."

They walked across the dusty road to a small café, two wobbly tables on the sidewalk and a tattered awning. Most of the stores on the street were closed and shuttered. The trees were full of black birds. The other bowlers kept playing under the trees.

"I'm looking for a place," Adam said.

"That's what bowling is," the captain said. "A way of looking. See," he said, leaning close to Adam across the table, "the English and the French play bowls differently." He had a brush moustache and drew his forefinger across the bristle. "Two different logics, you see. The English play a nice precise tailored green and get closest to their little white ball that never moves and that's their logic, English logic, while the French, in *boules* you just throw the white ball out there and go and get it and wherever it goes you follow it, fiercely, and that's French logic ..."

"And ...?"

"And men like me, we just blow the ball to kingdom come and that's an end of it ..."

He called out for two beers and clapped Adam on the shoulder.

"Now, where's this place you're off to?"

"*Village lumière* ..."

"Why in the world would you want to go there?"

"A woman I know."

"It's lepers," he said and drew away a little. "It's a jeezly leper camp off by the hospital."

"I know, she's a white woman, Gabrielle ..."

"Haw. I've got a gander at her."

"You have?"

"Sure. Crazy as a bedbug. She zoomed in here one day a year ago on a bicycle, if you can wrap your mind around that. I'll never forget it. There's tanks and snipers down the road and she just bicycled past and pedalled into town and I saw her and yelled at her – Doctor Livingstone, I presume – and she waved and bicycled on up to the hospital camp. Crazy as they come, but good-looking, I'll give her that." He took a long swallow of beer. "Terrible shame really. Good-looking and up there lost in a daisy chain with the lepers. You ever seen lepers, real lepers? It's the light in the wounds, that's the *lumière* business, it looks like there's this glistening light. The light's the rot ..."

part NINE

This must be the sky that fooled old Ponce," Adam said. "It doesn't look like it's dying. It's just ripe. Everything gets ripe in Puerto Rico." There was a strange dark sky out over the Caja de Muertos, a cobalt blue and violet sky, but also there were pure white clouds hanging low on the horizon. Though it was hot and humid in their hotel, there seemed to be an ice-blue haze over the water and a wind lifted sweet grass tufts away from the roots of shore pines, old pine cones lying like charred birds, circles of wind-blown sand around their bodies. Adam and Gabrielle walked along the shore toward the town, past broken lobster cradles and torn nets, rusted oil drums and stone houses with cats slumped in the roof gutters waiting for rain.

"It kind of makes me nervous," she said.

"It's not going to rain."

"Why not?"

"Those white clouds."

"They look like ladyfingers."

"I like that," he said, "I should write it down."

"Why?"

"That's what my father always told me. If you like it, write it down."

They went up a narrow, sloping road inside a high wall of mottled sandstone blocks and stone sentry turrets with finial crowns and lean eyeholes looking out over the water. By a hook in the road, they turned into a street of bluish-grey cobblestones made from foundry slag, houses of lime green and carmine, wrought-iron balconies, and windows with wooden spindle grilles. At the cross streets, there were carved icons bolted to the corner walls – Francis enraptured by his rapport with little animals, Sebastian stuck with arrows and wearing a gold hat for a halo – and as they went by a beggar man sitting on a stone bench, eyes the color of his amber worry beads, Adam said, "You know, I've got this dream that attacks me."

"How can a dream attack you?"

"I wake up sopping wet and shaking, I've been dreaming and I never dream like that, but I dream that all these years I've blotted out of my mind the night I killed a man, a faceless drifter I just walk up to, sometimes in a parking garage or sometimes on the street and kill and in my dream this dead man I hit with a tire iron while he is waiting to cross the street at a red light at three in the morning, he comes at me with his shrunken little face turned away while I wake up absolutely sure that if I stayed sleeping I'd see his face, because I've been hiding out with him inside my head all these years in my sleep so I wake up absolutely sure I've done it, so afraid I can't stand being alone …"

"Maybe you can dream your way into someone else's life."

"... but this dream keeps coming back on me, so now in my sleep I see it coming and I talk to myself in my dream and I try to head it off."

"I think you can dream your way in ..."

"... and I've had that damned dream playing chopsticks on my bones for years and sometimes during the day, all I worried about was being attacked by this dead man I don't know, but maybe now it'll all turn inside out because I thought I saw Mio standing in the shadows of my sleep last night, looking for me."

"Don't be ridiculous."

"What do you mean ridiculous?"

"Mio's not in your sleep."

"He's in my life."

"I'm in your life."

"Right. But now I got him betting the DON'T COME line on me, a stone angel with his gimpy fist, and it beats me how you ever made love to a guy with killer eyes like that."

"I looked him right in the eye," she said, pulling away angrily. "Did you ever kill anybody?"

"No. Of course not."

"How come you want to?"

"What're you talking about?"

"You're dreaming about it."

"You're crazy."

"No, you are. Mio's survived things you'll never know about, they stuck his hand in a fire trying to get him to tell where his parents were and he refused because he said if anyone was going to kill his parents he was going to kill them, so believe you me, he doesn't go in for fooling around over nothing."

"Thanks a lot," he said, curling his lip but moving closer to her, trying to touch her.

"What do you want from me anyway?" she cried. "You looking to dip your toe in a little nostalgia?"

"I'm not looking for anything."

"Sure you are, but you're not going to find it with me. You're not going to turn me into some kind of trip."

"So what are you here for, laughs?"

"When life's funny I laugh. This is not funny."

"No it's not."

"Can we lighten up?"

"Only if you kiss me."

"Look, you asked for that."

"No I didn't, I asked for a kiss."

"You can't just pop into my life and pretend I've had no life, pretend I'm not who I've been since we were kids."

"I'm not pretending. I'm telling you what I see. That's the problem."

"So let's pretend," she said, taking his hand, "that you didn't say what you said."

"Okay, but I didn't ask for what I just got."

"You did. You absolutely did so. Some cock-eyed connection between you and your night sweats and a man who lived through a nightmare."

"That's what I can't figure out. How you ended up wanting to live with a nightmare."

"Because I always live with a nightmare," she said grimly.

"I didn't mean that," he said.

"But I do. Mio understood. I killed my child, my own father's child. I could have killed myself. That would have been easier but I didn't, and Mio lives with a dead child, his own childhood, buried alive."

"So you love him."

"You're pigheaded, you are. You like to think you float through things just rolling with the punches, unscathed, and maybe you do. Maybe you're lucky. But you're pigheaded. You think Mio wants to be in your life? You don't know what alone is."

"I've seen it in his eyes."

"Take a look in your own. Who've you got in your life?"

"You."

"Me. You know what my uncle used to call me? The firefly. He was going to try and catch a firefly in a bottle. You know what happens to a firefly in a bottle? You get this drab little speck you blow off the end of your finger. No thanks."

"The only bottles I've got are bottles of wine," he said, waving his hand, trying to dismiss what he'd been doing to her, "good wine to get warm with you."

"I love these days, I love the warmth, feeling like there's a little girl alive in me again that I'd forgotten all about, but there are some wounds Mio and I never had to talk about, and that's a kind of love."

"You mean I should shut up."

"Yes, you should shut up."

As they came into a street crowded with cafés and stuccoed walls with big palm trees outlined in pink neon against the grey stucco, a dusky boy with long braided black hair, hooded black eyes, and wearing a coat down to his ankles rose up out of a doorway where he'd been sitting crosslegged and he began to follow them. Filthy, he was carrying an empty beer can and a wire coat hanger. When he came close, Adam offered him some coins but he shook his head. He kept following them, and then he jammed the hanger wire into the can and dragged it up and down against the open mouth of the tin can, making a flat scraping sound, a raw screech, keeping a ragged rhythm, falling into step behind them and then closing in, shadowing them down the street and around the corner. Adam turned and waved him away but the boy kept sawing his jagged music, shaking his braided hair, staring at them, his black eyes mournful and menacing.

"What the hell's he want?"

"Who knows?"

"It sounds like strangled birds."

"Maybe he's got a knife?"

They passed an empty baby carriage abandoned by the curb. It was missing one wheel. The wind was flapping in the boy's long coat, and then the boy, working the hanger like a rasp against the tin, circled ahead and waited beside a high stone wall, the veins standing out on his neck. There was a doorway in the wall.

"Let's dump this kid."

They pushed through heavy creaking wooden doors and found themselves standing beside an empty porter's gate-house in the town cemetery, looking down narrow avenues of tiny stone and marble houses, obese little cherubs with stubby wings cradling each other on wrought-iron porches and two effete angels holding avenging swords alongside a relief carving of a young socialite in her dressage jacket and cap as she stood over the open sunken room of her family's tomb, the bunks for six caskets inexplicably empty.

They looked back. The boy had not followed them. "Imagine, a kid like that giving us the willies. You'd think we were kids."

"We were once, we made love after going to communion, with Harry and your mother asleep in bed upstairs, and I tried to tell a priest that our making love was a prayer."

"Priests are fatheads. What do fatheads know about prayer? What does Harry know about singing? It's something he gets other people to do. These are the houses," she said, walking between two tombs, "of beheaded prayer."

"The what?"

"That's what Mio used to call cemeteries."

It had begun to drizzle.

"I think you've got that guy in your bones."

"No. I just knew how to sit silently with him, between his rages, though they weren't really rages. They were astonished laments that sounded like rages against god, but then, he didn't believe in god either. Would you believe in god if you had been buried alive by your own family because your hair was black?"

"Why'd they do that?"

"Because everybody was blond, blue-eyed and blond. They thought he'd brought them the plague and the war. And when the other peasants dug him up his hair was white. He dyes it black now."

"So now he only brings the war."

"Now he co-operates. He's a very co-operative man. The most intimate thing he ever shared with me was he let me see his white hair, he washed it all out, and there he was, like a ghost of himself. And I didn't have to love him, or want to love him, and I never knew if he wanted to love me."

"Well, nothing says you've got to love me either."

"Is that what nothing says?"

"That's what the skewbald sky says, I don't know what skewbald means, I just always liked the sound of it, it sounds like it's all screwed up."

"You are too sad, Adam, for a man who says he's happy."

"I am happy."

"Then you've got no right to act sad."

"I'm more than happy."

"If you're happy, then so am I, except I know men like you, intimate as hell as long as they're just passing through. It's all a dance, for three minutes, for three years, it's still a dance. That's okay. But you know what makes dancing beautiful, it's the right space between two people holding on to each other. Mio and Harry try to dance but they don't hold on and they don't know anything about space," she said, stepping away from him and holding out her arms. "We've never danced together."

"Here?"

"Why not?"

She was wearing low-heeled sandals and with her hands on her hips she beat her heels against the gravel, then bent her knees, pivoted, and shook her hair. Her blouse came undone as she spun and held her body straight as a candle, her nostrils flared. She took his hands and together they danced slowly between the tombs, erect in each other's arms, and then they rocked to a standstill and he sang quietly in her ear, pressing his body against hers, aroused by the thrust of her pelvis:

> *There's a line between love and fascination,*
> *It's hard to tell them apart,*
> *For they give the very same sensation,*
> *Take care my foolish heart.*

"Look," she said, "You don't need to know this, but I'll tell you the day I knew I didn't love Mio, he was holding my hand and he told me he saw a grave in my open palm. That was it, so here we are. We're in a graveyard. You see my hands. No wounds, no graves. When you kiss my hands I feel the sun, the heat. I love that ..."

"Look Ma, no hands," and he pretended he was throwing something high into the air.

They walked to the end of an avenue of small, narrow houses. "I feel like I'm in a tiny town," he said and kissed her neck. Then he rubbed his shoe against his ankle. Suddenly, his ankles were itchy and he bent down and scratched under his trousers, inside his sock. He thought he could smell urine in the gravel. She bent down, too.

"When we're quiet," she said, "like when you were singing, my ears sing in those silences ..." He was bent over in front of a white marble tomb, an angel with a leering smile sprawling across the roof, holding a harp in one hand, his other hand dangling over the edge of the roof.

"Jesus, it's fleas."

"You're kidding."

"It's goddamned fleas," he said, scratching his ankles.

"The graveyard's full of fleas."

"The kisses of the dead," she said and laughed.

"The dead, my ass," he said. "This is living. Come on," and he took her hand and broke into a loping run to the other side of the burial yard, away from the gate where they'd left the boy with the coat hanger and tin can. "Come on, maybe we'll be lucky and it'll pour rain and we can go for a swim in the sea." He felt suddenly hemmed in by the walls, by the darkening evening sky that seemed swollen with rain.

"Have you ever swum in the rain?"

She shook her head.

"Okay, we'll swim in the rain, we'll drown the damned fleas."

* * *

On a cloudless afternoon of sunlit-crusted snow in the yard, Adam and Father Zale sat on the back porch. The priest wore a heavy woollen muffler around his throat. He had grown paler and thinner, as if his silence were slowly starving him, yet he smiled continuously, his eyes sparkling. Once, Adam had seen him walking down the street with Harry, who was dapper in a double-breasted suit and straight-last shoes, carrying a silver conductor's baton under his arm. Excited in his conversation, Harry had stopped to make a point, standing on the sidewalk in front of the nodding priest, crossing the air with his baton, and Adam had heard him say firmly, "… the seventh angel sounded the trumpet …" They had walked on, Father Zale still nodding, taking Harry by the arm, just like he now reached out on the back porch and took Adam's arm. The priest came once a week in the afternoon, sitting with Adam on the porch, sorrow in his eyes because he could not say a comforting word when Adam said, "I can't somehow get it out of my mind, seeing my mother's body slip into the fire, and I know it doesn't make much sense because it's probably better than rotting away in the scummy earth, but I kind of see her exploding into a cocoon of ashes. It's hard for me to see that she really wanted it that way, though she wouldn't have said so if she didn't want it, that was the thing about her, honest as the day is long, too honest. I remember sitting right here a couple of months before she died, with her looking up over the roofs because sometimes she thought she saw an angel moving his lips over there, and she wasn't crazy or anything like that, it just amused her to think she was getting a visitation from outer space or wherever her dead cousin was since it was the stone statue over her cousin's grave that kept coming around, but then she turned to me, solemn, with this pleased kind of glint in her eye, and she said that one day she had told me that the less I knew about her and Web the better it was because that would let me love them longer, except now she was going to tell me something about them so I would understand them as well as love them."

Adam stood up. He pulled the lapels of his coat across his chest against the chill wind. The sun flared off the snow, cutting his eyes, so that he stepped down a stair, tucking his head out of the glare. He turned back to the priest, who had edged forward in his chair.

"And she said, you know, she and Web always treated each other the same way, accepting who they were, just the way they found each other, and Web, she said, was a driven lonely man who loved her as long as he could be alone and feed off his own loneliness, and that's where any greatness he had came from, his loneliness which took him off by himself all over god's country trying to fill it with more loneliness, and like most people she could have said that if he loved her he'd have stopped being who he was and become who she thought he should be, betraying himself, which is what she said most everybody mistakes love for, your lover has to betray himself and you call that love. But Web didn't betray himself or ask her to be anybody but who she was either." Adam turned away, stepping down the stairs into the snow, through the crust, tears in his eyes, and Father Zale came down the stairs after him. "Since she was a woman with her own loneliness, her own darkness, she said she gave him no real gaiety at all, the blind gaiety he needed to lift himself out of his gloom, and so they disappointed each other but never made each other betray themselves, and she thought they loved each other better that way, better than anybody else she knew." Adam stood out in the deep snow in the sunlight, tears in his eyes, with the old priest breaking through the crust behind him. They stood with their arms around each other, the priest weeping, too, because he could not say a word.

△

1842–1896

▽

To the memory of Annie Waters,
Who was the water in everyone's wine.
She punished the earth upwards of 40 years
To say nothing of her relations.

He was often alone. Web always called, especially on the day marking his mother's death, but they didn't talk well on the phone and Web said, "Don't let the dead get you down, they're supposed to give you a lift," and that always left Adam more lonely, and for a while one night he walked around the house humming mournfully to himself, drinking Web's whisky straight from the bottle, and soon he was drunk and decided to walk over to Harry's because he felt sorry for Harry who lived all alone, and he was going to stand and sing on Harry's porch, but when he got over there and before he could start singing, Harry opened the door and said, "Come on in," so Adam said, "I didn't come alone, I brought you a bottle."

They sat across from each other at the dining-room table. There were french doors between the living and dining rooms. The doors were curtained and closed. They seemed to have been closed for a long time. The table was covered with music scores, old bills, unopened envelopes, ashtrays full of ashes and butts. The scores were coffee-stained. There were no pictures or photographs in the room. Harry smiled in the yellow light from a small brass chandelier, took a long swallow, blinked, and said, "How about some music?"

There were four big old box speakers in the corners of the room. Each had a vase on it. The vases were filled with plastic swizzle sticks.

"It takes hold of you," Harry said, as the sound of trumpets rose in the small room, "trumpet voluntaries ... at the right hour they sound like crystal coming apart at the seams."

"I never thought about it," Adam said. He was sure the trumpets were causing a sudden pain behind his eyes. Harry lit a cigarette. He cupped the cigarette in his hand, hiding it. Adam had always believed Harry hid his cigarettes in his hand because he was smoking in church behind the altar, but here he was in his own home, hiding.

"This isn't the right hour," Adam said.

"*Now is the hour*," Harry crooned in a mock tenor, "*when we must say goodbye* ..."

"We just said hello."

"I know, but we gotta take any chance to sing a song ..."

"Come on Harry ..."

"Come on where, there's nowhere to go."

"Let's go in there."

"Where?"

"Where the doors are closed. What's in there?"

"I never go in there," Harry said and began to croon again.

Adam sat hunched forward, his head down, troubled by how rumpled Harry looked, his clothes unclean, singing "*Now is the hour*" even though a full choir with brass and strings boomed from the corners "*Kyrie, kyrie eleison*" and Adam, puzzled – but also because he was quite drunk – rubbed his face with both hands – thinking *there's your doomed gentleman songster mother dear, our old singing horseman and the only horses he hears are coming over the hill high in the sky* but then he realized Harry was sitting very straight in his chair, eyes closed, listening, with his hands folded on the table, and though the cuffs of his coat were frayed and his wrists looked bony and thin, he had beautiful hands ... long tapered fingers, and the skin was pinkish-white, scrubbed clean, the nails carefully clipped, cleaned, and the cuticles cut back. In the dim light Adam was so fascinated by Harry's hands that he leaned forward, trying to pour himself another drink at the same time. Then he realized Harry was smiling at him.

"It's all in the touch," Harry said, "the laying on of the hands," and he laughed and lifted one arm with an elegant gesture, the hand hanging bent from the wrist in the air for a moment as if it were a flower that had just died on the stem, and then he began to conduct, the hand caressing the air as voices of surpassing sweetness rose, saying, "Now this, this is the real trumpet stuff, this is it, *Dies Irae*, and you gotta listen to this, and if you're drunk and you're a lucky drunk who knows how to hear, you'll hear it ... all of Verdi's easy equilibrium, what your father would call good rocking, and yet it's such a complex complexity, every note, every syllable as precise as a raindrop ..." and he lifted both hands, seeming to hold a moment's silence between them, "and contrapuntal on your brain and little parallel lines all flowing like it was under water except it's bold, right out front, the boldest thing ..." Harry stopped conducting and filled their glasses, hearing deep in the corners of the room a bass voice, *Mors stupevit et natura, cum resurgit creatura* ..."the boldest thing," he said, pointing his finger at Adam accusingly, "is what Verdi called the *parola scenica*, he sculpts the situation, makes it clean, and evident ... and just when you think things are clear, he takes you into zones, neutral zones where there's no clear word, just a blur of voices, and sometimes the voices hiss at you ... it's wild, like something someone would do now, and you sit in there in those zones, neutral ..."

They sat across from each other at the table, saying almost nothing for an hour, letting the music fill the gaps until the bottle was empty. Then Adam got up and Harry, with his arm around Adam's shoulder, walked out with him onto the front porch.

"I really came over to sing on your porch," Adam said.

"So sing ..."

"I was going to sing you a song old Edmund taught me up at the Black River ..."

"Sing ..."

Adam hollered with a nasal twang, to the tune of "What a Friend We Have in Jesus":

> *Life presents a dismal aspect,*
> *Full of darkness and of gloom,*
> *Father has a strictured penis,*
> *Mother has a fallen womb.*
> *Brother Bill has been deported*
> *For a homosexual crime,*
> *Sister Bette has just aborted*
> *For the forty-second time.*
> *Cousin Sue has chronic menstruation,*
> *Never laughs and seldom smiles,*
> *Oh, life presents a dismal aspect,*
> *Cracking ice for father's piles.*
> *Amen ...*

They stood together on the top step, howling *Amens* into the night, and then Adam went down the walk and Harry lit a cigarette and when Adam turned to look back he saw the red tip of fire disappear in Harry's cupped hand as Harry called out, "Come to mass tomorrow, you'll really hear something ..."

The next morning, when Adam crossed the cobblestone square and entered the church, he found it was the feast of Corpus Christi and the pews were crowded, but the first three rows on both sides of the centre aisle had been cordoned off with white tasseled ropes. A priest in a black surplice and white mitre was sprinkling holy water over the altar. The choir filed onto the altar, the choir much smaller than it used to be, only seven boys and seven men, and Adam realized there was a wooden music stand in front of the choir stall. The choir, dressed in red robes, waited.

Then, outside the church, there was a drum roll, followed by a steady drum beat. The central doors opened and the De La Salle Drum and Trumpet Corps, in their black uniforms and silver capes, marched in single file up the aisle to the front rows. As the last drummer turned into his pew, Harry, robed in red, came onto the altar, to the music stand, and as he lifted his baton the priest appeared, his chasuble scarlet red with a white cross. Someone hidden was playing the organ, the choir began to sing.

Harry conducted the *Kyrie*, and the small choir sang with precision, each syllable clipped and as clear as Harry's flicks and turns of the baton. During the sermon, he did not leave the altar but stepped back to sit in a chair set aside from the stall. He sat very straight in the chair, his legs crossed beneath the red robe.

Then, at the moment of consecration, when the people in their pews all knelt, the drum and trumpet corps stood as the priest lifted the host over his head for the first time and Harry slashed the air with his baton. There was a rising drum roll and then trumpets blared, a piercing, rending note that startled and threw those kneeling back against their seats. The choir joyfully sang *Sanctus* into the echo and as the host was lifted again, Harry lifted his arm, too: drums rolled, the trumpeters blew the silence open, the note resounding and hanging in the air. *Sanctus.* Harry stood with his arms raised, waiting, a little lopsided grin on his face, and then as the priest lifted the host for the last time, Harry hunched his shoulders and slowly swept the air with his arms, urging a heavier and deeper drum roll, and then he almost leapt as he stabbed the baton toward the front pews of forty silver trumpets. *Sanctus. Sanctus. Sanctus.* The triumphal crescendo caromed through the church. Adam stood astonished. Harry, in rapt concentration, stood with his arms thrown back, turned away from the choir to face the crowd as the priest passed down to the altar rail, to the people slowly coming forward to take communion, and Harry, staring, his teeth clenched in an ecstatic pain, reached up, grasping at the ceiling, the gold stars.

* * *

"I'm always afraid that things like fleas get right into the blood," she said, as they drove through the black and tan hills south of the hotel.

"The dead are the plague, they're always touching us," he said. They saw below them, in a cove, mangrove like huge water spiders poised on the water.

"The old old farmers," Adam said as he drove the twisting road toward docks in the cove, "they thought these mountain streams were the white magic urine of spirits who spoke to them out of the tree trunks, and Ponce, crazy old Ponce, it was my father who first put me on to Ponce, he came along and set up a sundial so they'd know what time it was when they were dying."

She had her hand on the inside of his thigh. She began to sing "*It's three o'clock in the morning,*" but he paid no attention, pleasured by the flow of his own words. "They all thought that Ponce, with his face the ash color of dead fires, was supernatural, but he knew no matter how many tattooed ladies he had on his arm, no matter how often he called himself the *adelantando*, you know what the *adelantando* is …?"

"No."

"The front runner, Old Ponce the plunger thought he was the front runner …"

"You're crazy …"

"And then they ambushed one of his scouts and held the poor bugger head first under the magic water where he drowned so they killed some more white faces but they kept coming back so they figured the white men could only be coming back from the dead, resurrected *coming back and hammering the keys, always letting out a nasal moaning cry of pain with the earth pushing up a stone into the loneliness in the silence between notes,* but then Ponce picked up his mirror and winced at all his wrinkles and remembered something about a fountain so he went up to where that was and blew the crowd a kiss and went rooting around in the rivers and streams for his fountain and the old farmers up there with their hair cut like acorn tops stood inside their stag skins waving their antlers at him and he was stupid enough to wave back and so they shot him with an arrow and old Ponce, delectable, irrepressible, impeccable, and sensational, said, 'God helps those who help themselves and I couldn't help myself,' and he wept because he only wanted to be young again, to be loved, to be the *adelantando* ..."

"He did not."

"What?"

"He didn't say god helps those who help themselves."

"No, he didn't, but he died and he didn't come back."

At the docks, a man hunched up under a wide-brimmed floppy straw hat agreed to rent them a light aluminum boat that had a small outboard motor. The water was calm in the cove. The boat crossed the water slowly. He was full of satisfaction. "I liked telling you that story," he said, "I liked it a lot." The boat eased by the first mangrove trees, stragglers out on the edge of the dark web-work of root branches looped and hooked in the air, their leaves blocking out more and more of the sun the deeper they went into the grove, in under the tangled grey veining, the oily water the color of the leaded side of a mirror, only broken by sudden mirror-like flashes of light through gaps in the foliage as they snaked through the tunnel channels, hundreds of water bugs leaving swollen silver lines on the surface.

"Why did you want to come out here?" she asked.

"I don't know. Because it's here, I've never been in a mangrove before."

"Do you always go where you've never been before, just because it's there?"

"Maybe. Maybe most of the time."

"Strange."

"Why?"

"Because you're so attached to your home, it's in your head all the time, your memories."

"I used to think that's what immortality is."

"What?"

"Being alive in someone else's memory."

"And now?"

"I'm not so sure. I know now that I love you very deeply."

"Do you," she said, the overhead roots shadowing her face as she sat upright in the bow.

"I woke up this morning," he said, "and I couldn't remember what we'd done yesterday, or the day before. I just felt this quiet forgetfulness, like a complete loss of memory, and I couldn't even remember the names of some people. It was as close as I've ever come to bliss, or what bliss must be, or suicide."

"Suicide?"

"It crossed my mind, maybe love is something like suicide, you just leave off from yourself so you can't remember, you don't need to, you just are, like this mangrove or a flower at the back of a garden ..."

"It's pretty spooky in here."

"Maybe love's spooky?"

"You're cornering the market on morbid today."

"No, no, not at all. I couldn't be happier."

"Sure you could."

"No, I couldn't, could you?"

"Probably not. I'm not prone to happiness."

"Why not?"

She reached up to touch the roots.

"I can't forget."

"You told me you don't remember anything."

"That's right, but it's like what died in me is alive. Every day it's more and more alive. That's what I can't forget."

"But you've been happy here."

"And I'll always remember everything. You're immortal already, you see."

They came out of a channel, out of the grove into late sunlight, pale pink and mauve through layered clouds, the sun sinking. There were hundreds of black-and-white frigate birds with long tails that looked like open shears, and though the frigates fed on flying fish farther out to sea, the wind was wrong for feeding, so they were hovering overhead, over the boat, low-flying, and the males had a flash of startling scarlet red. Lying back in the boat, Adam cut the motor dead so they could watch the drift of the birds in the air currents, their undulation, funneling into line for a moment and then flattening out into a huge sickle shape, and the only other movement was from floppy-winged pelicans suddenly lifting out of the trees, their throats of heavy loose flesh like old bags, "Like the old gladstone travelling bag my grandfather used to carry," he said.

"I remember something your grandfather said."

"What?"

"Don't eat the red berries or you'll die. I just remember it now looking at the red on the black wings of the birds."

The light went down in the hour before the moon rose. He started the motor and swung the boat around toward the bay beyond the docks, the heaving water in the shadowlight of dusk like ebony glass, except after a while, as they entered the mouth of the bay, an effervescent foaming light began to appear in their wake and waves rippled away from the boat's bow like ribbons of glowing confetti.

Suddenly a fish leapt in the dark, luminescent, an arc of inexplicable light, and as the boat moved, small schools of fish skittered away leaving faint trails of glowing hand-stitching under the water. He trailed his hand, a foam of light churned around his wrist, and as she began to laugh gleefully he scooped up handfuls of light-loaded water and poured it back into the blackness and then dipped his arm up to his elbow in the water and held it open-handed, extended to the pin-holes of starlight in the sky, and light like illuminated balls of mercury rolled through his fingers over his palm and down his forearm.

"Stop," she said, "stop the motor."

The boat rocked.

"I've never seen anything like it," she said.

"Me neither."

They sat watching beaded trails of fish.

"Let's take off our clothes, let's go swimming," she said. "It'll be wonderful."

"We don't know what's in these waters."

"And you," she said, pulling her blouse free of her skirt, "you're the man who's always supposed to go where he's never been."

He undressed. They sat in the boat facing each other. "The night air's always so damned clean when you're naked," she said and dove into the water and he dove after her, cutting swaths of light down through the water, their bodies rising to the surface, shouting, and they thrashed the water, smacking the heels of their palms against the water, driving sprays of light into their faces, beaded shawls streaming over their shoulders as they kissed, kissing droplets of light from their cheeks, trying to touch and raise bursts of light all over their bodies. He lifted her so that her breasts were against his face, and then he fell back with the current of the water, covering her with quick kisses behind her ears, on her eyelids, her throat. They sank under, hanging in the water, and she locked her legs around his waist, scissoring light as they rose, each kiss tasting of salt, and she felt for his hips under the water, but he was drawn away in the swell of a wave and then she reached again and took hold of him, settling down on him, her other hand pushing against the small of his back. Riding the heave of each small wave he kept his mouth on hers. She moaned like a woman complaining, locking her legs around his hips. He angled back into the incoming waves, carrying the weight of her body, and she pushed down and with her fingers she opened herself so that they were locked, adrift in the pulse of the sea, straining, fondling and spinning, with a rush of light burning through their loins as they fell under a wave, and they broke, unbelieving at the release of weightlessness. They dove again and rolled under water, reaching out, kicking back to the surface for air, a wild cavorting of shadows, falling back down into the water, seeking to go as deep in the darkness as they could so they could make light, a turbulence as they came back up, as she arced into the air, a necklace sparkling and breaking apart over her breasts, and he held her, turning and swimming on their backs so that they lost sight of land and saw only stars and then, suddenly, the moon came up over the hills and the sky brightened, the stars dimmed, and with the brightening sky the beads of light in the water disappeared, all trace disappeared, leaving them swimming in the black water, reaching for the boat.

part TEN

He walked down a narrow logging road by a sign staked in the long grass that said CAFE LUMIERE, but there was no café; only a winding dirt track through high brush, and at the end of the track, rows of small plastered one-room white shanties tinted by the red dust so that it seemed a village of gentle ochre and russet and sienna, the doors and windows closed, and close to a communal water tap, a sheltered wall with long benches in front of it. There was no sound. And then, as if a signal had been given, the doors opened, dark oblongs like coffins, and staves and poles reached out into the light like antennae. Stumps of arms, feet in cloth bags, old men and women lepers, heads down, poling themselves forward as if the air were water, saying nothing *poling into the deep slow corruption of the body, not a secretive and sudden cancer but a prefiguration of death itself, dry yet glistening white and yellow wounds eating away the softest parts, fingers, toes, the disfigurement of a whole hand coming off, a foot, hobbling in the sun, alive in disease, living rot, cordoned, cut off. A* man draped in a worn grey shawl hunched toward Adam, his hooded eyes wide open and his hand held out, *the hand one man extends to another*, thumb, forefinger, and little finger gone, a creamy white scar in the black flesh where his thumb had been, a stub hand, almost a club, and in the still, hot silence of the afternoon, before Adam could recoil, the leper had left him no choice: a refusal to take his hand would recognize only his rot, his corruption, his death, and yet as the man's two hard fingers went into the palm of Adam's hand he felt a shudder of recognition, a bond with the leper, with himself, and also a welling inevitability, *as pressing as that two-fingered leper's kiss, deeply felt, wanting to weep for myself, for him* but the man was smiling, his eyes filled with laughter and some enormous satisfaction that seemed so simple, so open, and Adam stood on the edge of the village shaken as he looked over the leper's shoulder and saw her, pale with cropped hair, wearing a white skirt and white running shoes. She was spooning mealy-mealy into a child's mouth. There was a strong wind and she was holding her skirt between her knees. As she stood up and stopped at the water tap she saw him and stared, her finger to her lips. She closed her eyes and said, "My god, my god, my god," standing with her fists jammed into the pockets of her smock. "So, you really have come ..."

"Yes ..."

There was a stillness in her almond eyes and a lean energetic ease in her body that he'd never seen. She suddenly called to the leper women and men and they called back, laughing, throwing open their arms. Two women helped each other toward the water tap, carrying buckets, the pipe painted red and white. Their ankles were bandaged and one woman's cheek was pinched by creeping leprosy of the eye but as she hobbled up to Gabrielle she giggled coquettishly and shielded her eyes, shying away from Adam, letting out a low moaning cry. Gabrielle kissed the woman and they draped their arms around each other. Then, Gabrielle walked down the slight, short incline to Adam. "Well, I can't leave you standing here all alone, can I," she said, taking his hand, "not like you were a leper." She kissed him on the cheek, paused, and then said, kissing him again, "What can I do, I don't know what to do, what are you doing here?" She let his hand slip and went back up the incline, calling out toward the shanties, graceful in her own effortless momentum, waving, and men and women kept wobbling toward her out of the dark. She turned down a narrow alley, bending forward in the shadows in front of an old grey-headed man wrapped in a frayed brown blanket, and she touched his cheek with an intimacy so entirely open that Adam stopped, taken aback as the old man crossed his stump arm over hers and rested his head against her hand. Her eyes were wide open, some fixed locus of effortless enthusiasm in her, engaged in constant touching and cradling as she went along the alley, rewrapping loose bandages, squatting in the doorways to fondle watery-eyed children, looking back to see if Adam had followed, smiling shyly as she waited for him with an openness that seemed to invite pain, and he began to laugh at himself because he wanted to hold her hard and bite her, but she said, "I am so lucky, they give me so much, they fill me with joy."

"But you give to them," he said, surprised and offended

that she didn't ask him how he was or how he'd got there, surprised that she saw herself that way. "You open yourself up to them, you come to them …"

"Perhaps," she said, "but I'm the lucky one. I come away filled with the joy they give me." She took hold of his forearm. "You see," she said, an intensity in her eyes that gave him a little shiver, "it's a disease I love. I hate something like tuberculosis. Dead, it's a dead thing, but this is alive, you can surround it with love, with your mind."

At the end of the alley in the long grass, he saw a shaded clearing under tall palm trees, a small cemetery, and tilted in the grass, old stones carved in Muslim crescents with fetishes suspended from sticks. "That's where I live," she said, pointing to a cinder-block house painted white with a pink tiled roof. She took his hand as she opened the door.

They stood in the dim light from five small windows along one wall. There were wooden crossbars and beaded screens on the windows, and in the single room, a small table covered with a white cloth. White wall shelves and boxes held books and papers. There were letters and a silver pocket watch on the table, and beside the watch, a kerosene lamp with a tin shade. In the centre of the room, a graceful iron bedstead painted white, draped in white mosquito netting.

"Do I look very different?" she asked.

"Thinner, that's all. And me, do I look the same?"

"Yes."

"I'm not."

"Why?"

"I killed a man two days ago."

"My God."

"Otherwise, I'm the same old me" *whispering open up I got more sins* as he drew her close, surprised at how easily she nestled into his arms, her breasts bare beneath the smock, *a kindness taken away in the dark*, wondering why he could always remember the little oval mole beside her nipple.

"Now that I'm here, I hardly know what to say."

"There's nothing to say."

"That's crazy. For nearly a year I've wanted to say something to you."

"What?"

"I don't know," he said, stroking her hair. "I was hoping it would come to me once I got here."

"You don't have to say anything."

"Something's haunted me, that's all. Maybe we stepped on the sunlight."

"What?"

"It's just something my mother warned me about."

"My mother never warned me about anything. She had a wonderful dignity. She could swallow anything."

"Look where it got her."

"Don't be silly."

"If I wasn't silly I wouldn't be here, I wouldn't be haunted by you."

"Are you?"

For a moment he wanted to bitterly tell her how hurt he'd been to wake up and find her gone from their hotel room, and how he had looked for her in the casinos and made a fool of himself with Mio, waiting for him in the casino lobby. Mio had smiled knowingly and said, "I feel for you, but if she's gone she's long gone. That's the way the angel spreads her

wings." Mio had taken the rose from his lapel and given it to
him, like a flower for the dead. Adam had turned away, about
to crush the rose in his fist, but then he'd stood apart from Mio
in the casino lobby, plucking the petals ... *she loves me, she loves
me not* ... then he'd shouted, "She loves me," dropping the
stripped head. But Mio had quickly picked it up and had laid it
in the crook of his taut gloved hand. "I hear you're a
photographer. Photograph this," and he had held out the
dead hand to him. Adam had shuddered and scowled,
muttering, "You're an angel. A real angel, Mio." He had
hurried from the lobby, going on to New York, but not finding
her there either, finding only the plump brown woman who'd
said, "She be going to the village of light." Now, here he was,
dismayed by the forsaken village, but then he said, "Yes,
when I was in Cairo ..."

"Oh, I'd love to see Cairo ..."

"I woke up one morning and I could see the gull sails on the
old boats on the Nile and I thought you should see that with
me ..."

"I'm happy here."

"You are?"

"Yes. Very happy."

She put two fingers to her lips and then touched her fingers
to his lips and stepped back. The sun was almost down, a last
lurid streak of lemon, like a rip in the air. She lit the kerosene
lamp. There was only a pale glint in the five small windows.

"And I'm so happy to see you."

"But surely you're not going to stay here?"

"Sure I am."

"You can't."

She looked up sternly, letting the silence weigh between

them, and then went on adjusting the flame, saying, "Tell me about the man you killed."

"Shit, I never really saw him. Just a spinning face in a stairwell, and the whole time I was driving through the bush his face kept spinning away and I kept trying to hold on to it till I thought I was losing my mind, with only the terror in his eyes clinging to me like it was the terror I should be feeling, except I don't feel it. I'm sorry I shot him in the back."

"He didn't see you?"

"I don't know. They were shelling the hotel downriver. It was quick, too quick, and I got out quicker."

"It's a wonder you didn't get killed. Are you so unhappy?"

"About what?"

"That you had to come here."

"I'm not unhappy."

"I don't believe you."

"You know what W.C. Fields said?"

"No."

"They asked him what he believed in and he said he believed he'd have another drink so what've you got to drink?"

"Palm wine."

"Jesus."

"No, that's Palm Sunday," she said, giggling. "Besides, it's very good."

She parted the mosquito netting that hung from a ceiling clamp in a cone around the bed, and she reached under the bed and then sat down with a jug in her lap. "I sip a little at night. There's always a chill, and the noise. I don't think I'll ever get used to the noise of the night."

He sat beside her and tilted the jug to his lips.

"Do you think your friends are outside the door listening?"

"Oh no, not at all. You're the first white man they've seen in my house, they'll assume we're in bed."

"We should be."

"You look exhausted."

"This is crazy, you're out here in the middle of nowhere and right away you're carrying on just like it's yesterday between us, like you didn't pack up and disappear."

"You look bushed so lie down," she said, and went to the door. "Lie down and get undressed." When she came back she was carrying a bucket of water. He was naked under the sheet but she pulled the sheet away and began slowly to sponge his neck and shoulders, his stomach, thighs, and feet. "You're so tired you can hardly keep your eyes open," she said, and wet his erection and washed him and then held him hard at the root so that he seemed even more erect in the shadow of the kerosene lamp. "You know, it's almost a year since I washed a body that wasn't sick with a wound somewhere," she said. "Your body is very strange."

* * *

Eugene Euclid Waters
1901–1967
He died
in
public relations.

* * *

It was early December. The clouds were low, the sugar maples bare. Adam got out of a taxi and set his bags down on the sidewalk. He thought the homes seemed narrow. The rooming-houses were gone, and nearly all the verandas, too. The verandas had been torn down, the ivy torn away from the walls, and the bricks sandblasted. Because there were not enough garages behind the houses, hedges had been uprooted and railroad ties sunk into lawns to shore up new driveways. The front lawns were staked with big red signs with black letters:

RE-ELECT ITZAK KLEIN
TO
BOARD OF CONTROL

There were also photographs of Itzak. He looked stern, wearing rimless round glasses, and he had a goatee. Almost every lawn had a KLEIN sign. He began to walk slowly up the street. A woman wearing a cloth coat with a grey fox neckpiece, the head of the fox peering over her shoulder, said, "I wouldn't leave your bags there like that. The new people on the street are better off but they're better off because they know how to steal."

"I don't remember you," he said.

"I don't remember you either."

"Waters, I live right over there."

"Do you now?"

"Yes."

"Well, at least you don't have a sign for that Klein person."

"No."

"He's not one of us, though I must say I don't remember a Waters family ... though the city's not the same, I hardly go downtown, all those black faces, I hardly know who I am. And to think this Klein person sits on the Board of Control. My father would have a conniption."

"Would he?"

"Oh yes. He was a fine man."

"What did he do?"

"Professor, professor of economics. Worked with Stephen Leacock. Why, Leacock used to come to the house and he was an amusing man, I'll tell you. He thought the blacks were all black because they were too stupid to move north and get bleached by the Aurora Borealis, and for all we know he was right. Anyway, that's certainly what he says in his book. He wrote a book on economics. My father helped him."

"You're sure we never met?"

"No."

"And I can't believe Klein, I can't believe he's on the Board of Control."

"Neither can I, but he is, since last year, but there was a big scandal and now there's new elections. I don't understand these scandals."

"No."

"Socialists stirring up trouble, there's always someone stirring up trouble. Can't leave well enough alone."

"No," he said. She held out her hand. He shook it and then picked up his bags and said, "It's good to be reminded where we come from."

"Yes," she said, straightening her fox neckpiece, "we forget too easily."

The next week, he went in the evening to an all-candidates meeting held in a convention room at the Harbor Heights hotel. With the cold winds, ice was beginning to build up inside the breakwater. He hunched up against the winds, wondering why he'd walked instead of taking a taxi, and he was glad to get to the hotel, riding the escalator to the second floor, to the broad windows facing the water. The sun was down, but in the light cast from the tall towers he could see choppy water inside the breakwater.

The long convention hall was crowded, tacky and shabby, and he had to sit at the back of the hall in a row of leatherette chairs. There were several hundred people sitting under the high ceiling, the chandeliers and gold mouldings. Then, seeing a blue banner along the side wall, he realized he was in the wrong room: WOMEN'S WORLD BODY BUILDING CHAMPIONSHIP – QUARTER FINALS, but before he could leave he was asked to move along by two men who'd also come in late, two portly and flush-faced men. A recorded trumpet fanfare announced fourteen oiled women who strode out onto the stage – tall, tanned, their eyes and teeth shining, one of them black – to be judged, the female master of ceremonies in a tuxedo said, "For muscularity, shape, and proportion in the following categories ... hit poses, the relaxed state, and free posing to music."

Adam decided to stay, surprised at how beautiful some of the women were. "How'd I ever miss this?" he wondered, pleased to have ended up, if only for a while, in the wrong place, fascinated by their glistening flesh as they flexed into knots and bulbs, a rococo skinscape that was neither male nor female. "This is not the tits, teeth, and tiara set, I can tell you," a young man sitting beside Adam said. "This is your auto mechanic's view of the body, all chrome and bumps and lumps," and he smirked and looked pleased with himself, applauding a new contestant. There were constant bursts of applause from people who were mostly pudgy, and the men, if they stood to clap, were wearing trousers too loose in the seat. Adam forgot the time as each woman went through her poses, each having the strange guise of power but no potency, an oiled sheen of sexuality but no sensuality, and then he realized that he'd stayed far too long and he forced his way out along the back row, thinking *so this is where baton twirlers end up*, knocking against the knees of grumbling men.

When he opened the door to a smaller convention room, he found the meeting was almost over and very few people were still there. A group of women were chatting by the door, one wearing an emerald-green cloth coat and green felt hat with a green veil. She told Adam the other candidate had not bothered to come. "Got cold feet, facing the likes of Mr. Klein, I should think," she said.

"Tell me," Adam said, seeing Itzak Klein, who looked bent, bonier, and determined, standing with campaign workers, all of whom held a KLEIN sign, "what does Mr. Klein stand for, I mean how'd he get onto the board?"

"Your law and order ..."

"Really?"

"You surprised?"

"Well, a little," he said modestly.

"You should vote for him if you care for anything decent."

"Yes, decency," he said.

"Yes," another woman said, turning her squat, broad-bosomed body toward Adam, bristling with hostility. "It's not as if his daughter was out on the street where any man might easily get at her, but in her own home ..."

"And Itzak?" he asked, astonished.

"You know Mr. Klein?"

"Only years ago, years ago."

"Mind you," the woman in green said, "he hasn't exactly got the police on his side either, though they should be."

"Why's that?" Adam asked.

"Because he said in no uncertain terms that all women should carry ice-picks in their purses."

"Well," Adam said, "the police just don't understand, do they?" Itzak had not moved. He stood with his fists clenched, dwarfed by signs and balloons, the light catching his round rimless glasses, and all Adam could feel in the room was a stilled animosity, a chill of disappointment, as if everything were in place but all wrong, and Itzak looked firm: KLEIN FOR CONTROL. He had wanted to tell Itzak he'd met Gabrielle, to say he'd heard about his brother, and wondered if he knew where Gabrielle was, but he smiled at the two women and said, "Well, it's over, isn't it."

"It's just beginning," the broad-bosomed woman said.

He backed out of the room. The women quickly turned because one of the balloons had broken with a loud pop over Itzak Klein's head.

Adam went down the escalator, crowded because the WOMEN'S WORLD BODY BUILDING CHAMPIONSHIP was over. "Who won?" he asked the man in front of him. "The wrong one," the man snarled. As Adam went through the revolving hotel doors, he saw a very thin black man wearing a scarlet coat and a scarlet top hat standing by the curb. The man was flagging taxis, one foot in the gutter, the other on the curb. The coat was too short in the sleeves for his long arms. Dudeman Wicken's suits had always been too short in the sleeves. Years ago, he had been doorman for an after-hours booze can and brothel across the road from Hercules War Surplus Sales, and he had also been a small-time pimp. Seeing a blonde wearing a luxurious wolfskin coat looking bewildered and anxious, he spun into the cruising traffic, his arms wagging for a taxi. He opened a taxi door for her, ushering her in, tucking the door shut, smiling, a pimp's handyman in a hotel top hat out in the street, and Adam cried, "Dudeman, remember me?"

Dudeman narrowed his eyes, looked hard at Adam, and then said, holding out his hand, "My man, gimme skin. Long time no see ..."

"I'm home for a while."

"Afterwhile, child, let it be afterwhile."

"Dude, what're you doing down here in that hat, how are you?"

"Fine as wine, baby. How's your poppa?" he asked, opening a taxi door.

"He's coming home in a couple of days. You okay, Dudeman?" Adam asked, getting into the taxi.

"Oh man," he said, taking off his hat and leaning into the back seat, "I got my whisky, I got a little pink booty, and I got my slave that paves my way, now how can't I be happy? I got everything under control." He closed the door, put on his hat, and strode back to the waiting crowd at the curb, calling out, "Don't want your custard, don't want your mustard, just want your lean green ..." and the crowd laughed as Adam drove away.

* * *

In the early morning, ragged fog lay in the air between the leper houses. He parted the beaded window curtains, staring at the fog, listening to whistling parrots. She made coffee, boiling water in a small pot, pouring it through a filter in a funnel into two cups.

"I hear you bicycled into here," he said.

"Only from downriver."

"You just grabbed a bike?"

"The consul's, he tried to stop me because of the shooting." She handed him his coffee and stood staring out the small window, too. "That's one thing I never understood, they were shooting everywhere into the forest from the roads and it was as if I wasn't there, they didn't even look at me, I don't know why they didn't shoot me."

"Some poor soldier," he said, laughing, "was sitting there scared shitless in the middle of all that machine-gunning and he looks up and sees you coming, a white woman on a bicycle, I'd pretend you weren't there, too. Otherwise, I'd think I was crazy."

"Maybe," she said, buttoning her white smock.

"This where you looked after your girlfriend?"

"Yes."

"Where's she?"

"Killed herself."

"So you came back?"

"No."

"You going to tell me why?"

"No."

"And you even showed up with no hair dryer."

"Right," she said, primping her hair, laughing.

"So, who runs this place?"

"There's a tinker-toy hospital between here and town, a couple of doctors and nurses living in chalet houses that look like Switzerland."

"Why not live there?"

"You want to live in Switzerland? I want to live here," she said. "I came back almost absent-mindedly, not knowing why, or at least not sitting down and telling myself why, and I live here in this house the same way." She smiled. She always smiled. It unnerved him. Her even teeth seemed whiter. He thought, *there is something absent in her*, and then with sudden dread, as if he'd made a terrible mistake and had misunderstood her completely, *it's me, I'm absent in her while I carried her around in me all this time*, yet she gave him an affectionate hug around the waist and opened the door. He put a camera in his jacket pocket, and as they walked through an alley, the sun dropping down the walls, she said, "That gun, it's still under the bed, leave it there till you go."

"Who said I'm going?"

"Adam, don't be ridiculous."

"But I am ridiculous."

A blind old man sat on the stoop of a house. She let out a girlish cry and hugged the old man and then stepped back. As he felt for her, waving his hands like flippers in water, she stood coiled with energy, an absorption in herself so intense, so filled with delight, that she was able to enter into everything around her, and she stepped back onto the stoop, embracing the blind man, whose hands fell limp into his lap. "He's one of the first," she said. The man, his head tilted, gave her a toothless laugh, his eyes the lustre of mercury. She held his dead hand in hers. Then, he settled into a dark corner of his doorway.

Farther along the alley, a young man with copper-colored hair wove a sleeping mat from thin papyrus strips. He was working on a raised platform in front of several cells with heavy wooden lattice bars on the doors. Solitary men and women sat inside on litters. "They're bound hand and foot and dragged out of the bush by their families," Gabrielle said. "Whatever's inside their brain is too evil and too deep for any drugs we have. We keep them in there, otherwise they'd be thrown into the river, or poisoned." It was stifling in the cells, even in the early morning. She moved from cell to cell, peering in and talking quietly, and she unbolted one of the doors although the weaver warned her: "He want to kill ..."

He was about twenty-two and naked except for trousers sheared at the thighs. There was a bowl of uneaten mealy-mealy beside him. He was very black and thick through the shoulders and he stared out into the light, a shrouded gleam in his eyes, the whites a greasy brown. In the darkness, each dart of his eyes was a warning of an impending lunge out into the light, but she lifted the bowl and told him to eat. He didn't move. He stared at her, kneading his knuckles. She leaned forward within reach and quietly said, "Yes ... yes ..." They stayed that way, silent, staring, and the man began to laugh, a playful clucking at the back of his throat, but when Adam, standing behind her, began to laugh too, he scowled and turned the bowl upside down. The mealy-mealy spread across the floor. She backed out of the cell and closed the door and the man lay down.

"You have to be very careful," she said.

"Look who's talking!"

"I know what I'm talking about."

"And I don't?"

"No."

"Maybe, but that guy sees something you know nothing about."

"We don't understand their minds," she said, suddenly going forward with a masculine stride he'd never seen in her, going toward a small square. "We don't understand their purity and power. I've been in the forest with them, you'll believe this if you've ever had a vision ... I've seen an old man, they initiated me, you see, they have such a feeling for trees, he concentrated so hard for so long that a tree bent down toward him ..."

"Hey," he said, as she strode on ahead of him, "you trying to lose me?" She stopped and tucked her head into her shoulder *just like Harry used to tuck his head behind the glass waiting for the sermon to be over*, yet she was laughing, excited by the attention from the lepers, and she paraded him into another alley. He didn't know whether he should be exasperated or strut as her man, except he suspected she wasn't thinking about him at all, and hadn't thought about him, and had let him make love to her shadow, leaving him in easy possession of something that didn't matter. Still, she had clung to him, she had moaned. Sometimes she seemed to be all shadows. He hurried, putting his arm around her shoulder. "Remember our tree," he said. "The tree in the back yard, Dad's Dead Dick?" She turned, staring so intently into his eyes that he thought she was somehow wounded, trying to look into his eyes, wondering why he had wounded her, but then she threw her head back and laughed.

"Thank you," she said, touching his cheek.

"For what?"

"I had forgotten Dad's Dead Dick. I sometimes forget I was a girl. You're the only guy who's ever given that back to me, I was almost never a girl."

"When I was a kid I said your name over and over ..."

"I'm not her, not the person who had my name."

"Sure you are."

"Names don't matter."

She gave him a quick kiss. Her lips were dry. She looked radiant but she had a sour breath.

"I'm sure they'll find the cure," she said.

"For what?"

"It'll be in the mind, the disease comes from the mind, some unbearable stress, the blacks are so spiritually alive in a way we don't know about, and the stress ..."

Her fists were closed in the pockets of her smock.

They entered a courtyard of plastered houses. The plaster had been painted coral, the benches by the door turquoise. The yard was empty except for several large enamel, aluminum, and plastic bowls on the ground and a machete between two of the bowls. Then, the doors opened and men and women came out, timorous yet fearless, and sat down on the benches, a mournful lineup, some crossing their scarred legs, pulling pieces of colored cloth across their throats, resting a forearm stump under a chin, a head tilted with haughtiness.

"This is awful," Adam said.

"No, no, they're not the worst. They have their families, they can do a little work, but it's the handicapped ... children born with a withered leg, or no colon, they're like reptile children dragging themselves through the dust ..."

Facing the men and women, their repose striking him as an entreaty, he said, "How did this happen?"

"It's in the mind ..."

"How'd you ever end up here?"

She took his face between her hands, as if they were alone and could be intimate, and her voice was faint, full of pitying annoyance. "You only wonder why we end up where we do if you've never been anywhere, if you figure there had to be a plan because all you ever had was plans."

A clucking pigeon flapped toward the forest and a flock of *queleas* hovered over the tree line and then scattered in all directions. It was hot, but from another courtyard they heard a man complaining of the cold. A wizened old woman turned toward him with weary, expressionless eyes, and she limped forward, blinking dully, but then she hesitated and tottered back to her bench.

"You got your camera?"

"Sure."

"Take their pictures."

"They don't want to."

"They'll love it. That's why they've come out, so you can see them. This is their vanity, they want you to see them ..."

As he circled around the benches, focusing, shooting, he

felt them quickly yield to his presence, and he also saw an assertive audacity in them, as if they were measuring him, and a young woman with a pinkish-white scar inching into her eye even looked at him with an amused lascivious glint, and he thought, "I could never make love to her," and then he was ashamed – not because he felt he should be able to make love to her, but because he heard Father Zale saying, "Shame is when you can be all alone and still happy," or was it Father Zale? He couldn't remember and suddenly turned from the men and women on the benches, stricken *doing the dead man's float, and all I want is an easy getaway or loose shoes* at the sight of Gabrielle standing against the sky in her white smock, alone on a knoll, self-assured, and he hurried to her, taking her arm.

"I had this sick feeling," he said.

"So don't look at them."

"No, no, when I turned around I didn't think I'd see you there."

"Maybe I disappeared in your dream," she said, "that's what love is."

* * *

Just before Christmas, the day after Web came home from Copenhagen, it snowed heavily. That evening there was a party in one of the houses on the street. The sandblasted house belonged to Arthur, the missionary's son. The missionary had died on holidays in a car accident in the south of France. Arthur, who had become a successful lawyer specializing in speculative properties for people in show business, buried his father in Provence rather than bring him home, saying, "After all, that's where he met his maker." Each year, Arthur held a sing-along of Yuletide carols in the house, and when Web and Adam were taking off their coats in the front hall, he said, "Come on back outside, look at this." He was wearing fleece-lined flight boots and a pin-stripe suit. He hurried Web and Adam back down the walk. Web began to shiver. He was thinner, his skin tighter on the bone, and his eyes seemed bluer, almost translucent. "There's something about you," Adam said. "I mean, we haven't seen each other for a year, but it's not just that." Web smiled and said, "You never know, you never know," but he was shivering as Arthur turned them back toward the house and said, "How d'you like that? It's dynamite." There was a big pink plastic Santa Claus face lit up in the front window. The left eyelid dropped a wink. "Just like Myron Cohen," Arthur hooted and clapped Adam on the shoulder. "We saw it already," Web said, cold and uninterested, and he went up the walk. Arthur put his arm around Adam. "Do you know, Web," he called out sourly, "I almost shot your son when we were kids."

In the hall, Web said, "I took the liberty of inviting two old players, pals of mine, Rueful Paillard and Slim Ottis, I hope you don't mind."

"No, no. Not at all," Arthur said, "the more the merrier. Merry Christmas."

Two waiters wearing black velvet smoking jackets and brown shoes were serving the guests. There were too many people, the house was narrow and smoky. A dozen men and women had linked arms around the upright piano and they were singing, "*O little town of Bethlehem, How still we see thee lie.*" Someone opened a side window. The cold air coming in cleared the smoke but some guests huddled against each other, and then a fleshy woman with auburn close-cropped hair slammed the window down. "I didn't come here to catch my baby a cold." She had once been runner-up in a national beauty contest and she was married to a professor of political science. She carried her two-year-old girl in her arms because she had read somewhere that women in ancient Athens had suckled their children till they were three; she wore loose, low-cut evening dresses and suckled the child whenever the child woke up. Her husband, who had the nervous habit of patting his head with his fingertips because he wore a cheap hairpiece, picked up the phone in the hall. He'd been to a requiem mass that morning and now he was writing down hockey scores on the back of the embossed mass card. He nodded hello to Adam and then put down more bets on the west-coast games, which were just starting. "Certainly I bet," he said to Adam. "Some guys bet to check out how they're doing with the world, whether they're up or down. Me, I bet to win. It's all attitude, you see. Like Quasimodo, you've got to go with your hunch. It's all a question of attitude."

He excused himself and joined a television talk-show host who was leaning against a red-brick retaining wall that the architects had broken up with a series of oval openings filled with indirect blue lighting "*O holy night, the stars are brightly shining.*" "It gives a sense of space, don't you think?" the professor said. The talk-show host, who carried a blackthorn cane, said, "No, it looks like a fish tank. I expect to see Esther Williams go by any minute. Then all the sharks in here can synchronize their watches." He went into the kitchen, using his cane as a wedge, and the professor's wife, upset by his tone, hurried after him, but before she could speak, he said to her, "What's your name? Never mind. It doesn't matter. Image is more important than ego, the image you have of yourself." The woman, hollow-cheeked and thin-lipped, shifted the child in her arms. He stared for a moment at the sleeping child and then lifted his cane. "When I perform on television," he said, "I'm not for real. I'm John Harding dressed up as John Harding, I shine in your eyes like a star." He let out a whoop of self-deprecating laughter. "*Joy to the world, the Lord has come.*" The woman said, "I hate men like you." Harding, taken aback, as if he couldn't imagine how anyone could dislike him, said wonderingly, "Why?" He turned to Web. "I just don't know how that kind of hatred is possible."

Adam eased past the man and put his arm around Web. He saw that Rueful and Slim were sitting at the kitchen table. There was a bottle of Chivas Regal on the table and Rueful was holding a pert white girl's hand.

"You sure you're up to this?" Adam asked Web.

"Sure. What's to worry?"

"I was just thinking, after coming from Copenhagen ..."

"Hell, on the road's my second skin."

"Yeah, but the bones get weary."

"It's only when your mind gets weary that you've got to worry."

"My mind," Rueful said, looking up, "gets weary all the time."

"That's why you look so down, Rueful," Slim said. "You was born weary, you will die weary, I even figure you makes love weary."

"Now don't you go upsetting this little lady here. Web, will you tell this man I am a lover of high renown."

"He is a lover of renown," Web said, winking at the girl, "who sometimes has to get high."

"Come fly with me, baby, come fly with me, 'cause I be dying to fly with you."

They all laughed and filled their glasses and Adam said quietly to Web, "You know, I was kinda hoping Harry would be here."

"I wonder how old Harry's doing now."

"Still on the organ."

"Harry's Harry ..."

"Yes and no ..."

"Come on, old choirmasters never die, just their wives do."

"And their daughters disappear."

"Well, we've all got our disappearing acts."

"I ran into Gabrielle."

"His daughter?"

"Yeah."

"Where in the world ...?"

"I spent ten days with her in Puerto Rico."

"Harry'll go out of his mind."

"So he should."

"Tell Harry."

"I can't tell Harry."

"Come on, we're all too long in the tooth for him to care about you being with his daughter ..."

"It's not that, she doesn't want him to know where she is, ever, and the truth is, I don't know where she is now either, she just up and disappeared. Took off. No word, no nothing."

"And she still doesn't want to come home to Harry."

"No. I don't think she ever wants to come home."

"I tell you, the world don't stand repeating."

Arthur appeared between them. "Remember me," he said, "the old sharpshooter." He was now wearing a Red Wing hockey sweater and carrying an empty champagne glass. A bellowing roar went up around the piano and men held their glasses high, their fists clenched to their breasts, singing "*Adeste fidelis, laeti triumphante – venite, venite* ..." "You know," Arthur, who was drunk, said, "I'll let you in on a little secret, it was better before we were grown up, you put on funny hats and broke balloons and everybody loved you." He tapped his cigarette ashes into his empty glass, smiled winningly, and went back to the living room.

"Well, we've all got our secrets to tell," Web said.

"You've got secrets?"

"I've got a couple left. So what was she like?"

"Gabrielle?"

"Yeah."

"It was like looking at the moon."

"You can go bonkers looking at the moon."

"No, no, it's like she was a sliver of light, a beautiful curve of light, except she was always only that curve of light, and you feel the rest of her is there, the full moon is there but it's all in darkness and there's never going to be any more light on the darkness."

"Boy, we're two peas in a pod."

"Why so?"

"We do like to dance on the dark side."

"Well, I figure the moon's still out there," Adam said, hugging his father, "so I should go to the moon whenever I can ..."

"The moon's okay in June," a tall man with pock-marked cheeks said, interrupting impishly, "but I don't see the need for travelling, not these days, my dear." He was wearing a stylishly cut robin's-egg-blue safari suit. "The whole world's coming to us, if we can afford it, and anyone who cares can afford it. Everything comes to we who wait. I mean, isn't that the global village? We sit in our huts to hear what's going on everywhere."

By two in the morning, almost everyone was gone, including the professor whose wife, the beauty queen, was asleep in a chair, the child in her lap staring wide-eyed at the ceiling. Arthur had taken off the hockey sweater. "I ain't no Red Wing," he said, "though all things in life are possible," and then he slumped to the floor, mumbling, "The trouble with holding parties is you get left with the leftovers."

In the kitchen, on a shelf on the wall beside Slim, there was a small soapstone sculpture of a bull seal and a filigree-silver letter opener. Rueful had the white girl on his knee. He was singing quietly:

> *I'm gonna leave here early*
> *in the morning,*
> *people because, just because I'm 'bout to go*
> *outa my mind,*
> *I gonna find me*
> *some kinda good woman*
> *even if she's dumb*
> *deaf crippled and blind.*

And then he started talking about how he used to be as bad as Jesse James and how he always carried a black cat fetish-bone in his pocket because he was a seventh son. "So did Lil Son Jackson," Slim said, "and he got his self dead from seven stab wounds in the back." Rueful laughed and lifted the hand of the white girl, pried open her fist, and kissed the inside of her hand and said, "You know, my daddy he was white, I mean plantation white, man, ivory snow, and owned all kinda lumber tracts in the delta, and he laid one day his eye on Momma, a black little darling, man, and he says to me years later, he say, 'Rueful, you my seventh son and when your daddy die he gonna leave you lumber, you be rich boy, you got good white blood, you got mojo from your Momma, you is the hootchie-kootchie man.'"

Slim, pocketing the silver letter opener, said, "Web, ain't I know'd this man all his natural born life?"

"I believe you have," Web said.

"And you know'd a lucky man," Rueful said.

"You got no white father, you be a no-name nigger through and through."

"No, I ain't," Rueful said, holding on hard to the white girl's hand.

"Then who you be, black boy?"

"Man," he said, thrusting out his chin, "I is the resurrection of the dead."

As they broke into loud laughter, Slim put the small soapstone seal in his other pocket. Arthur appeared at the kitchen door, bleary-eyed, but he winked and cried, "Dynamite."

Adam and Web left arm in arm, and they all went down the walk a little drunkenly out into the snow, a brilliant white snow under a full moon in a clear sky, and Web said, "See, there she is, your full moon."

"Yeah," Adam said, "but she's gone."

"Oh well," Web said, "oh well oh well," and began to sing, holding on to Adam, growling and moaning, and Slim and Rueful and the white girl did a little strut between the banks of snow:

> *Ow ow ow,*
> *Momma cooked a chicken*
> *She thought it was a duck*
> *She put it on the table*
> *With his legs cocked up ...*

* * *

It rained steadily for days, torrents of rain. The alleyways between the leper houses turned to deep mud and pieces of plaster fell away from the house walls into the muck, revealing the ribwork of the walls. Their clothes were clammy. She held on to him in the house, speaking brokenly, as if she were distracted, her nerves taut. She knelt to make love to him and then suddenly laughed and said, "No, there's no future in that ..." Then she insisted that his muscles had to be massaged in such dampness and she stood behind him for an hour kneading his shoulders and neck, saying nothing, shushing him when he spoke as if he were a child being sent to sleep. Once a day, just before noon, she went out into the rain, bent under a heavy canvas umbrella, refusing to let him come with her. "You didn't come here to catch your death of cold ..." When she returned, white-faced, drawn, her eyes shining, she immediately went to bed and slept for several hours, and she slept through the night in his arms, sleeping so soundly that he lay awake, fascinated, and when he asked her how she could sleep so much, she said, "My dreams make it possible for me to sleep ..."

"What dreams?"

"The future ..."

"And ...?"

"Nothing ..."

She smiled and looked out one of the small closely set windows at the grey rain falling in sheets.

"Those are absolutely useless little windows," he said. "They don't give any light."

"A missionary built the house."

"So?"

"The windows face east, he thought he was looking through the five wounds in the morning light."

"Jesus Christ."

"The very same, wise guy," she said, laughing.

"And what do you see?"

"The damn rain."

"It's a wonder everybody around here isn't nuts."

"Everybody is, a little."

"Don't you ever want to get out of here, don't you want to know anything about back home?"

"Not much ..."

"Why not?"

"Well," she said, lying down on the bed and closing her eyes, "it wouldn't make a lot of difference."

"To what?"

"To the future, and you're as much of the past as I can think about." She held out her arms to him. He sat on the edge of the bed, suddenly aware of a terrible fragility in her, aware that whenever they were together she always reached for him, even in her sleep, even as she drew farther and farther away into her own world, refusing to let him or anyone else see the faces of her demons. She fell asleep with one arm hooked behind her head and he sat for a long time listening to her breathing and the rain running off the tile roof, staring at her face, her legs slightly parted *a burning light cold as ice stinging in all my veins*, so at ease in her sleep that he got up and shifted the lamps closer to the white cone of mosquito netting, loaded his camera, and began to slowly and quietly, almost stealthily, move around her, *you tek me when I sleep, you steal me inside*, standing still for long moments – not reflecting but staring at her, somehow from a great distance, though he could constantly feel how close and clammy the room was, how close she was as he focused again, trying to capture a light in her that had eluded him, as if she had surrounded and shielded herself with shadows, shadows that fell away like petals in his hands as he tried to take hold of her *she loves me she loves me not* until at last he leaned very near to her so that he could hear her breathing, and he whispered, "You've got the face of a saint without god," and then he said aloud, caustically, causing her to stir, "No god, no saint, so there you are," and fully dressed, wanting only to comfort her, to shield her, he got into bed and held her and she pressed against his body and murmured warmly and he said, "Don't worry, I won't let the bogeyman get you."

"I don't believe in the bogeyman," she whispered.

"What do you believe in?"

"God, except he can be very cruel, though if you believe

that you're a bigger fool than I am because maybe it's true and maybe it's not but that's for God to know and me to find out."

"I don't know who's loonier, you or me."

"You. I know what I'm doing here and you don't."

part ELEVEN

He lay in his boyhood bed with his eyes closed but with the bedside light on. "A house," he thought, "even more than a woman, should not be left alone." He could hear his father snoring in the next room *and how's he dealt with his own loneliness, his own emptiness?* and he opened his eyes as if he expected to see an answer written on the walls *always expecting to see the writing on the wall when there's only slogans and dayglo shit in the sky* and he closed his eyes and fell into a half-sleep, dreaming that he was still awake walking in the shallows of the Black River with Gabrielle, except the river was leaking away through a huge iron pipe into Christie Pits where the tattooed man lay spread-eagled on his back across second base, alive and trying to embrace frigate birds circling overhead, and when Adam turned, Gabrielle was standing naked at home plate, her body stencilled by blue dots, and he joined them together, drawing his finger across her collarbone and breasts, her belly and hips, and with each joining, snowflakes took off from her body like winged stars, the ceiling in his room covered by stars, the ceiling creaking under a weight until the stars broke apart and a huge cross fell through and his mother said, "You'll see, we all carry a cross." But the cross kept falling and falling until it became so small he caught it in his hand and when he kissed it, it became a bird, a bigger and bigger scavenging seagull sitting on Father Zale's head as he sat in a lawn chair snoring. It was his father's snoring that woke him and he pulled his covers close to his chin, glad of the quiet of his room, the easy stillness of home, though he'd always slept well wherever he was, unafraid of sleep except for the dream that invaded him, but he felt no invasion coming, only the incessant snoring of his father. Then the snoring stopped and he heard a woman weeping and he sat up, quickening but confused, wondering whether he'd really heard weeping ... listening, and then his father appeared in the doorway and Adam said, "Did you hear her weeping?"

"What weeping?"

"I heard it."

"I didn't hear anything. I woke up and I didn't hear anything."

"We've left this house empty too long."

"Maybe we should sell it, I've wondered whether we should sell it."

"Not on your life."

"It might be better."

"Better for what?"

"For whatever," Web said, coming into the room.

"What're you doing up? You were lying in there snoring to beat the devil."

"I woke myself up snoring."

Web was carrying a furry little bear in the crook of his arm.

"What in the world is that?"

"Your teddy bear. When I woke up I suddenly remembered it's been up with the hats in the closet all these years."

"I never had a teddy bear."

"You played with it in your crib."

"That doesn't count, I don't remember anything from my crib."

"Exactly. So how many fathers give their sons back their childhood in the middle of the night?"

Adam laughed and took the bear and looked into its face, its amber eyes, its slightly torn red felt tongue flapping beneath a battered snout, and he tossed it into the air.

"That's what you did as a kid, I spent half my life picking up that bear. You'd fire it out of the crib like you couldn't wait to get rid of it and I'd pick it up and bring it back to you and then one day I just picked it up and took it away and you howled and howled so I never knew what to do with you, whether you were coming or going as a kid."

Web sat on the end of the bed, bent forward, his elbows on his knees. His forearms and wrists were still muscular, powerful.

"You know," he said, "I've got friends who've got sons all over the world, and they talk about this one and that one and having a lot of sons is a kind of protection against bad luck, against all the evil out there in the air, all peasants understood that, but you're it, you're all I got."

In the morning, Adam gave Web a glass of freshly squeezed orange juice. "It's a habit I got into in Cairo," he said, "sunlight on the tongue to start the day."

Web studied the glass. "If you say so," he said, but did not drink the juice.

They sat across from each other in the living room, facing the leaded windows.

"Kinda nice, being together again."

"Yeah."

"It's strange," Adam said, "the room doesn't seem smaller, there just doesn't seem to be as much light."

"It's the ghosts," Web said. "That's what ghosts do, they suck up all the light, they swallow so much light that they disappear during the day and glow at night."

"What crazy night hawk told you that?"

"My father, when I was a kid, and you're sitting in his chair, the chair your grandfather always sat in. He was a frightened man, scared of his wife at first, but she died young, so he kept on being afraid without having anything to be afraid of, he was such a nice quiet man no one ever wanted to do him any hurt. That's why he had those off-in-the-distance-looking eyes – like he was always waiting for someone he could be afraid of to show up ..."

Web sat with his chin in his hand, staring out the window into the bare black branches of the sugar maple tree by the front hedge. In their silence, they heard the old wood scantling snap in the walls and the hot water pipes clank with the cold wind blowing against the east wall. There were little linings of frost along the inside of the leaded windows.

"I keep thinking I should hear Mother's step in the hall," Adam said.

"Yeah," Web said.

"Except I don't. I mean, I think I should hear her but I don't. I don't know whether to be disappointed in myself or her."

"For what?"

"For not showing up."

"Oh, she's here."

"I guess she is."

"And we're here."

"It's strange though."

"Not so strange, it's just the way time goes by."

"Yeah, but it kind of stands still, too."

"Only in your head."

"No, that's what's strange. There's a stillness in the house I never knew was here."

"There's probably all kinds of things we don't know are here."

"But I know what's missing."

"Maybe so. But maybe we only know what we're looking for, like your grandfather always knew what he was looking for but it was never there."

"He told me never to eat the berries on the bushes ..."

"He had a lot of nevers, and he went where we're all going, straight to never-never land."

"You thinking of dying?"

"No. No, not at all. You'd be surprised."

"I go through my whole life surprised."

"There are worse ways to go."

"I think we need a drink, except there's nothing to drink. No one's been here for months."

"How little you know," Web said, standing up.

"You've got a drink?"

"You think if I can find your teddy bear I can't find a drink?"

"I looked everywhere."

"You only looked where you looked and that isn't every-where."

Web went down the hall, Adam slumped in his chair and found himself seeing things as if for the first time: the frayed hem to the window drapes and a dead begonia stem in the big blue porcelain bowl on the radiator lid, the face of a Renoir woman Flo had cut from a magazine and glued to a board and varnished so that it looked like old canvas in the light from the windows or the soft light in the evening from the beaded shade on the lamp on the piano, the sheet music upright on the rack *what night was that?* Adam wondered, squinting, trying to read the title but not wanting to get up from the old easy chair as Web came back into the room carrying a bottle and two glasses.

"Single malt, my boy, and so," he said, handing him a glass, "you haven't got your ass shot off yet?"

"It's not from lack of trying."

"It's a funny thing that, trying to get yourself killed."

"That's not what it's all about."

"No, I'm sure, but I've tried thinking about it, worrying about you getting shot up in the middle of someone else's war, which has got to be a lonely way to go."

"I'm not going anywhere."

"Maybe that's true, too."

"You have been thinking."

"I try it on for size every now and then."

"Look, I've got a gift."

"We've all got gifts."

"I see what I see, not many people can actually see what they see."

"We all see what we see."

"No, I can see what's there, actually there, not what I'm supposed to see. It's like you used to say about the silence between notes, that's where all the music is, except there's a silence for me when I hear that click and I know I've got a moment right in the middle of everything all going to hell, and that's my music and it may be a lonely music but it can't be much lonelier than you knowing that what people listening to you hear and love is not what you hear and love, and what's worse is you've got to love your fans for loving you for all the wrong reasons, or at least not the reasons you'd like to be loved for ..."

"Boy, you've got your mouth working this morning."

"Sorry."

"Nothing to be sorry about."

"I wish that were true."

They sat saying nothing for a long time, and though Adam could see that Web was thinner, his skin drawn, his body bent, there was something eager, intense, in the way he leaned forward, coiled in his stillness, and then Web said casually, "You got your legs on?"

"Where you want to go?"

"I thought we might go up by the graveyard."

* * *

The day it stopped raining in *village lumière*, brilliant sunlight broke through the high branches, smearing light on the leathery trunks, and rain water that had been held by broad leaves continued to drip from the branches. Heat poured down through the trees, the damp earth turned spongy. The shadows were thick with translucent flying insects.

They walked out of the village. She stood on a grassy rise behind the block houses and he sat by her feet on a flat stone in the long grass, looking at her standing above him, her face in the light but her body shadowed by leaves and overhanging glistening green tendrils, and he told her that standing in her own stillness she was beautiful, as if she were exulting in the luminous fact of her own existence, and as he told her again that she was beautiful, he heard a monotony in his own voice, a toneless fragility that had no conviction, no resonance in the humid growth, growth voraciously feeding off itself in deceptive stillness, and when she reached down and tenderly touched his cheek, he jumped, recoiled, and stood catching his breath, filled with a dismay that was inexplicably, physically, painful, and when she then touched his hair he was filled with a sense of irrevocable loss because they had begun to hesitate, to watch each other, and as he kissed the back of her hand, her fingers, he thought, *this is absolutely false*, and he blurted out, "This is false." She smiled, the paleness of her lips distressing him, and took his hand, leading him along a narrow track that skirted the village, going toward a wide clearing where there were several white wooden buildings.

"Nothing is false here," she said.

"I suddenly thought," he said, "that I don't love you, but I know that's not true."

"Maybe it is," she said, "but I can always smell a rat, and there's no rat."

"Then what is there?"

"Didn't you take pictures of me? You have your pictures."

He felt helpless, felt for the first time that whatever pictures he had were irrelevant.

"We have to decide," he insisted, "what there is."

They walked between two long clapboard buildings raised on piles, ducking under the morning's wash, ragged colors hung on lines between the tribal wards.

A fleshy man lay sprawled on the steps, his head bobbing, eyes staring, mouth open. His thick hands fumbled with a robe that hardly covered his thighs, and just below his knees his skin was encrusted, greyish, wrinkled like animal hide, and the calves were swollen down into enormous ankles; there were no ankles, only huge pink-bottomed hoofs, the toes like bulbs, the toenails black, a big man weighted down by his feet. They went into a waiting room off a small pharmacy where there were open shelves of jars, vials, and bottles, and boxes of pills stacked on a long, low checkered table, a flat pillow on the end of the table, and behind it, a blackboard. In the next room, with plain plank cupboards along one wall, there was a simple A-frame steel stool, a grey steel operating table, and a big round overhead light *a dead moon*. To Adam's surprise, the old priest, wearing his frayed white soutane that seemed even shorter at the ankles, was standing beside the operating table.

"No one's working today," he said, and then stepped behind the table so that it stood between them. He offered to make tea. There was a teapot sitting over a bunsen burner and he turned up the flame. "Sit, sit," he said to them, "the doctors are in town at the dispensary. When the doctors go there I come here."

They drank tea. Gabrielle sat unsmiling as the old priest closed his eyes, tugging at his grey eyebrows, and he said, "I cut timber and dug postholes here, you know."

"No, I didn't."

"You can't escape it," he said, "life leaps out at you here, out of the rot, the forest purging itself so that it can live ... acceptance of this process," and he cocked his head as if he were listening for something on the air, and then plodded on portentously, "and a reverence for that reach toward the light must lead us to a compassion for all those who are trapped in pain, and this compassion allows a man to purify himself, to atone for the rot at the heart of life, the rat in the hair ..."

Faintly, they heard CDEF ... DECF ... the dispensary bell ringing through the forest. He opened his small sunken eyes and stared at them, holding the cup to his lips but not swallowing his tea.

"Oh Roland, cut it out," Gabrielle cried.

"Roland?" Adam asked.

"He's no priest," she said, "or maybe he was but he's no priest now, though they all think he is and he says mass for them ..."

"And you are lovers," Roland said with a wry smile that wounded Adam.

"Sure," Adam said defensively, and then wished that he had said nothing. Gabrielle ran her hands through her cropped hair and laughed at herself. "Not enough hair there," she said, so Adam stood behind her, enfolding her in his arms, resting his cheek against her hair, as if he were protecting her, protecting them, from the old man's wry laughter. Yet, even during the months when he'd wondered why she'd gone away without a word, he had never felt so separate as he did now, distressed by her happy possession of herself, not needing him at all though she was totally and unselfconsciously, almost tauntingly, open to him, especially in their bed where she felt free to give him everything but what he wanted, any sense of dependence, so that her inner light remained her own in a darkness he could not touch, could not enter. "You can swallow my sins," she'd said, "but you can't have my darkness, no one can."

"Christ," Roland said, scowling in the stillness of the operating room, "is the heart, the broken heart ..."

"Keep Christ to yourself," she said, speaking so quietly that Roland did not seem to hear her.

"Think of it," Roland said, "a child Jew who heard a voice tell him he was the Son of God, a child who knew that in this life of attrition, pain, and suffering, he was doomed to be the Messiah, the man who would tie his life to death in the actual moment when cosmic catastrophe would signal final judgement and deliverance ..." He lifted the teapot away from the flame and turned up the flame so that it was a hissing blue-orange jet in the air.

"You're wasting gas," Gabrielle said drily.

"You see," Roland said with a sardonic shrug, turning the flame down and pouring more tea into their empty cups on the operating table, "in his messianic consciousness, so obsessed with pain, affliction, disease ... Jesus must have seen his miracles as a prefiguration of the kingdom of deliverance to come, and through atonement, his voluntary sacrifice, his chosen death, he would save those who believed in him ..." He handed them cubes of sugar and went on with a grandiloquent wave of his hand. "The only trouble is, the cosmic collapse didn't come after Calvary, Jesus deluded himself, there'd been no deliverance and affliction remained everywhere ... but one profound truth emerged, and only St. Paul saw it ... in this terrible vale of sickness, a man could lead a life of sacrifice, in this web of darkness such sacrifice might help to bring to pass the final liberating event, we might renovate the future and death would die and there might at last be the light of joy ..."

"Joy ..."

"Yes, joy."

Adam sat very quietly. "So, that's what you're up to," he said, "renovation ..."

"We live in the House of the Lord," Roland said.

"Where tradition is a trend," Adam said, stood up and offered his hand in goodbye.

As he and Gabrielle went down the stairs to the walk between the wards, he said, "I can't stand that old son-of-a-bitch ..."

"He's harmless," she said.

"He's got no light in his eyes, it's frightening, there's no light ..."

They went up another set of stairs into a ward, into a dark long room of cots and pallets on a board floor, and as she took down a chart board from a wall hook, she said, "The fact is, he's afraid of the sun, afraid of sunstroke, the only relief he gets is in the night, in the moonlight ..."

"That's for lovers," he said, "and he's no lover."

"It's hard to love like a lover here," she said, standing at the foot of a bed, a scarred black face on the pillow watching her.

"So why the hell stay?"

"Has the light gone out of my eyes?" she asked.

"No."

"I'm happy."

"You're all alone."

"No, I'm not. I'm surrounded."

"Jesus Christ ..."

"We just went through that," she laughed.

"This might be the loneliest place on earth."

"No, that's where Harry is now. I'm not where Harry is."

"You're not where I am either."

"I was thinking about you last night."

"I hope so."

"The way you've got of looking at things, each thing so separate it makes you seem like you're looking for some kind of root, like you're very lonely, but you're not lonely at all."

"I'm not?"

"No. You're the least lonely man I've ever known."

He was afraid to speak. She was watching him intently with her satisfied smile, a smile he now resented.

"You're fascinated," she said, "fascinated by everything around you, including yourself, and maybe even aroused by your own intense feeling for things, but maybe that's not love ... it's wonderful but maybe it's not love ... Maybe it's your moontan."

"That's you."

"It'll wear off."

"You think you know me that well?"

"I didn't say I knew you."

"Do you think I know you?" he asked.

"We've known each other since we were kids."

"Yeah, but what does that mean?"

"Kids'll be kids," she said, kissing him lightly, and suddenly he was aware that what he knew was not her, even when they'd been together, ecstatic in the sea.

*   *   *

He stood with Web at the entrance to the old cemetery. The street frontage had been sold so that the burial yard was like a park enclosed inside a city block, and there were shops along the street: Aviva's Adventures in Bamboo, Christen Birger Unisex and Creations, Baghdad Fine Carpets, Harvey Adelman's Quick Quiche Cuisine ... and between two tombstone shops, a laneway leading into the burial yard, pathways of family plots, with the domed crematorium in the centre of the yard. There was no one else walking in the yard.

"I used to like coming here with you as a kid. Nobody else's father took them to a graveyard."

"No, I guess not."

"Sitting out here under the trees eating hot dogs for lunch."

"We're sure not sitting down in this snow."

"We could lie down and make angel wings like when we were kids."

"Oh yeah."

"Yeah."

They turned down a walk between weeping willows.

"We're not going to see much in this snow."

"Maybe not."

Web walked ahead, past the cluster of Waters tombstones to an oak that stood away from the path, broad dead leaves clinging to the branches. The snow under the tree was unbroken, the crust glittering in the sunlight.

"So what's up?" Adam asked.

"Come on," Web said, and broke through the snow crust till he stopped by a lean slab. He brushed the blown snow away from the face of the stone and stepped back a pace, standing beside Adam.

BABY

Still
Waters
Run
Deep

"There," Web said with his arms folded across his chest, "lies your twin brother."

"My what?"

"Your twin brother, still-born. We never really named him, but we had to have a name on the papers so we called him Still. There's no date because he was never alive."

"Jesus Christ ... you mean I've got a brother?"

"No, you never had a brother. He was dead in the womb."

"And now you want to tell me ..."

"We thought it was better ..."

"Better what?"

Adam grabbed Web by the shoulders.

"Better not to carry around a dead brother all your life ... nobody needs to live with a dead twin who was never alive. Nobody does."

"You did."

"And so did your mother. It was no fun giving birth to a child dead."

"You're crazy," and he shoved Web and Web stumbled, falling backwards, his arms wide open as he fell into the soft deep snow under the oak tree.

"Man, I tell you," Adam said shaking his head, "it's not safe being alive."

Web lay flat on his back, staring straight up into the clear cold sky. He seemed strangely at rest, open to the whole sky.

"It's not safe, you never know what's creeping up on you," and Adam put his hands on his hips and began to laugh. "You're a wild old son-of-a-bitch," he said.

"Well," Web said, stretching out, smiling, "we all got secrets that've never been told."

"You got some more to tell me?"

"As a matter of fact, I do."

Web began to wag his arms and legs in the snow.

"I'm going back to Copenhagen, for good I think."

"You're what?"

"I got a new woman, a young woman ..."

"Holy sweet Jesus," Adam cried, throwing up his hands and spinning so that he too fell into the snow, with Web still sweeping his arms excitedly.

"She's beautiful, she loves me."

"Where'd you run into this?"

"She's a painter, she was having a show in a gallery by the canal and I heard this guy say to her, 'Your new paintings, they look like fields of pollen, bursting flowers, they make me happy,' and she said with her sweetest accommodating smile, 'They're faces, faces from where they were shot, my family, explosions of blood,' and I thought right then and there, there's a woman I want to know, so now I know her ..."

Adam, saying nothing, began to wag his arms back and forth. Then they both lay still.

"Fucking peaceful, eh?"

"Yeah."

"So you're in love."

"I guess so. Old guys like me don't cross-examine their emotions too much. I'm excited, I'm happy, I'm flattered, I can't wait to get back."

"And here we are lying in a goddamned graveyard."

"It's nice. And besides, I got to straighten up with you and say so long to your mother."

"It's awful in there, that damn crematorium's all-day sucker music."

"I'd like to get her out."

"You can't do that."

"I dunno. I'd like to sprinkle her ashes on the snow all over our graves. Let her melt down into us ..."

"She might like that."

"When I die ..."

"Yeah."

"You bring me home," Web said. "There's two empty plots, one for me ..."

"Okay."

"So just stick me in, and if you want ... it'd be good if you're not against it, since she went the way she wanted to, you could plan on the other for yourself, right there beside your old dad, if you still love your old dad with all he's done after all these years ..."

They lay quietly for a long while and then got up and brushed the snow off their coats and stood staring down at the two angels in the snow, both bare-headed, the sun shining on them through the black branches, and then Adam put his arms around Web and held him close and whispered, "I was born into sweet waters ..."

*　*　*

In a dark place under tall palm trees where fetishes hung from stakes driven into the soil, light filtering through the leaves was soft on her face. "This is where I want to be buried," she said. "You're sewn into four palm leaves and the hole is very shallow, that's why those mounds are there, and in four days they're gone. The ants get right in and clean you out."

"This is crazy, you know," he said, "we may never see each other again ..."

"But that's what dreams are for," she said.

"You going to hang your dreams beside one of those things?" he said, pointing at a fetish, trying to be jocular.

"I've got one of those things."

"You do?"

"Sure ... and Roland's got one, too. I mean, he's crazier

than crazy, but he takes it with him walking at night, it's his little fear bag with lots of things in it, hairs and two pieces of a skull, dyed red …"

"And yours?"

"Well, I wish I had my braids."

"Your pigtails?"

"Never mind. But what I've got is an antelope horn, see," and she took a horn out of her pocket. It fitted his fist, carved into the figure of a kneeling man, his chin in his hands, mouth open, a little zero, staring wide-eyed.

"I don't know," he said.

"You don't know what … ?"

"Did you ever go home and start looking up names in the telephone directory?"

"I never went home, only once …"

"Didn't you do that, looking to see who was still there, who'd flown the coop …"

"No."

"Almost nobody's ever there, my father's off in Copenhagen with someone I never met and all those people who said 'give me a ring' are gone, and look at you …"

"Unlisted …" she said, and looked at him with a sad, knowing little smile, smiling at herself.

"And you're walking around with a fetish, and Harry's singing holy, holy, holy …"

"Don't be hard on Harry."

"I'm afraid to see Harry now that I know what I know."

"Just leave him alone when you go home."

"You're the one who won't go home."

"You go home for me."

"And what are you going to do?"

"Lie down and look at the stars."

During the night, the old widow in the dispensary had died and now she was laid out on a bier in the centre of the village, wrapped in white except for her face and hands, with a rosary strung through her black bony fingers. Women, their own bodies wrapped in wild, colorful cloths, sat around her, their hands and feet bandaged, silent for a moment, and then they took up the soft chanting of a litany for the dead, the call and answer. In the distance, children were laughing and playing in a ditch near the town road. Old Roland, holding a furled black umbrella and wearing his white soutane, stood in the shadows of a doorway, looking surprisingly disconsolate, as if he had been impinged upon.

"You know what's funny about the stars?" Adam said as they walked around the clustered women.

"No, I never laughed at the stars."

"All through history people have tried reading the stars ..."

"Don't you want to know what's going to happen to you?"

"Sure. But the stars are the past. What you're looking at has actually been over for a million years. You think you're looking into the future, but the best you could ever do is find out where we've been, where we began. We never know where we're going."

"You're going home and I'm staying here."

"God knows if I'll ever get home, I nearly got killed coming here."

"Go to Copenhagen."

"One Waters walking the canals is enough."

"You could go arm in arm."

"Walking the waters two by two."

"Well you came here, and I'm glad but you shouldn't have."

"That's the way love is."

"I wish I knew what love is," she said, "I wish I knew what evil is."

"Evil," he said testily.

"It's in us, it's our inheritance stumbling out of the bush all the time," she said. "You leave that dead old widow out in the sun, and watch the worms in her hatch. The worm is alive in us from the day we're born, in our cells, and it kills life, and Roland's right – poor Christ, trying to prove a little healing could prefigure a great big healing when what we know is no matter how many cures there are, new plagues break out … Harry's not evil, he's just a sore that broke open, and we all carry a dead child, genetically, and there's no cure, only clean bandages and a little comfort, because the wound's too big, big enough to dance on, to love in like we loved in, and wash like we washed each other, washing our wounds …"

"You'll lose your mind here," he said.

"No I won't."

"Why not?"

"Just to spite you," she said, putting her arm around his waist, "and I do love you, but if you ask me to explain, I'll hate you."

"Maybe if I could make you hate me …"

"Never …"

"Maybe if I'd never swallowed your sins …"

"Remember that kid with the coat hanger and the tin can?"

"Sure."

"He sticks in my mind."

"I'm not surprised."

"I wish I could hear whatever music he was hearing, I sometimes think ..."

"What?"

"That he was sent to us, that if I could hear that music, I'd hear what my own dead child hears ... the music Harry never hears."

"Harry's got his eye on heaven, he's got stars in his eyes."

"Oh yes," and there might have been tears in her eyes, "Harry's in his heaven and all's right with the world." She opened the door to her house. Several men, two of them leaning on peg-leg crutches, stared, lethargic smiles hanging on their faces. Gabrielle and Adam went in and she closed the door.

"I want to make love to you," she said, and knelt beside the cone of white netting. "I want to swallow your seed."

In a while, they heard the dispensary bell.

"Give me a ring sometime," he said, and opened his bag and took out a pair of shoes. "These are yours," he said. "I didn't let you leave them behind in our hotel."

"So," she said, "you knew all the time that I'd never be back."

"No," he said, "I just hate to see empty shoes."

"Don't ever forget me," she said, taking the shoes.

"Are you crazy," he said, "you're alive in me." He picked up his camera case and took out the deck of cards. "Here, you keep these. I've played solitaire with them half-way around the world."

"Aren't you forgetting something?"

"What?"

"The gun. That's the real world out there."

He put the pistol inside his belt and they walked down the road to the river. They stood in the late afternoon light on the sandy shore close to the cement pier and the pirogues, the leper boatman with the bowler hat waiting for him. Suddenly, her face glowing, almost joyful though she had told him that she felt stricken by sadness, she said, "I must get you something," and she turned and loped back up the hill path, disappearing between buildings. He sat down to wait, brooding about her fierce inexplicable joy and the swell of happiness she aroused in the village, and then she came back down the hill. She was carrying a big, white-faced mask with long, loose straw hair and a straw beard. The eyes were little lopsided gouged holes and it had a pug nose and a pursed mouth. "It took me a time to get it," she said. "It was filled with lizards. It was here when the missionary was here."

"The white face," he said.

"Yes, it's good against evil."

"Will you promise me something?"

"Whatever you want."

"Get one of the lepers to make you a little sign and hang it on the wall by the bed."

"What kind of sign?"

"Two equals one ... that's all."

"You mean like numbers?"

"Yeah, $2 = 1$ ... it's something Father Zale taught me."

"We are one," she said.

"I can't write you any more," he said.

"No. Make sure you sit still in the pirogue. The water is dangerous, electric fish." She kissed him on both cheeks and on the mouth. "Thank you for coming again," she said. "To part once more," he said, and the boatman helped him into the pirogue, his leper hand streaked pink by the wound in the dark flesh. They pulled out into the river, clouds coming with the falling sun. There would be more night rain. There was an Uzi on the bottom of the pirogue between the boatman's feet. When Adam looked back, she was standing on the cement pier, her arms up in the air, extended to the sky. She stood there with her arms high as he passed out of sight around the headland.